In his presence, every sound was dynamic...

Carla loosened the frozen soup from its container, and it plopped into the pan. The blaze of the gas jet whooshed.

"I wish you'd just go sit down in the living room until I have your food ready," she said nervously.

Brigg moved from his position at the door, but toward her instead of away. She stood motionless, her hands hanging at her sides. Even before he gently clasped her shoulders, she could feel the warmth of him all along her body. When he drew her against him, she felt that intensity engulfing her. She tried to fight the pleasure, tried to quell the thought that this was what she'd been waiting for—perhaps all her life!

ABOUT THE AUTHOR

Sharon McCaffree began her writing career at the age of sixteen when she took her first job as a newspaper reporter. Reporting and playing the piano professionally helped finance her college education. She now holds a master's degree in American history and teaches the subject on a college level. Sharon lives in Missouri with her husband and three children.

Books by Sharon McCaffree

HARLEQUIN AMERICAN ROMANCE

4—NOW AND FOREVER
87—MISPLACED DESTINY

HARLEQUIN TEMPTATION

36—ONE BRIGHT MORNING

HARLEQUIN SUPERROMANCE

85—PASSPORT TO PASSION

These books may be available at your local bookseller.

Don't miss any of our special offers. Write to us at the following address for information on our newest releases.

Harlequin Reader Service
P.O. Box 52040, Phoenix, AZ 85072-2040
Canadian address: P.O. Box 2800, Postal Station A,
5170 Yonge St., Willowdale, Ont. M2N 6J3

Misplaced Destiny

SHARON McCAFFREE

Harlequin Books

TORONTO • NEW YORK • LONDON
AMSTERDAM • PARIS • SYDNEY • HAMBURG
STOCKHOLM • ATHENS • TOKYO • MILAN

To Irene McDaniel,
the "Jody" in our family

Published January 1985

ISBN 0-373-16087-9

Copyright © 1985 by Sharon McCaffree. All rights reserved.
Philippine copyright 1985. Australian copyright 1985.
Except for use in any review, the reproduction or utilization of
this work in whole or in part in any form by any electronic,
mechanical or other means, now known or hereafter invented,
including xerography, photocopying and recording, or in any
information storage or retrieval system, is forbidden without
the permission of the publisher, Harlequin Enterprises Limited,
225 Duncan Mill Road, Don Mills, Ontario, Canada M3B 3K9.

All the characters in this book have no existence outside the
imagination of the author and have no relation whatsoever to
anyone bearing the same name or names. They are not even
distantly inspired by any individual known or unknown to the
author, and all the incidents are pure invention.

The Harlequin trademarks, consisting of the words
HARLEQUIN AMERICAN ROMANCE, HARLEQUIN
AMERICAN ROMANCES, and the portrayal of a Harlequin,
are trademarks of Harlequin Enterprises Limited; the portrayal
of a Harlequin is registered in the United States Patent and
Trademark Office and in the Canada Trade Marks Office.

Printed in Canada

Chapter One

The errand in the country was a nuisance. As Carla Blake paused a moment to survey the overgrown cemetery, she couldn't help wishing her father had taken up genealogy *before* he had retired and left Illinois. Then he undoubtedly would already have located the tombstone that might help him prove five generations of his family tree. And therefore Carla would at this moment be happily drinking beer in town with her old friends who, like her, had come back for the Shelbyville High School fifteenth reunion. She wouldn't be in this eerie place with the stranger to worry about.

The man was a tanned, balding giant with a fringe of silvered brown hair that matched his luxuriant beard. He had arrived when she was examining the stones in the west section of the deserted churchyard, and had nodded politely at her as strangers do in the country. Carla had dutifully nodded back, but when he began to remove a wheelbarrow and several heavy tools from his station wagon, something about the athletic way his superb body moved had looked poignantly familiar.

She had watched him load dirt from a mound near the abandoned church, all the while trying to dredge his name from the past, but somehow his face didn't match her recollections of that body.

She hadn't even realized she was staring, and that was her mistake. When he glanced up and caught her puzzled concentration focused on him, his answering grin was wicked and audacious. Immediately Carla had flushed and torn her eyes away, but the damage was done. He kept watching her.

In some recess of her memory she could recall feeling similar uneasiness a long time ago, but she couldn't place when or why. She only knew that then, as now, she was uncertain what was going to happen next.

She tried to continue her search and think of other things: of the way the sun had filtered through the haze when she had left her Chicago apartment at dawn that morning; of her excitement when she had entered Shelbyville and seen the Welcome Seniors banner stretched across the main street from the hardware store to the bank. Her body, stiff and tired from the drive, had known she was thirty-three years old, but her brain had responded to that sign like a young girl.

Thinking about the reunion didn't help distract her much. She wished she were back in town at that tavern near the high school that she used to believe was so temptingly evil, the place where her classmates would already be gathering informally. Anywhere but with this man. Nervously Carla glanced over to where the stranger was supposedly trying to straighten a tilting headstone. He was leaning on his shovel, obviously staring and doing his best to intimidate her. Carla's urbanized instincts warned her to leave. But her habit of trust, nurtured in this very community, told her she was being silly and that she had invested too much time on her father's request to give up now.

Trying to convince herself that her adult imagination was as overactive as those of the two spinster sisters who used to write outraged letters to the Shelbyville newspaper, she kept doggedly at her task. Picking her way around a family plot whose headstones were of too modern a style for what she sought, she searched for the tall, narrow markers that her father had said were typical of the early 1870s. It was slow going; the white stone of most of them was aging into gray, and the grit of time had made the crude markings on even those that were still standing almost illegible.

Sighing, she stole another glance at the man and was relieved to find he had returned to his work. She supposed she would have felt less ill at ease if he weren't so big. Few men were bigger than Carla herself. An Amazon, Charles used to call her.

The day had grown warm, unseasonably so for a November weekend, and Carla unbuttoned her down jacket and removed the paisley scarf she had tied bandanna-style around her hair. The man was apparently feeling the heat, too, for he had tossed his jacket to the ground and rolled his shirt-sleeves high on his muscular arms.

The springlike weather was unreal. Carla well remembered the Thanksgiving in Shelbyville when she was about eleven; they had had four inches of snow, and she and Suzannah had enjoyed sledding so much they had almost forgotten to show up for the turkey dinner their families were sharing.

Distracted by the memory she walked past a dozen or so more graves before realizing she had missed a promising gray-white headstone leaning precariously sideways in a plot closer to where the man was working. There were so few likely markers left for her to check that she forced herself to walk over to examine it, despite the proximity of the audacious stranger. And, for once, her courage was rewarded. She had found the burial site of Jonathan Cannon, her father's relative.

Relieved, Carla drew a pad from her purse and quickly wrote down all the information:

> Jonathan Bryce Cannon
> Born Nov. 21, 1840
> to Cecil Wm. Cannon & Mary Jane Bryce
> Died Aug. 1872 of intemperance
> Grieved by wife Constance and ten children

She grinned at the inscription. Her father would be upset. Although he had hoped the tombstone would prove this known ancestor was the son of Mary Jane Bryce, he would not be pleased with the intemperance. Her father was an avid teetotaler.

"Intemperance? They didn't say if it was from drink, or the kind that led to those ten children by the time he was thirty-two."

The man was standing at her shoulder, and Carla jumped involuntarily, wondering how he could have moved behind her so silently. When she looked directly at his face she had to tilt her head. He was staring at her hair.

His fascination left her breathless. Her hair was a coarse mop, lush brown and curling almost to her shoulders, but certainly not worthy of that much attention. At one time she had worn it quite long, but Charles had complained that it gave her too much of an earth mother look, with the angular bones of her face and generous proportions of her body, so she had obediently kept it cut. After three years it was just beginning to grow out to a length she liked.

"I had expected you to have some gray by now," the man said, still looking at her hair. "What are you, Giant Child? Thirty-three, -four?"

Her emotions churned in confusion. *Giant Child?*

There was only one family in the world that knew her by that name. But this man couldn't be....

He was smiling at her like an old friend.

"Mr. Carlyle?" she ventured uncertainly, then reddened upon realizing that this arrogant stranger could never be Suzannah's father. Not only was the personality wrong for that dear, quiet man, but even fifteen years ago the hair fringing Ambrose Carlyle's balding scalp had been solid gray, not this dark natural brown, silvered at the temples. And Mr. Carlyle had been pale and hunched with age, never tanned and athletic.

The man's eyes narrowed speculatively. "I've looked this way for ten years. Didn't you expect me to grow bald, too?" he asked.

Suddenly all the vague recollections fell into place. His teasing arrogance, the staring. Even her own embarrassed discomfort. Her body had remembered what her mind had forgotten. Suzannah's brother.

"I'm surprised you recognized me, Brig," she said weakly, finally understanding her peculiar awkwardness in his presence.

Brig Carlyle had always been able to make her practically fall apart, with a simple, knowing grin or a speculative tilt of his head. Everyone else in Suzannah's circle had idolized the brazen brother who was nine years older than they. Only Carla had disbelieved in his deity, and he had cheerfully made her suffer for it.

"I suppose you know how nervous you were making me." She felt about ten years old again.

"I figured it was worth a try. I knew you right off. You've changed some, though, Giant Child. You always used to have a grown-up head on a *child's* body." He looked her over thoroughly, bringing even more redness to Carla's flushed cheeks.

"People always used to tell me that came from being

born to middle-aged parents," she snapped, not denying his description. Even her proud parents admitted she had been a gangling, ugly child. But at about twenty-two she had suddenly seemed to grow into herself; the big eyes had darkened to a deep blue, the complexion had bloomed, as had her body. Her rather mammoth beauty was, however, a mixed blessing. Although Charles had been pleased that his clients found her appearance fascinating, he had never been able to adjust to the fact she was taller than he.

Looking Brig over cautiously, Carla felt as if she were going into a time lapse. Now she'd know him anywhere, even balding and with the beard. The intense gray eyes in the bony face were the same, the sardonic quirk of his mouth, the broad shoulders and chest, huge hands. And he moved just the same, like a panther. Unexpected for such a big man.

Suddenly Carla wanted to hear him laugh. There had never been anything so wonderful as making Brig laugh. She had always felt a sense of supreme accomplishment when she managed that.

She realized why her subconscious had not let her recognize him, even though all the Carlyles had been almost like relatives. Although Brig was only home from engineering school sporadically by the time the girls were in junior high, he had always treated Carla as an equal, assuming she could take as much as she handed out. In self-protection she had managed to hide the hurt and confusion his antics would stir in her, but it was no wonder she had tried to forget him. There had always been fireworks when they were together. Even when she had moved to Chicago, where Brig headquartered any time he happened to be in the country between construction jobs, she had never bothered to look him up. And Suzannah had eventually quit mentioning him in her letters.

Carla finally snapped out of her reverie, determined that she wasn't going to let him get under her skin anymore. She was a grown woman who could handle anything. She had had enough practice.

"You've changed, too." She finally broke the contemplative silence. "I thought baldness was a sex-linked chromosome from the female side. You're not supposed to look like your own father. You're supposed to take after your grandfather Harris, who, I know for a fact, died at eighty-five with a full head of hair."

The taunting words came easily, just as in the old days.

"I should have expected that sort of unkind observation from you." He didn't laugh, but his grin was heartlurching enough. "You were always the only one of Suzannah's friends who had the nerve to talk back."

"Someone had to. You had the rest of the girls intimidated with your fifty-foot size advantage."

"Never fifty feet on you, dear Carla. Carla—?"

"It's Blake now."

Again he looked approvingly at her firm body, clad in the paisley blouse and soft wool skirt. "I always knew you'd grow to be a magnificent woman, Giant Child." He used the pet name that he had long before coined for her and that the rest of his family had taken up. "And you've learned to stand up straight. Good."

"Marriage to a perfectionist teaches one to make the most of one's questionable assets," she said unthinkingly, then was immediately ashamed of her bitterness.

"Surely your husband doesn't feel he has completed the job of perfecting you?" Brig feigned disbelief. "I always thought your tongue was the worst problem."

"He gave up on that when we divorced three years ago."

Carla wondered if it had actually been a flick of sympathy she saw in his eyes. Perhaps. She had never been able to decipher what Brig was thinking, even though he could usually read her thoughts.

"Come over here and talk while I finish reseating this stone," he said abruptly, not taking her by the arm, but his old magnetism forcing her to come along with him just as certainly as if he had. "I know you're in town for the reunion, but what are you doing out in this graveyard?"

She followed him reluctantly. "My father's gotten hooked on genealogy since they moved to Colorado, and he wanted me to track down a missing ancestor."

"Was this ancestor the intemperate one with the long-suffering Constance for a wife?"

"The very same." She laughed, suddenly feeling better. After all, there was no reason for her to continue reacting so violently to Brig. He was just a man, not some powerful devil-angel as she had once believed. "My mother will be happy. She likes her little glass of wine at bedtime despite Pop's telling her it's not good for her. This should give her some ammunition to hassle him."

Brig chuckled and returned to his work, so she settled against a sturdy stone nearby and watched him. His muscular arms bulged when he shifted the heavy marker from side to side, letting the loose soil he had piled around it level the base. There was something strangely companionable about being with him while he worked. It came back to her how often she and Suzannah had done that as little children, before Carla had gotten old enough to begin the fights.

"I've been behaving in the oddest manner ever since I got into town," she said introspectively. "Even though I've been gone fifteen years, it's almost frightening how easily I'm falling into childhood habits. When I drove in, I almost stopped at Dad's old lumberyard to tell him I was safely off the highway. He was such a worrier whenever I had the car."

"Maybe you've stayed away too long. When did you come down?"

"This morning. I left before dawn so I'd have time to drive through downtown Chicago. I love to see the hulking shape of the skyline when the mist is first rising off Lake Michigan."

"Wasn't that route a little out of your way? I thought Suzannah said something yesterday about your having a condo in midtown."

"Don't bug me about going out of my way," Carla objected. "In seven years of marriage I could never take a side trip without a major argument from Charles. It is now my greatest luxury to go where I want."

She lifted her face to enjoy the sudden coolness of the soft breeze. The countryside was beginning to smell peculiar, and instinct not totally destroyed after years of urban living told her that there would probably be a heavy rain soon.

"When I recognize people, I start acting the same age I was when I last saw them." She returned to her explanation of her reactions to Shelbyville. "I stopped at the drug store counter to get a sandwich, and when that woman who's always run it waited on me, I ordered a chocolate soda instead. It was crazy. I haven't eaten one of those gooey things since I graduated. Do you revert whenever you come home?"

"No, but then I've returned frequently enough to not lose contact completely." He again tugged on the heavy stone, but this time it stood straight and firm, his job well completed. She watched him gather up his tools and dump them into the empty wheelbarrow.

Still caught up in the past, Carla felt no compunction about enlarging her musings to a frank appraisal of him. They had always been recklessly blunt with each other. "Of course you know that the baldness is just right for your personality," she said. "Now you look more piratical than ever, a regular Captain Ahab, which means that I was wrong." She sighed dramatically.

"What are you talking about, woman?" he asked, not at all offended by her rambling remarks. But then, he never had been.

"Didn't Suzannah ever tell you that her friends had bets on what *Brig* stood for? We were in about fifth grade, I think. I'd forgotten about it until just now." Her voice was merry with the recollection. "Caroline was in a religious phase at the time and swore your mother named you after Brigham Young. Most of the others felt you were a perfect pirate and that your name was short for brigand. And I'm convinced now they were right."

"But those weren't your guesses?" Apparently he had never heard the story.

"No. I thought someone as dictatorial as you had to be named for a brigadier general."

He laughed out loud, throwing his head back in amusement.

Carla flushed with childish satisfaction at his reaction. That gorgeous laugh! "So what is Brig short for? Suzannah swore she didn't know, and somehow I never found out."

"Actually all of you were wrong. My name is Brigg, with two g's. Which is why I'm out here today." He set the wheelbarrow back on the ground and laid his jacket on top before indicating the stone he had just reseated. "I'm named after my mother's favorite black sheep cousin, and when she discovered his stone was tipping she couldn't wait for me to get back for a visit so I could fix it."

Carla looked at the inscription. "Hezekiah Evelyn Brigg?" she read disbelievingly.

"Mother hardly expected any son of hers to be the Hezekiah type, and Dad set his foot down against Evelyn."

"What on earth did they call him?"

"He was the youngest of eight and the only boy. You figure it out."

"Not Sonny?"

"You've got it. Mother tied that on me for a while, but I talked her out of it."

Carla was certain he had. He must have been a terrible child for the gentle Mrs. Carlyle to raise. She started to say as much, but a sudden onslaught of rain stopped her.

While they were hurrying to their cars, Carla noticed that water was clinging to Brigg's beard in little, perfect droplets, and she wondered fleetingly how he survived in cold weather when moisture probably froze in the thick growth.

"I grew the beard on a long construction project in Brazil this spring. I'll probably shave it off soon."

He could still read her thoughts. She frowned at him belligerently while he loaded the things into the back of the station wagon.

"Hurry up woman, you're going to get soaked." He grabbed her arm and rushed her into her own car, then surprised her by scrambling in on the other side. She twisted her head to study him. He was soggy and disheveled, but still magnificent. Some things just wouldn't change.

"Brigg with two g's. That's going to take some mental adjustment for me. It gives you a whole new personality."

He laughed again, that hearty, pleasing sound.

"What are you doing in town, anyway?" she asked. "I would have thought you'd try to avoid Suzannah's friends at all costs." Immediately she realized the question was foolish. It was the day after Thanksgiving, and since Brigg had been a widower for many years, he had probably brought his twin daughters down to spend the holiday with his parents.

"I wasn't thinking," she added hastily. "Of course you brought the girls to see their grandparents."

"No, I didn't. Their boarding school in the East planned a holiday field trip to New York City, and they wanted to go. I let them, since I'd seen them a couple of weeks ago, anyway. I was looking forward to a lazy weekend at home alone in Chicago, and it's your fault I'm here instead."

"Mine?" Carla objected, feeling some of her old childish rebellion at his humorous accusation.

"Suzannah broke her right foot. Her husband is in England this week, but she was determined to make it to the reunion, since you were coming. The folks don't drive anymore, so I was elected to go get her and her kids."

"That's not exactly a solitary weekend, is it?" Carla laughed, visualizing what the trip from Kansas City to Shelbyville must have been, with talkative Suzannah and her three school-age children along. Add to that the long drive to Kansas City from Chicago, and no wonder he was upset. "I wouldn't mind taking them back," she offered, "but we'd all have to miss the family party your mother invited me to Saturday night. I have to get back to Chicago in time to teach Monday morning."

"That's okay. The folks have already arranged something for her, so I can return to Chicago tomorrow." He looked at the muddy parking lot speculatively. "I suppose we'd better get out of here while we still can. Are you staying in a motel?"

"Yes, the Downtowner. There are fancier places out on the highway, but I figured that would be handiest."

"I'll be dropping Suzannah off for the reunion dinner tonight. We'll pick you up at seven." He was out of the car before she could respond.

It was impossible for him to hear her shouted objection.

Carla decided to call the Carlyle farm and offer to pick up Suzannah instead, but once she was back in her room, dried off, and relaxing with her feet up in a chair, she changed her mind. It would be nice to accept a little TLC for a change, even from Brigg.

Gradually the storm passed on, and as she looked out her window at the uncomplicated pace of life resuming on the streets nearby, her lips quirked in a sentimental smile. She was home again. Meeting that terrible Brig—Brigg with two g's, she corrected—had confirmed it.

And soon she'd be seeing Suzannah for the first time in three years. And Caroline. Most of their old gang was planning to be back. She almost laughed aloud. They'd probably all get so steeped in nostalgia they'd be just as obnoxiously immature as all the other reunion groups that arrived year after year.

So what? For the first time in years Carla was in a mood to enjoy herself.

The first three hours of the reunion were marvelous fun. Carla arrived at the party feeling as if she were a grown woman with the id of an eighteen-year-old, and soon discovered that most of her classmates were undergoing the same emotional metamorphosis. They all joined in enthusiastically singing the high school alma mater at least three times, gaily posed for pictures with each other, and behaved reasonably decorously throughout the dinner and speeches, intimidated by the presence of their former teachers.

Once cocktails and dancing started after the formalities, Carla looked at what seemed like hundreds of family snapshots, and genuinely enjoyed meeting her friends' spouses and hearing about how absolutely marvelous their children were. Surprisingly she even found it painless to explain, if asked, that she was now divorced, and that she had no children. If the reunion had been five years earlier her feminine pride might have needed to explain that she had lost a child. But by now the old miscarriage after she had had a severe case of influenza didn't seem worth mentioning.

She had visited with almost everyone, and danced with more men than she could attach names to. Then, all of a sudden, while standing in a small, chattering group, she seemed to run out of steam.

"Any chance you can scrounge us up a couple of chairs in a quiet corner?" Suzannah limped to her side, looking even more exhausted than Carla.

"We're getting old," Carla groaned as she pulled three chairs into a relatively secluded nook behind a Coke machine and helped Suzannah hobble over to them. "Want to put your delicate foot up?"

"Delicate?" Suzannah snorted, using both hands to drag the bulky walking cast onto its resting place. "Ahhhh!" She settled back and looked at her foot disbelievingly. "Wait till my kids see all the stuff that's been written on this thing tonight. They'll think I've been to an orgy."

"You mean everyone's been signing it? Well, if they can, so can I. Where's a pen?"

"Keep it decent." Suzannah handed her a pen from

her purse, then sighed. "I'm glad you rescued me. It's been a ball, but I don't think I could stand up another second."

"I wish you had colored pens." Carla bent over the cast.

"What kind of picture are you doing?" Suzannah asked suspiciously.

"An American eagle. Don't panic."

"An American eagle? Good Lord!"

"Do you want another dog at a fireplug like Pete—"

"He told me he was doing a teddy bear."

"Hmmm. Maybe it's a teddy bear at a fireplug."

"Just do the eagle."

"When do you get this thing off?" Carla bit her lip as she concentrated on her artwork.

"Not for six or seven weeks. It makes me furious. I was having so much fun helping Bob program his computers at the office."

"Can't you still do it?"

"It would mean someone having to leave the office to drive me home before the kids get back from school."

"Knowing Bob, he'll arrange it. Okay, the eagle's done. How about Uncle Sam, too?" She straightened and looked at Suzannah.

"Thanks, but no thanks. I remember the quality of your artistic ability."

Carla shrugged good-naturedly and returned the pen before leaning back to look around the noisy, crowded room. The dance floor was small, and several of the celebrants were already so enthused from their second cocktail session that the party was beginning to look like a circus.

"If one more person asks me to dance I think I'll die," Carla mused, grateful that she and Suzannah finally had a chance to talk. "You're lucky you have an excuse."

"Oh I danced once. Brigg asked me for a slow one—being nice to me in front of my friends for a change. Isn't that hilarious?"

"At least he's big enough to help you drag the cast around," Carla laughed. "I was surprised he decided to attend tonight."

"Me, too. He hadn't been planning on it. I'm even more surprised he has bothered to socialize. I half expected him to sit around looking bored as he always used to."

"As he always used to." Carla finished the sentence with her. And they both grinned. "Ah, memories."

"I've loved this evening," Suzannah reflected. "But I think by the end of Mom's party for all the relatives and old friends tomorrow I will have had enough reliving of the old days. I'll be ready to get the children back to Kansas City and watch for Bob to get home from England."

"What are you going to wear tomorrow? I know you wrote me to bring something sophisticated, but—"

"*Do* wear something sophisticated," Suzannah insisted. "Quit underplaying your looks. You know how people here always dress to the hilt for special parties. And Mom has had invitations out for a month. I remember the last time she did that, and I wore a cotton sundress to her garden party, thinking I didn't want to show up the poorly dressed country folk. Was I ever embarrassed! I'll swear they'd all been up to the designer room of Marshall Field's with their year's paycheck."

"All right, all right. I'll wear my sophisticated dress. I promise I won't look like a poor schoolteacher."

That was the wrong choice of words.

"I'll have to agree with Charles," Suzannah said with sudden assertiveness. "Not about your going back to work hurting his image. But, really, Carla, to return to school and get a teaching degree?" As always Suzannah jumped from one subject to another with no regard for the comprehension of her listener. "If you wanted to work, you would have been better off in your old job as an executive secretary."

"I wanted to be around children." Carla racked her mind for a change of subject. Suzannah on a mission could be formidable, and the telltale signs were there.

"You were crazy to let Charles get off without a settlement or alimony." Suzannah was not going to be easy to distract. "I hope you're insisting that the school pay you a decent salary. After all, your reading students have been making the highest scores in the district the past four years in a row."

"How did you know about the reading scores?"

"Mom sent me a clipping from the Chicago papers. Now, seriously, you should tell them that if they want to keep your excellent services they have to pay you enough."

Carla laughed aloud. "Suzannah, you are the nosiest person I know. I'm lucky you don't live in Cook County. I can visualize you carrying a briefcase full of testimonial letters up to my school board."

"You laugh. But I just may see what I can do about your problem. After I get Brigg's taken care of."

"Where's Brigg now?" That ploy worked. Suzannah frowned and began searching the dance floor, forgetting for the moment Carla's supposed financial difficulty. Carla hoped whatever problem Suzannah thought Brigg had would keep her occupied for months. She dreaded to think what her friend might do if she learned that Carla's job this semester was a temporary appointment. Staff cutbacks in her suburban district had been intense the past few years as enrollment had declined. Carla had not been teaching long enough to be tenured, and would already have been laid off had not an older teacher taken a semester's sick leave. If the woman decided to come back in January, Carla would be out of work.

"Look at him!" Suzannah's disapproving snort disturbed Carla's reverie. "I'll wring Brigg's neck. He's pulling that condescending stuff with Caroline again."

Carla located Brigg's head above the other dancers'. "How can you tell what he's doing? I can't even see Caroline, she's so short."

"I just know by the expression on his face; that holier-than-thou, bored smirk he always used to give me. Why would he act like that? Caroline is so cute and sweet."

Carla grimaced, thinking the description was a little inappropriate for women of their age. "Brigg looks all right to me; he's smiling. Really, Suzannah, what do you expect? People have been lionizing him all evening: the well-known Brigg Carlyle of the ultra successful Carlyle Construction Company—offices in Chicago, Toronto, Paris, Bombay. Under the circumstances I think he's been wearing his best manners."

She would have said more, but just then one of the Pettis twins grabbed her hand and began dragging her to the dance floor. "Can't have you a wallflower back in that corner," he quipped, his eyes already a bit bleary.

"So kind of you," Carla sighed, before loosing her breath in a gush when he hugged her against his chest. She wondered which twin she was dancing with.

"Hasn't this been the greatest party?" He had to look up slightly to locate her eyes.

"I feel like Miss Popularity," she agreed, trying to

draw away from him a little. "The only boy who used to ask me to dance was the basketball center."

Encouraged by his cocktail consumption, the twin leered at her. "But grown men like their women gener-ous-ous-ly built," he stammered, punctuating his statement with a swat on her rump.

Carla jerked in surprise and was embarrassed to see that Brigg and Caroline were dancing next to them and had seen the whole thing. Mercifully Caroline didn't make any clever remark; she was too busy draping herself against every inch of Brigg's body she could reach. Since Caroline had always been a flirt, Carla probably wouldn't have thought anything about it, had not Suzannah made her comment. But she glanced at Brigg to see how he was taking it, and what she perceived made her quake, forgetting her own problems with Pettis's groping hands. Suzannah was right; Brigg *was* in his old condescending mood. She would not have wanted to be Caroline for anything, for he was making no attempt to hide his disdain. Carla was embarrassed for her.

She glared at Brigg, her old protective ire up. There was no telling what outrageous things he would encourage Caroline to do, letting her dig her own mortifying grave in front of all their old friends.

Brigg saw Carla's expression and, in answer, leaned his head even more attentively toward his partner's chattering mouth. Caroline's response was a delighted kiss full on Brigg's sardonic lips.

Carla didn't see his answering expression, for that was when Pettis began kissing her.

The switch happened so smoothly she never realized how Brigg had done it. One moment the two couples had bumped, there was the usual apologizing and back slapping, and the next minute she was whirling away in

Brigg's arms, barely hearing his explanation that his sister would kill him if he didn't dance with her giant friend at least once.

"You're one to be calling me a giant," Carla protested as she tilted her head to see his face.

"Do you want me to turn you back over to Pettis?"

"No! And I don't intend to unleash you on Caroline again. It's unfair to lead her on; she's just a harmless flirt."

"Flirt! She's a woman seriously on the make. Forget her. Let's get outside; this noise is killing me."

It was a relief to move to the tiny patio, even if a good bit of chatter was going on around a snack table there, too. Carla drew a grateful breath of the cool night air, only then realizing how stuffy the dance hall had become.

"Nice out here," Brigg said quietly, lifting his head to look at the stars. "Is it just me, or have I heard the same boring questions and answers in there dozens of times?"

"It's just you," Carla lied calmly, deciding for the moment to let him divert her from Caroline's defense. It was nice out there under the bright fall sky, and she didn't really want a fight. "I found the conversations scintillating. Especially my own. Do you know that I have told one hundred seventy-five of my classmates that I live in Chicago now, which is rather amazing, since there were only ninety in my class."

"And such an interesting statement: 'I live in Chicago.' I do, too, you know."

"Do what?" She was distracted from Brigg's remarks when she noticed Caroline appear at the patio door, then begin threading her way forcefully in their direction. "Dance time again," Carla said hurriedly, grabbing Brigg's hand. He let her lead him through the other patio door, only once looking back over his shoulder in puzzlement.

"I have a hunch you're trying to keep me away from the delectable Caroline," he murmured into her ear as he drew her unnecessarily close.

"Suzannah doesn't like you treating her so condescendingly," Carla grunted, trying to loosen his hold.

"Suzannah doesn't like many things I do. Caroline loves it."

"Caroline's too stupid to know you're letting her make a fool of herself!"

"You said that, I didn't."

"Brigg!" Carla tried to struggle loose of his intimate hold, but with no success.

"Do you want to dance with me or not?"

"I want to go home. Suzannah's tired too." She had the wild feeling that this innocuous party was about to explode and that she would go with it.

"Well, in that case—I always like an honest woman." He released her readily and began elbowing a path for them. But somehow they got separated, and Carla reached Suzannah without Brigg.

"When your brother extricates himself from our intoxicated classmates, he's going to take us home," Carla explained belligerently, still feeling strangely ill at ease since discovering Brigg's mood. He had always been trouble when his hard, inquisitive mind started dissecting the superficialities of Suzannah's friends.

"Oh, great!" Carefully Suzannah lowered her heavy cast to the floor. "I've had fun, but enough is enough. My only regret about this party is that you and I haven't had much chance to talk. Are you certain you can't spend tomorrow out at the farm?"

"I promised the folks I'd call on several of their old friends and I just didn't have time today."

"Well, at least come out a little early before the party. We can talk while we help Mom. I'm absolutely going to break Brigg's neck!"

Carla began collecting the sweaters they hadn't needed, and didn't even try to decipher that change of subject. She had a desperate urge to get out of there before disaster struck.

"You know what his attitude reminds me of?" Suzannah mumbled, incensed.

Carla didn't answer, hoping Suzannah wouldn't go on.

"Don't you remember that time we were all dreaming of becoming actresses and we put on that play out in our barn?"

Suddenly visions of a party scene from a playlet flashed across Carla's memory. It was hazy—a bunch of adolescent girls dressed up in mothers' gowns and makeup, laughing shrilly and wiggling in what they envisioned as glamor personified. "We wrote that horrible play ourselves, didn't we?" she responded, momentarily caught up in the past. They had thought their depiction of a sophisticated city cocktail party was glorious.

"Don't you remember when we talked Brigg into seeing us rehearse, and he told us with a perfectly straight face that we were unparalleled at being vapid and vacuous?"

"I remember. Too well." Carla felt a terrible urge to giggle. It *had* been a horrible play.

"And we all thought he was complimenting us, Caroline especially," Suzannah continued angrily. "You were the only one who knew what vapid and vacuous meant. We couldn't believe it when you threw that ear of dried corn at him."

The glow was distinctly coming off the party. Other

memories were rushing up: her rage that Brigg had not liked their play, her frustration that even hitting him in the face with the corn had not made his hurt match hers. Instead he had seemed pleased that she had understood his barbed comment. Carla shook her head, unable to remember more, feeling suddenly flat. It was definitely time to go home. Finally she got Brigg's attention and held high their wraps, indicating she and Suzannah were ready to leave.

"I can't understand why he looks so bored with Caroline." Suzannah couldn't seem to leave her pet subject alone. "Mother and I thought they might get together, since Caroline divorced her second husband this summer."

"Brigg and Caroline together?" So that was the problem Suzannah was working on. Carla was shocked. A more unlikely combination she couldn't think of.

"Doesn't she remind you of Nancy? Just like her, I always thought."

"Nancy?"

"Brigg's wife. She was three years older than we, but surely you remember her arriving in town her senior year? She was little and happy, like Caroline."

Images of Nancy whirled in startling array. A tiny girl, features indistinct, but laughing, always laughing. Pretty—no, beautiful. And totally self-centered. Yes, very like Caroline. Except that in her young days, Caroline had been a loyal and honest friend.

Carla remembered one of the few occasions she had spent much time around Nancy, the year or so Nancy's family had lived in town. For a few months they were in a literature class together, mismatched because of the three year age difference, but Carla was stretching her capabilities beyond her grade level, and Nancy was making up a graduation requirement she had missed in frequent moves around the world with her military father. Nancy had groaned at Shakespeare, laughed at Jane Austen, and rebelled against reading *Silas Marner*. That did not distinguish her much from the rest of the students, except that she never voiced her boredom in class, only privately among the brighter boys. They devotedly completed her assignments for her, coached her for the tests, and she made a great impression on their charmed, elderly teacher without ever having read any of the required books.

Carla had figured out early that Nancy was one of the lovely takers of the world. On one occasion Nancy had made friends with several of the senior girls, helped them plan a huge bring-a-date party, and accepted money and responsibility for bringing the food. Then she had not shown up at all because she and her mother had gone clothes shopping at a new suburban mall in Chicago instead. Her own invited date had been stranded at her doorstep in his new suit, with flowers in his hand; and the party had proceeded solemnly, without any food or drink to help break the ice. Later Nancy had laughed off her friends' complaints by offering to show them her three new cashmere sweaters and two cruise dresses garnered out of her trip.

Carla remembered that she had tried to reserve her own judgment about Nancy's supposed predatory habits, because she knew high school girls resented any new, attractive competition; jealousy could create vicious, unfounded gossip. But it had seemed unnecessary, even to Carla, for Nancy to have systematically taken away the boyfriends of four of the cheerleaders and two of the senior class officers, only to drop all her male acquisitions when college students began arriving home for the summer, and pickings improved elsewhere.

And there had been Nancy's mother, too. She had shown up at every parent function that year, dressed fit for a Parisian embassy affair. Even after all these years Carla's face burned with indignation as she remembered the efforts of many well-meaning Shelbyville homemakers, her own frail mother included, to make the grand lady feel welcome. They had all been dismissed with vague, condescending smiles from both Nancy and her mother, who had laughed and visited together like best friends, apparently choosing self-imposed isolation as the only way to survive in the boonies.

After the first few months of getting acquainted with Nancy, Carla had accepted the obvious and avoided her. It had seemed to Carla that, unlike their group's own vapid and vacuous Caroline, friendly overtures from Nancy usually meant the girl wanted something done for her. But Carla had kept quiet about her own misgivings, for many of her friends, Suzannah included, had remained charmed by the beautiful, effervescent young woman.

To the adult Carla, the hazy memory of Nancy was still troubling. She had never thought before about Brigg's marriage. It had taken place in late summer after Carla's sophomore year, and by then Nancy had been gone from town for several months, and Brigg had rarely come home from his job. Carla and her parents had not even attended the wedding because they were vacationing in Colorado.

Brigg had seemed to pass out of Carla's existence after that, and she had never before questioned the logic of the new life he had chosen. But now it semed to her that such a marriage was totally out of character for the man she perceived Brigg had become. As she watched him approach, her thoughts rambled in an excruciating mixture of adult understanding and youthful censure.

Nancy, dead at twenty-one in a horseback riding accident, the girl who never grew up. But an adult Nancy would have been the epitome of vapid and vacuous; Carla was certain of it. She would have made Caroline seem selfless and brilliant by comparison.

Bizarrely it occurred to Carla that Brigg had probably been lucky that the vagaries of reality had taken Nancy from him; he hadn't had to discover what a bland and pointless home life they would have shared together. Carla knew from experience that such a discovery could be insidiously self-destructive.

Walking toward her, Brigg seemed to be looking into her soul, trying as in the past to read her thoughts. She tore her eyes away from his stormy ones, her face red with the embarrassment of her own mental temerity. How had she dared to pass judgment on this man's personal life, even in the quiet recesses of her musings?

Brigg and Suzannah took Carla home first. And Caroline was along this time, having attached herself to Brigg's arm to beg a ride for herself. Hoping to avoid a scene Carla hopped out of the back seat the instant they reached her motel. But Brigg was too fast for her—he sprang from behind the wheel and caught her hand.

"I always see my woman to the door," he said smoothly, his hand warningly tight on her protesting arm.

She didn't rise to the bait of "my woman." Brigg was up to something, she knew. She had her key ready, but when she tried to shove it in the lock, he stopped her.

"You haven't kissed me good night yet," he said mockingly. "Caroline has already kissed me good night three times, and we're not even at her front door."

"Go to hell."

His response was to place a hand on each side of her body, effectively trapping her against the shadowed doorframe. Then he slowly levered himself against her, his look intimate.

"You're being cruel. Caroline doesn't deserve this type of humiliation, especially not in front of Suzannah."

"Early in the evening I tried to turn Caroline off, and she ignored every tactful discouragement I made. She deserves anything she gets. And so do you, with your pious censure."

His kiss was heavy and long. When Carla tried to struggle, he turned her just enough so that her efforts would not be visible to the two women in his car.

Her mouth should have felt bruised and scratched from his beard, but he had been careful. It was a kiss for effect, and he had put nothing of himself in it. She felt emotionally violated.

Afterward he framed her face with his hands and began running his fingers through her hair, setting up a convincing picture of a fascinated man who couldn't stop handling her. Carla knew Suzannah and Caroline would be bewildered at his interest in her, for they could not feel his fury as she could.

When he kissed her again, Carla's adult composure completely left her. She felt as helpless as when she had been a child. Although Brigg had never touched her romantically in the past, he had so frequently outmatched her wits that the trapped feeling was equivalent. And, as always, she instinctively struck back the only way she knew—with words.

"Why take it out on Caroline because she's so much like your wife?" she snarled thoughtlessly when he finally freed her lips. "Or have you finally realized how lucky you—"

She was aghast the minute the foul statement began forming in her mouth. She was not a child anymore; she knew better. You didn't encroach on a man's privacy just because you were upset.

"Brigg, I didn't mean that," she stammered.

"You've never said anything you didn't mean, Carla," he snarled, his face set in ice. "So you're going to resume our old fights with the gloves off? Then you'd better be set for some hard punches yourself."

His hand went to the back of her neck and she felt his inescapable strength as he pulled her close once again. His kiss was long and almost ardent, like a lover's. But she gave him nothing of herself in return, too ashamed and hurt to react. She expected him to stalk off once he released her, but instead he brooded beside her, coldly watching her fumble to open the door, nodding politely as if nothing were wrong when she stepped inside, never unbalancing the intimate picture he had been creating to discourage Caroline.

His adherence to his original goal, even under stress, alarmed Carla. Her eyes were glazed with confusion as she watched him go to his car, and it was only when he had driven away, that she carefully closed and locked the door. She knew he was not through with her yet.

Chapter Two

"Mother, you've really left too much until the last minute this time," Suzannah observed with barely contained irritation. "You must have fifty slices of bread here for us to prepare, and there's the salad to make."

"I guess I'm just not as organized as I used to be, dear," Mrs. Carlyle soothed pleasantly, not at all perturbed that her menu was still not ready and her guests were due to arrive in twenty minutes.

Carla smiled to herself as she began trimming crusts off bread for finger sandwiches. Several hearty casseroles were already cooling on the back of the stove, their tempting odors filling the kitchen. It seemed exactly like old times. Mrs. Carlyle always had large and marvelous parties, but she did have a way of leaving many last-minute details undone, knowing that her guests would come expecting to help out.

"I got an extra pound of coffee, didn't I?" The frail woman looked absentmindedly around the room.

"Mother!" Suzannah appeared near the explosion point.

"If she really does intend to use the crystal goblets she has on the serving table, no one's going to want coffee, anyway," Carla whispered reassuringly. "The champagne will be too tempting in those lovely antiques."

"And there's that, too," Suzannah's worry was undiverted. "Mother, you know how rowdy our family and friends can get. Are you certain you want to use those goblets?"

"What's the value of having beautiful things if I never use them? I want to celebrate—it's been too many years since my son and daughter have both been home at the same time—"

"I thought Brigg had already gone back to Chicago." Carla didn't even realize she was interrupting as she fought to keep the distress out of her voice. Brigg hadn't been at the farm when she arrived, and she had avoided letting Suzannah corner her to talk about him.

"No way, Carla dear," the mockingly caressing words came from behind her as Brigg entered the kitchen with two bulging sacks of groceries in his arms. "I decided to drive Suzannah back to Kansas City myself."

Carla whirled to stare at him, her skin going suddenly cold. She hadn't counted on confronting Brigg this soon, and her mind whirled desperately, trying to anticipate his intentions. While she knew some sort of reckoning was inevitable, she wished she could have waited to face him in Chicago, away from this pervading nostalgia.

It must have taken only a few seconds for him to set down the groceries and begin strolling nonchalantly toward her. Speechlessly she watched him approach, her eyes focused on his bittersweet smile. Yet it seemed like a lifetime, with all sorts of desperate plans of escape fleeting across her consciousness, before the warmth of his mouth brushed her open lips.

"Oh, that's what I did about the coffee." Mrs. Carlyle seemed oblivious of the tension in the room while she pulled a can out of the sack. "Now I know what I really forgot. I wanted to cut some pyracantha and money plant for the hall table."

"I'll do that," Carla stammered, slipping from under Brigg's enveloping arm.

"But how are we going to get that salad done in time?" Suzannah was too concerned about the party to tackle the obvious undercurrents between her brother and her friend at that moment. "Mother doesn't even have the lettuce washed."

"Her guests will do it, as always." Brigg walked over to pat his mother on the shoulder, his challenging look at Carla notifying her he was only allowing her to escape him temporarily.

Carla grabbed some shears and a box that had apparently been laid out for the forgotten task, and swept past him without even a remote glance.

It was dusky and quiet outside, the hum of traffic from a highway two miles away only a faint whisper, little disturbing the normal night sounds of the country. The air was frosty, and the scent of wood smoke from the three fireplaces in the old farmhouse made Carla realize she had been foolish not to grab a wrap. Her soft silk dress had long sleeves, but the clinging material was thin and the neckline low, ill adapting to the cooler temperatures brought on since Friday's rain.

She hurried to the north side of the house where she remembered having seen the huge bushes with their bright orange berries. Then, pulling on the gloves which were in the box, she began to trim off long boughs of the thorny shrub. It was a slow process, for she had only the dim yard light and the glow from the farmhouse windows to guide her.

Although she was shivering as she worked, the task

felt comfortably familiar, and she wondered idly how many other times she had done odd jobs around this farmhouse after the sun had gone down but before the moon and stars had become bright enough to light the way of hesitant children. She and Suzannah had loved to play nighttime hide-and-seek under the trees to her right, feeling quite daring to be outside so late among sinister shadows, but enjoying the fact that their security was only as far away as those lighted windows.

How nice it would be if adults had that same security nearby. Annoyed at her thoughts, Carla decided that she had cut enough of the pyracantha. But Mrs. Carlyle had asked for money plant, too. Carla well remembered the transparent coinlike blooms, but she couldn't recall where they grew. Slowly she followed the bedding areas around a corner of the kitchen and toward the front of the house. The Carlyle family home was basically a two-story white frame structure, but its design defied architectural description, so many wings and screened porches having been added through various generations. It was near one of those jutting porches, the addition of which Carla herself remembered, that she found the plant.

Six or eight stalks should be enough, she thought as she set down the box and began feeling for long stems.

"What are you trying to do, freeze yourself?" Brigg's voice came from the darkness at the edge of the porch, just as she cut the last stalk. Startled, she jumped to her feet.

"Here, I brought you Dad's jacket." He touched her shoulder briefly to pinpoint her location before draping warm wool about her. Gratefully Carla shrugged into the coat, hugging it to her to calm her shaking. She had become very cold, but whether it was from the fall weather, or her own sense of doom, she couldn't honestly say.

"I should have finished before now, but I couldn't find where the money plant was."

"It doesn't matter. Mother's not too worried about the bouquets. She's drinking champagne and having fun while everyone else works."

"I have enough now. I'll get them arranged for the tables." She tried to move past Brigg, anxious to avoid any verbal confrontation on the night of Mrs. Carlyle's long anticipated party, but he was having none of her machinations.

"Surely you don't intend to avoid me all evening," he said tersely, blocking her way. "There must be several women coming tonight who will need your protection from me."

"Stop it, Brigg."

"Stop it, Brigg!" he mocked, raising an eyebrow. "You can dish it out, but you can't take it, is that it?"

"I've already admitted I was way out of line last night." Carla tried to keep her voice under control. It would never do for him to realize how terribly he unnerved her. "I apologize again, Brigg. Most sincerely."

His jaw was clenched as he stood close to her, taking in every detail of her appearance in the soft island of light amid the autumn blackness. He studied the way her hair fell in soft waves against the roughness of his father's jacket, the flow of her dark blue dress, dark as the night, along her curved thighs. His inscrutable gaze roved down the long legs to her delicate, high heeled Italian shoes, then back up to where the skillfully closed neckline suggested the fullness of her breasts. Too many people had complimented her whenever she wore the dress for her to doubt that she looked good. But Brigg's critical, cold eyes made certain she understood that he, personally, found her appearance lacking.

She drew a shuddering breath. "I feel as if you've declared war." The words came out without her realizing it.

"Perhaps I have," he mused cruelly, seemingly intrigued by the statement. She watched the way his lips moved within the irregular frame of his beard. Even in the shadows she could sense the unyielding planes of his face.

"Then I decline the declaration," she said. "You win. I have no war to fight with you, Brigg."

"I have no feeling, from reading those very expressive eyes of yours, that you disbelieve what you said last night."

Carla knew she should claim having had too much to drink. Anything. Yet she hesitated, her comparisons between Nancy and Caroline so real once again that her innate honesty stalled what should have been an immediate denial.

"Again, I'm deeply sorry for what I said, Brigg." That was the best she could get past her lips.

His eyes narrowed. "I may as well know the full extent of your ammunition, dear enemy," he said carefully. "Why don't you spit it all out, those ugly thoughts of yours?"

Somehow Carla couldn't imagine herself having a conversation like this with any other man in the world. His determination to understand her thoughts had always been his real power over her. She sighed in resignation.

"You want all the garbage on the table, then, to crucify us both? You want me to say I always did think Nancy was a vain and boring fool? That you deserved a life of adult hell, if you were such a simpleton to have married her in the first place?" Her voice was harsh, but she saw no quicker way to shock him into calling this subtle war off than to overstate the situation. There were tears in her eyes when she realized that despite her desperate audacity, he was not going to give an inch. "I at least had an excuse last night, Brigg," she said in ultimate weariness. "I spoke as an awkward girl reacting to a maturity she didn't understand. It was an automatic reversion to the old days when you could intimidate me. But—"

"You've changed a great deal since the old days, Carla." He slid his hand to the back of her neck, turning her so that he could see her better in the indefinite light.

"I would hope so—I'm thirty-three years old. I won't revert again, Brigg; you'll be dealing with a woman from now on, so don't expect me to play patsy to your self-destructive games."

She succeeded in pulling out of his grasp, and walked carefully back through the darkness to the kitchen, the box of cuttings clutched against the heavy jacket. She was proud of herself that she managed to move slowly, even though her heart was racing with anguished confusion.

Carla didn't plan to try avoiding Brigg throughout the evening. She felt confident that he would never create a scene that might ruin his mother's party. And, at first, her conclusion appeared accurate. He wandered in and out of the kitchen on various tasks while she arranged the cuttings into two bouquets. And when she placed one of them on the dining room table where he was serving champagne, he included her in the conversation with arriving guests as casually as if nothing cataclysmal was developing between them. Perhaps that was why she had her guard down when he found her alone.

Mrs. Carlyle had asked her to leave a platter of snacks in the all-weather porch off the family room. When Carla stepped into the glassed area, she realized that all the furniture had been moved out, apparently to provide room for dancing later. She set the tray back in the adjoining room, then went to the large closet, which had been niched into a corner of the porch, thinking she might find an occasional table stored there.

Brigg found her helplessly twirling the handle of the locked closet. "I'm passing out champagne," he said in his most civilized voice, as if nothing had gone on between them before.

Carla studied him in surprise, letting her hand fall from the knob. The dark porch was partially covered with thick vines that cast wavering shadows across the two of them from the reflections of the yard light, so it was hard to gauge Brigg's expression.

"I see your mother didn't change her mind about using the antique goblets," she eventually said softly as she watched him stroll slowly toward her, two of the lovely glasses Suzannah had been so concerned about in his big hands.

"Impressive, aren't they?" he asked, holding them up so the sparse rays of light could catch their rainbow prisms. The conversation seemed too civilized to be real.

"They must be family heirlooms." The comment was redundant, but Carla could think of nothing else. She was startled when he handed her both the brimming goblets.

"No place to set them," he responded to her questioning look. "I'll have to bring a table out later."

"What am I supposed to do with two?" She was feeling calm, since he was behaving so acceptably, but she could not stop herself from stepping back slightly as he moved toward her. The movement caused the two glasses to touch, and she flinched at the resulting golden tone only true crystal can produce. "I'd die if I broke these," she blurted, looking closely at the glasses in the dim light to reassure herself she had not caused a chip or crack.

"I thought you might feel that way," he said oddly, beginning to fumble in his pocket.

She felt awkward, having no choice but to hold the precious goblets while he pulled out horn rimmed glasses and put them on before looking her over carefully.

"Have I told you you look nice tonight?"

It was a reasonable statement. Although her dress was in its fourth season, the style was classic; and she knew the neckline, while designed with a self-bra so that it could be slit to the waist, also looked elegant closed, as she preferred. But she watched him curiously, suspecting that he thought nothing of the kind.

"You've become quite a woman, Giant Child." Brigg's eyes rested at the point on the neckline where she had tucked the tiny safety pin.

"And you look very professorlike," she said resentfully, thrusting one of the champagne glasses toward him. "As if you're an entomologist examining a bug."

He grinned at her, still not taking the wine she was offering. "I'll have the champagne in a moment. Actually I can't think of a tactful way to tell you your neckline needs some rearranging."

Carla was horrified, realizing that the pin must have come undone. The dress could be extremely revealing, and she had never had the nerve to wear it open, despite Charles's pressuring. She was not ashamed of her voluptuous body, but she preferred not to display it to the general public.

"Hold these goblets," she pleaded. "I'd better—"

"You can't see to fix it. I'll repair you." He reached underneath her thick hair to remove her gold necklace, which he slipped into his pocket.

Anxious to have the neckline corrected before any of the guests she could hear nearby joined them on the porch, it didn't occur to Carla to be suspicious. She stood obediently, carefully trying not to spill the two servings of champagne, as he slipped his fingers inside the dress and removed the pin.

"Yes, quite a woman." She could barely hear the whispered words before she felt his fingers slide all the way down to her waist, spreading slightly apart the folds of the dress. He studied the situation for some moments, and she impatiently waited for him to continue his task to reclose the neckline. But, instead, he pocketed his glasses before walking over to the entrance of the porch and called for a passing group of guests to join them.

Disbelieving, she watched him turn back and bring the others with him. The eyes of his guests widened visibly when they saw her standing in the shadows with a wineglass in each hand. She didn't dare look down, but the feel of cool air against her exposed skin told her that her shapeliness was well suggested in the inch or so gap he had created all the way to her waist.

"I think I have the clasp of your necklace repaired, gorgeous," he further shocked her by saying in an outrageously sensuous tone before moving close behind her and lifting her hair from her neck. All eyes followed the fall of the necklace as he slid it teasingly up and down her cleavage.

"That's the way that dress was meant to be worn,"

he whispered against her ear when he bent over to complete fastening the necklace. "You're so proud of being a woman, then be one!"

When he slipped an arm possessively around her waist, her hands trembled enough to spill champagne at her feet. Somehow she managed to acknowledge the introductions he made, and tried not to flinch when many expressed surprise at how sophisticated the girl they remembered as Carla had become.

"Ah, but you can see that she has grown up," Brigg commented with a suggestive warmth in his voice that had them all chuckling at his blatancy. His hand tightened at her waist when he finally took his own glass from her, and she knew he was warning her that if she tried to move away he would not be above keeping a hand on the fabric, widening the bodice opening in certain disaster. Defeated, she lifted her chin high and maintained a remote smile.

Brigg made the rest of her evening miserable. He gave her no chance to slip away to repair her dress. He was either hulking possessively at her side every moment, or holding her hand, leading her first into one room, then another, making certain that everyone at the party saw the glamorous Carla and knew he had staked a claim on her. The conversation in her presence became extremely awkward. Even the women couldn't seem to decide where to put their eyes. They focused on her forehead, over her shoulder, anywhere but toward the gold necklace or lower. Her flaunted sexuality with Brigg made them uncomfortable, for such things were just not done in Shelbyville.

Suzannah was openly amazed at the development. Carla had never seen her without words before. But Mrs. Carlyle, the gentle, trusting soul, seemed unaware of what was going on. She asked Brigg to bring out the polka records, but he said quite loudly that he would do so only if Carla would give him the first dance. And his mother had assured him enthusiastically that, of course, dear Carla would. That was when Carla knew she would have to leave.

There was no way she could polka, when even her slightest movement tested the determination of the silk to continue covering her quivering fullness. Her dancing would turn Mrs. Carlyle's party into a strip show. She would not let Brigg do that, even to satisfy his apparent need for revenge.

Suzannah had gone with him to get the records, thus giving Carla the ideal time to escape. She delivered her thanks and good-byes to Brigg's father and fled.

When she was back in her motel, she realized that it made no sense to remain in town any longer. She could not be certain that Brigg would not eventually come to her room to continue his battle, and she felt that she had paid enough for her presumptuous remarks of the night before.

It took her less than fifteen minutes to throw her things into her suitcase, check out, and start driving toward the darkened highway.

There were few stars, and the state road out of Shelbyville was almost deserted. Carla didn't begin to have her thoughts together by the time she had covered the nearly thirty miles to the interchange at Mattoon, so she drove right on past the busy service stations and motels to join the light stream of traffic heading north on the interstate highway.

Later she considered staying somewhere for the night, but when she reached Champaign-Urbana, which would have been a good choice, she had gotten a second wind and decided against stopping, even for gas.

All she could think about was Brigg Carlyle. She

couldn't say he had ruined everything about her reunion; she had to share some of the blame. But she cursed him for creating her predatory image at his family's party, an image that would not be easily forgotten in Shelbyville. Her flesh began to burn as she recalled how he had exposed her to his guests, casting her in a sensuous role she would never have assumed, and, in a vindictive game, taking the matching part for himself.

It was getting too warm in the car with the heater on, and gripping the steering wheel with one hand, Carla shrugged out of the coat she had thrown on so hastily. Her dress still gaped to the waist, and at that moment she was sorry she had not taken time to change. She was looking around the car seat for her purse, hoping she had an extra pin handy to fasten the dress shut for her own peace of mind, when she saw the gas needle out of the corner of her eye.

Empty? Not for the first time she wished she had kept her own smaller car when they had divorced, but Charles's business had been in financial trouble, so she had agreed to take over the hefty payments on his Cadillac. Gas guzzler!

She glanced at her watch, angrily castigating herself for being so careless. It was well after one o'clock, and many of the rural interchange stations might not be open this late, even on a Saturday night.

Easing her foot off the pedal to set her speed at the most gas conserving, Carla tried to relax, but within five minutes, sputterings warned her just in time to pull off on the shoulder before the engine died.

It was a bizarre situation, made worse in her own mind because she was still wearing that ridiculous dress. As the occasional car sped by, she decided that she had two choices: sit and wait for help, as experts advised women to do in this situation, or start walking. Carla was not a woman of inaction, and when she surveyed the countryside around her and thought she saw the glow of lighted buildings over the next hill, she decided on walking.

She pulled the coat back on, regretting that it wasn't practical to change her dress in the car. But she felt better once she unearthed a safety pin from her purse to pin her neckline up and changed into the flat shoes she kept under the front seat for bad weather.

It would have been easiest to walk along the shoulder, but she felt too exposed there, not at all certain that someone stopping would be a genuine Good Samaritan. So she climbed up to the fence line, where the brush left as forage for wildlife shielded her from the headlights of passing motorists.

She was in luck. When she got to the top of the hill, she could see a lone service station another half mile away at the next interchange. And it was open. Carla covered the remaining distance quickly and was relieved to find an elderly man still running the self-service facility. He was unable to leave his post to help her, but he called his grandson who lived on a farm nearby, and the young man quickly came to drive her back to her car. Carla's relief when her gas tank was finally refilled was immense, and she pressed generous wads of bills into their hands, agreeing wholeheartedly with the lecture the old man gave her on her carelessness.

Running out of gas probably cost her a couple of hours. And a good bit of new gray hair, Carla admitted, once she was safely back on the road. When she finally entered the outskirts of Chicago, she was exhausted and gained none of her usual pleasure in the night sights of her city. All she wanted was to get home.

She didn't even have the energy to look at the clock when she finally let herself into her apartment. But, blessedly, she also didn't have the energy to think.

It wasn't exactly a scuffling sound that woke her. Restlessly Carla tossed between the soft sheets, finding no comfort in her rumpled bed. She must have been half dozing when the sound came again, not exactly a knock, but at least a firm, pressured sound, perhaps a person walking softly? The doorbell clinched it. Someone wanted to get into her apartment.

Cautiously she slid out of bed and pulled on a robe, knowing from the way her body felt that she had not been asleep long. Perhaps only minutes.

Barefoot she padded quietly through the darkened living room, careful not to hit any furniture. She wasn't exactly afraid, for she told herself that perhaps one of her neighbors had seen her come in. Several people left for work quite early, and it was possible that they needed her help with car trouble.

"What's wrong? It's five in the morning," she called through the closed door.

"It's five thirty. And quit shouting, Carla. Do you want to wake all your neighbors?"

She froze, her whole body instantly identifying that voice. Damn him. Following her all the way back.

"Go away, Brigg," she ordered.

"You know I'm not going to do that." He began to knock louder. Carla was determined not to let him in, but she had second thoughts when she heard a man's voice from across the hall threatening to call the police.

"Go ahead and call them," she could hear Brigg respond. "I'm staying here until my girl friend lets me in. She sounded depressed on the phone and I'm afraid she'll—"

"Get in here!" Carla threw off the night latch and reached out to jerk Brigg inside. She started to close the door behind him, then, on second thought, looked toward the furious neighbor. Unfortunately he was one she had not met before.

"It's all right," she assured the man. "We won't bother you anymore."

"You're not committing suicide, are you, lady?" he asked anxiously, easing his door closed as if the thought might be contagious.

Brigg stuck his head out over her shoulder. "Don't worry about a thing. I'll take care of her now."

Carla pulled him back into her apartment and slammed the door, but said nothing to him, her anger making her afraid to trust her words. She stalked into the kitchen, not even pausing to light a lamp to help Brigg find his way.

The city lights visible from her window illuminated all the familiar things—her stove, the small booth for snacking, the work island. She had gone there just to get away from him, but it felt good to be in woman's age-old kingdom, and she decided to remain there to face Brigg. She would take any advantage she could get. Perching up on a stool near the island, she wearily leaned her head against the wall.

Carla knew he was looming in the doorway, because he had found a lamp in the living room to turn on, and it cast his shadow over her bare feet. But she refused to look at him.

"Planning to make me a cup of coffee?" he asked sarcastically.

"No way."

"Thank you, Brigg, for being so worried about me," he continued in the same mocking tone of voice. "Yes,

I made it home just fine, Brigg. Too bad you had to make the drive for nothing, with Suzannah still at the farm and needing a ride to Kansas City tomorrow."

Even with her eyes stubbornly down, she could still sense him coming toward her. The shadow of his bristly beard moved up her bare leg and across the fold of her robe. In fascination she watched that distinct shape of his profile halt just short of her waist.

"Why the sudden concern, Brigg?" Her eyes moved to the region of his knees.

"Are you all right?" He grasped her chin, making her look at him. The concern in his voice sounded genuine, and the fact that his fingers along her throat were trembling slightly made her believe he had actually been worried. That struck her as odd.

Abruptly she shook off his hand and moved from her perch. "I was fine until five minutes ago. I am a competent driver," she muttered. "Do you really want some coffee before you leave?"

"I don't know," Brigg exclaimed wearily and sank to the stool she had vacated. When he leaned his head back as she had done, closing his eyes, she studied him for a brief moment. There was a white break in his tan just under his chin, where the beard kept the sun from reaching. It made him look defenseless, and she found she didn't like that. Angrily she turned away, still making no effort to produce coffee.

"How did you know where I live?"

"For some reason I had gotten your address from Suzannah after I ran into you out at the cemetery. I guess I had decided I might look you up some day, since we've both been living here so long. The idea had never occurred to me before."

Carla had no answer for that; since her marriage she

had lived in Chicago except for one year when Charles was opening the branch in Detroit, yet had never asked Suzannah for Brigg's address, either.

"Driving back here alone at night was a stupid thing to do, you know." He still had his eyes shut. "I've been watching for your car along the side of the road—you could have had a flat tire, engine trouble, anything."

Warn me about stupidity, Carla thought wryly, knowing she would never tell him what had really happened on that unreal drive back to Chicago. Running out of gas was so preventable. She had never before let it happen to her.

"When I learned you had checked out and headed toward the highway, I figured you'd spend the night nearby."

"I thought about it."

"I didn't spot your car at any of the motels in the next three interchanges so I stopped at a phone booth to get your home number from information in Chicago, thinking I'd go back to the farm and give you a ring later to make sure you got in okay. Why is your phone unlisted?"

"Any divorcee can tell you. The minute the legal notice is public, you start getting kook calls and heavy breathing. It's a nuisance you don't need at a time like that."

It seemed an effort for him to lift his head from the wall to look at her. "What time is it?"

Carla glanced at the digital clock on the stove. "As you said, five thirty."

He leaned down and began pulling off first one huge brown loafer, then the other.

"What are you doing?"

"Heading for your couch. I told Suzannah I'd pick

her up at the farm around noon, so that gives me two or so hours to sleep. I'll lose an hour of that if I drive over to my house."

"How logical. Any chance of asking my permission, since it's my reputation you've been bandying about tonight?"

"I think we're a little beyond that, aren't we, Carla?"

She refused to answer. Instead she walked back into the living room to look at the couch. She barely fit into its length; Brigg would pour out both ends. She clutched her arms about her, frowning when he brushed past her and sank down into the deep cushions.

"Won't your family be worried?"

"You mean the folks?"

"Of course. Weren't you sleeping out at the farm?"

"Since I told Suzannah I was leaving the party to go to your motel, they'll undoubtedly assume I'm quite safe."

"You fool! You mess up my dress so I look like a predator before half the town, then you indicate I've invited you to my motel. My parents are going to love the gossip they'll be hearing from their old friends in Shelbyville."

He got up and followed her as she walked toward a hall closet.

"Does that really bother you?" Brigg appeared genuinely surprised.

"You mean at my mature age? Yes, it does bother me, since my parents, elderly as they are, still think of me as their little girl. I don't appreciate being put in the position of causing them embarrassment."

He reached a huge hand to her face to wipe at a tear with his thumb. "Good Lord," he said wonderingly, not quite believing the salty moisture he discovered there.

"It's too late to worry about it now." Carla thrust a pillow and a stack of linens at him. "You'll never wedge yourself into that couch. There's an extra bed in the room at the end of the hall."

He didn't argue with her offer.

Once he began thumping around in the guest room, Carla laid aside her robe and crawled back into her own bed, thinking how conflicting were the auras surrounding any association with Brigg. There was incredible tension, yet she felt secure to know he was there with her.

As she had been driving back from Shelbyville she had gone over and over the situation in her mind. And while she could not escape the conclusion that she had been terribly presumptuous to an old friend, there had to be more than that behind Brigg's explosive reaction to her words. She wondered if perhaps he had never sorted out his feelings about Nancy. Carla knew from experience that reckoning with old hurts and emotions could not be put off forever. The wounds festered.

She got up again and pulled on her robe, then thoughtfully sat down. Instinct told her she could help him. Hadn't facing the hurtful truth about her life with Charles been the best thing she had ever done? But on the other hand, she wondered if one should, or even could, force someone else to grapple with his own bitter thoughts. Indecisive, she remained poised on the edge of her bed.

It grew quiet in her apartment. Brigg had turned off all the lights except a small night fixture in the guest bathroom. Its glow made a vague fan shape across the hall carpet, a shape that she saw his shadow fill even before she heard him approach.

"About last night, Carla—" He was standing hesitantly in her doorway, and she could tell he was trying to adjust his eyes to the darkness within her room.

"Yes?"

"You know, of course, that it was more than just what you said?"

"Yes."

He stepped inside her door, but did not walk to her side. "You raised questions I had shoved to the back of my mind for years. They were painful to handle."

"I had no right to do that."

"Maybe it was for the best. I've bottled the guilt of how I felt about Nancy inside too long."

"It takes one to know one, Brigg," she said quietly.

"What?"

"I loved Charles—my husband. I still do in some ways. When we first married, he wanted me to keep working and pour everything I earned into expanding his office supply business. That made sense, but I looked forward to the day when we would be financially secure enough for me to stay home and raise our children. Gradually, though, I realized that when he could afford for me to quit, he planned to dress me in a style befitting his position and send me out socializing to enhance his image. I knew he loved me as much as he could love anyone, so I tried to become what he wanted me to be. But he was so insecure. It became apparent that no matter how hard or long we both worked, he would never feel successful enough."

Carla paused in her painful reflections, gathering her courage to continue. "About seven years after we married, Charles became seriously ill. It horrified me that when the doctors diagnosed leukemia, my first reaction was one of relief. I could hardly face that I would welcome the death of my husband as the only solution to my unhappy marriage. As it turned out, he had a rare form of anemia. I left him the day after the doctor told us he was completely cured. There had never been a divorce on either side of our family, and I don't believe my parents will ever understand my decision. It almost destroyed them."

Brigg had no doubt that the divorce had almost destroyed her, too. He realized, then, why she had been concerned what her frail parents might hear about her weekend in Shelbyville. They wouldn't understand that, either. Watching the shadowed sadness in her expression as her thoughts wandered, he suddenly wanted to talk.

"Nancy was so young," he began tentatively. He felt her eyes return to his face. "And she was cheerful all the time, which was what attracted me to her. Right after I finished studying engineering, my uncle had helped finance my partnership with two older friends, and our chemical plant construction business was going almost too well. I was working incredible hours and traveling all over the world. But I guess, to Nancy, that was appealing. She'd lived abroad herself before her father was sent to Shelbyville as an army recruiter. I met her at a party when I was home between foreign assignments, and she was ecstatic when I suggested taking her into the big city of Chicago for a date. She was advanced for her age when it came to men, but that suited me; I didn't have a lot of time for the getting-acquainted niceties. After her high school graduation, her father retired to Chicago, and I looked them up anytime I was back between jobs.

"I lived in a tiny apartment then and was refurbishing a town house I had bought when I was at the University of Chicago. A number of us students had invested in deteriorating homes and were fixing them up for rental. I had completed all the construction work to make it into two self-contained apartments when Nancy's father died. She began coming over to help me decorate it, and the relationship became extremely convenient. Before meeting her I had frequently come back from a job to learn that I would either have to placate my current 'neglected' girl friend, or look for a new, quick bedmate. With Nancy I never had that problem. She and her mother were close and did lots of things together, like sisters, so she wasn't bored when I was gone for long periods of time. We had been sleeping together almost from the first, and somehow we just drifted into marriage. The house was a perfect place for us to settle—her mother took the downstairs apartment, and Nancy and I the other two floors; I could do the work I loved, yet occasionally come home to a little peace and pleasure. It seemed the best of both worlds."

Carla shuddered, appalled that Brigg had expected so little upon entering marriage. "And did Nancy adapt to what you had to offer?" she asked curiously.

"Very well. She furnished the house to her taste and spent every dime I regularly deposited for her, but never asked for more. Neither did her mother."

"You supported her mother?"

"Someone had to help; her government pension couldn't maintain her life-style, and I knew Nancy couldn't be happy if her mother was in need. I even bought them a couple of horses and stabled them nearby because they missed riding at the army stables so much. They played around a lot together, but whenever I was home, Nancy spent most of her time with me. The life suited us both at first."

Carla shuddered again. That life-style would also have been perfect for Charles: an undemanding woman to stay out of his way, to entertain herself, wear gorgeous clothes while meeting all the best people, keep his house decorated and his bed warm when his sexual urge could no longer be denied. But for Brigg? She was surprised he had settled for that.

"We were careless, though. Nancy got pregnant just a few months after we were married, and I found my attitude changing. I tried to get home more frequently at the end of her pregnancy, but she didn't seem to need that attention. In fact, at times, I felt my presence was inconveniencing her social schedule."

"And after the girls were born?"

"We hired a day nursemaid; caring for them fulltime seemed too much for either Nancy or her mother. Nancy loved Jane and Ann, but more as if they were toys than her own children. She would have them all dressed up to show off to me when I would get home, and we would take them for a walk together. Then she would be through with motherhood for the rest of my stay.

"I began to think that since we had gotten ourselves a family, it was time we started acting like one. I finished up a job in Belgium and arranged to take a couple of months off, thinking Nancy and I could make some adjustments together.

"I suppose even though I offered to spend more time at home, I still expected Nancy to take most of the load of parenthood. Anyway she certainly didn't want to talk about changing our life-style. After I had been there a couple of weeks, Nancy insisted on going horseback riding with her mother. The doctor had just okayed resuming that kind of exercise, and she had bought a riding habit to show off her newly slim figure. I remember that it was a Sunday and the day maid was off. The girls were a little over three months old, and it was my first time caring for them alone, but I learned fast in those few hours. I was all set to show off my great baby-sitting abilities when Nancy returned home—" He stopped, his voice hardening.

Carla waited patiently, wondering if the ensuing argument had been so devastating that it still hurt to think about it.

"She never came home," he finally said bluntly. "Her horse threw her and she broke her neck. Death was instantaneous."

Carla's expression tightened in sympathy as she imagined his shock.

"It seemed impossible that such a young, vigorous person could die like that. I felt as if I'd done something to cause it. For years I couldn't erase from my mind how happy she had looked when she had left the house. I never really faced another memory of Nancy. That last morning she had thrown a hysterical fit, ranting that being around the twins was exhausting her, and begging me to get her a weekend maid and night nurse, too. Once I had agreed to look into it, she became perfectly cheerful again and made her plans to go off with her mother. I was furious all afternoon. I doubted that she'd ever grow up, believed she'd be as irresponsible and empty as her mother, and try to play me the rest of our lives. Show off my baby-sitting abilities to her when she returned? I was going to give her hell. When you started comparing her to that obscene Caroline, it brought all the old guilt to the surface."

Brigg ran his hand up over his scalp, an unconscious gesture from when he had had thick hair. Nothing could have emphasized more his aging and his maturity.

"She might have changed, Brigg."

"I doubt it. She was a carbon copy of her mother,

who certainly felt no adult responsibility for the girls. She cleared out the week after Nancy's funeral. Took all the furniture I'd bought her and went to sponge on a distant relative. I guess she was afraid that if she continued to live off me, she'd also be expected to help supervise the care of her granddaughters.''

"What on earth did you do?" Carla could picture how distressing it would have been to have such a problem so suddenly thrust on him. He had been relatively young himself then. Twenty-six or so.

"Mother and Dad came up and stayed for a few weeks. They wanted to take the girls back to the farm, but I felt that my daughters should have a home of their own, even if I wouldn't be there with them too much. By the time my vacation was up, I had been able to locate a good full-time nurse and a housekeeper. But if the folks hadn't been able to make frequent trips to Chicago and check on things those first few years I would never have been able to keep Jane and Ann."

He had sagged against the wall as he talked, and it hurt Carla to see him so drained.

"Brigg, I should never have said what I did about your marriage." She quelled the impulse to go take him in her arms. Already she had presumed too much on old childhood friendship, and she didn't want to repeat her mistake. This man, she gradually was realizing, was not dear old obnoxious Brig; he was Brigg with two g's, and almost a stranger.

"Lord, this has been some weekend." He swung away from the wall and looked at her bleakly. "I thought I was going to do a harmless good turn for my little sister. And then you showed up. I feel as if I've survived a match with an exorcist."

"I haven't exactly escaped unscathed," she pointed out bluntly.

"It's a mistake to stir up the past."
"Go to bed, Brigg."
He stood looking at her in the semidarkness for some seconds before returning to his room.

The next morning he was gone when Carla awakened. There was not even a note.

Chapter Three

Monday was the pits. Even worse than the dreary Sunday Carla had spent alone.

She realized later that she should have expected a bad Monday at work, because her body had tried to prepare her for trouble the minute she walked in the school door. She was too aware of things.

Carla's strangely acute senses had picked up the smell of fresh paint, an indication that workmen had finally redone the peeling auditorium walls during the Thanksgiving break. And from the warm air wafting out of the kitchen, she could predict that there would be chicken casserole in the school lunchroom that day, the kind with the sticky rice and the peculiar bits of artificial pimiento the children always left strewn around on their plates. She noticed the reflections off the vinyl floor in the secretary's office, and realized the heavily used surface had been recoated over the holiday. Her ears even told her that the level of giggling voices and shuffling feet on the back playground was too quiet, that the second bus must be late in depositing its children.

That increased sensitivity should have prepared her to expect disaster when the school's address system crackled overhead, and the secretary asked her to come to the principal's office before the children arrived. But it didn't.

It was still a shock to have learned that she had lost her teaching job. The principal had received the board's financial plans for the next semester; there was no money to create a post for the tenured teacher who was returning after illness, so Carla was being laid off at the end of December.

"I can't believe the board's stupidity in letting our best teacher go," her harried superior ranted. "Your students display the finest improvement in reading the district has seen in years, and yet the board won't change its tenure policy and decide this on merit. There's no other nontenured classroom teacher left in the district to bump, so out you go. It's insane."

Suzannah would agree, Carla thought involuntarily. "I didn't think they'd do it," she admitted aloud, the implication finally sinking in. "I knew it *could* happen, but—they're really going to change my little second graders over to another teacher in midyear?"

"Unbelievable, isn't it," the man agreed, sinking down behind his desk to look at her solemnly. He had been fighting the arbitrary cutbacks in his staff on the basis of seniority ever since the school board had issued its edict, and he had been especially anxious to keep Carla.

"I have one hope of keeping you," he said pensively. "There's a possibility I can offer you a nonteaching job for the rest of the year, which would buy us some time. I might even know about that by the end of today."

Carla was so devastated that she didn't even register his remark. Almost in a daze she returned to her classroom. Not teach anymore? The prospect was unacceptable. Teaching had been her salvation. Not for the money, of course. In the summers she made almost half as much as her entire teaching salary, just filling in as vacation executive secretary for her old boss. And he wanted her back full-time.

It was the children she needed, and the sense of accomplishment in seeing their young minds develop. Teaching had given her a feeling of purpose that her marriage had taken away from her, and if she lost that purpose she didn't know if she could pick up the pieces of her life yet another time. One could adjust only so much....

Carla continued through the day in that shocked daze. She did her best to conquer her dejection, but the children, always an accurate barometer measuring the reactions of adults, knew something was wrong. And they responded accordingly, becoming testy and noisy themselves. It was all Carla could do to keep classroom discipline without creating an unpleasant scene.

She had just dismissed the final lingerer, and was mechanically getting her things together to go home, when the squawking intercom called her back to the principal for another meeting. It was stiflingly warm in the outer office when she arrived, so while she waited for him to finish a conference with a mother who was worried about school bus safety, she loosened the collar of her shirtwaist blouse and contemplated the inefficiencies of public spending. It seemed to her reasonable to expect heating systems in schools to be as well adjusted as in commercial establishments; that children in one room should not have to be reaching for sweaters, while their younger brothers in another were peeling off jackets to escape the overheating. Yet such a situation was common in their supposedly well-designed school. And in the late spring, when the sunny days began to make the one-story box structure an oven, no air conditioning or attic ventilating system seemed affordable. Children were expected to learn despite the intense heat.

Carla's thoughts rambled on, recalling the many difficulties she struggled with daily from what she felt were unwise spending priorities, yet skirting the critical one, the very existence of her job. She scarcely noticed the children rushing in and out with their usual last-minute emergencies, or the strident voice of the upset mother in the office beyond. It all seemed somehow irrelevant.

It was another fifteen minutes before the mother finally emerged from her conference, apparently calmed at last.

"I couldn't save your classroom job," the principal explained with regret once they were settled privately in his office, "but—"

"I understood that this morning," Carla assured him. "I don't blame you."

"No, I mean this new position I'm trying to create. But I can offer you a three-quarter time job as a reading supervisor for the rest of the year. You would be getting somewhat less total pay, without benefits and accumulation toward tenure."

"Reading supervisor?" Carla asked curiously, for the moment setting aside the negative aspects of the job offer. "Since when did our school ever rate a reading supervisor?"

"Since the superintendent has been hearing your praises from me and parents of your former students. Any exception to tenure policy might open the doors for lawsuits from teachers who have been cut. But the board did agree to let the superintendent channel some of his government grant money into this position. No one wants to let you go, Carla."

But they're doing it. "I'm not certain I would want to remain as an adviser. I'm a teacher."

"And that's what I want you to do. Since the superintendent left your job description up to me, I'd like to assign you a regular number of students in grades three through five to work with."

"If you wait until they have problems and then just give them to me a few minutes each day, I don't know that I can help them. You know I incorporate reading skills into every aspect of my classroom instruction."

"Actually I was thinking more in terms of team teaching. One of the third grade teachers is particularly strong in math, and two of the fifth grade teachers lean heavily to social studies. I've already felt them out on this. They would welcome having formal reading instruction off their shoulders so they could work in smaller groups in their own fields. And all the classroom teachers would be willing to consult with you on ways your reading methods could be incorporated into their own classroom activities."

"That's generous of them," she stammered, genuinely touched.

"You may not be aware of how highly your skills are regarded by your colleagues. Several of us are pushing for the board to adopt a viable merit program to supplement tenure," he admitted. "Job security is important, but when we have to face letting qualified people like you go just because someone else has worked here longer..." He fiddled with the pencil on his desk. "Frankly, you stand to lose a lot with this temporary job offer. But the board promised me that if they can find the money they'll eventually upgrade you to full-time status with benefits and tenure accumulation."

Unable to shake her disappointment that her skills would be so little valued by those in charge of the district's financing, Carla was tempted to tell him that she preferred to return to secretarial work, where her contributions were appreciated. But he was so earnestly persuasive that she left the school promising to think about the supervisory job.

She was greatly shaken, and the drive home was equally as tense as the weekend's return from Shelbyville had been.

While Carla was fighting Chicago traffic and her own turbulent thoughts, Brigg Carlyle was making his second drive from Shelbyville to Chicago in as many days. This time via Kansas City. He was tired, but far from tense; more accurately, he was boyishly jubilant. All because he had discovered Carla, his Giant Child, again.

Discovered that little big girl he had never quite forgotten, yet never let himself remember, either. For he had thought she was married and out of his reach. Years ago he'd even quit asking Suzannah about her, for as he became more jaded and lonely in his maturity, he thought it better not to dwell futilely on the old friendship that had always threatened to be more than that—might have been, had she not been so much younger than he.

For some reason scenes from her tenth birthday party came to him, and he laughed aloud. Carla had been his devoted slave then. The intricacies of her adolescence had not yet fueled that strange, argumentative tension that later existed between them. He recalled that he had been home from college for the weekend, and Suzannah had wanted him to put up a tire swing for a surprise party Carla's parents and his own had planned to give her at the farm. The day before the big event Carla had come home with Suzannah to spend the night, thinking she would be attending a family luncheon the next afternoon. She had hunted him down in his father's workshop and announced that she was there to help him with whatever needed doing.

He remembered that all the time he was selecting the right rope and cleaning off the only big tire he could find, she had chattered on about the new dress her mother had packed for her to wear at his family's luncheon. She had been quite worried about whether the dress would look just right, because Suzannah had dishonestly told her that their Aunt Agatha was planning to be there, and Aunt Agatha intimidated everyone with her ideas of suitable fashion and behavior for young ladies.

Carla had been so apprehensive about making a social faux pas that he had envisioned her standing off by herself during the entire party, primly dressed in her new outfit and afraid to swing her leg up over that dirty old tire for fear someone would find such behavior unladylike. And so he had started his project all over again. He had found a wide, thick board, meticulously drilled the appropriate holes in it, then set her to work sanding it paper-smooth while he had checked out all the big old oak trees in their yard for just the right one in which to install a proper swing for a young lady—Carla's swing. It was still up, and he still thought of it as that, even now. Carla's swing.

Suzannah had been furious that he had had Carla help put up her own surprise; that he had ordered her to take careful readings of the measuring tape he had flung down from the sturdy branch he had chosen, and had insisted she hold the rope while he cut, then burned, the edges to keep them from fraying. He had even had her climb the extension ladder and help toss the measured rope up to his higher perch on the appropriate branch. She had solemnly watched him level the swing just so, and just as solemnly tested it out for him, letting him push her higher and higher, with no fear at all.

He probably shouldn't have done it that way. But it had been so much fun to watch her big eyes grow serious, and her lips purse in concentration as she readily took on each new assignment. And it hadn't ruined the surprise at all.

He didn't believe that any greater happiness could possibly have shown out of her eyes when she had shyly glanced over at him after the party was well under way and his father had announced that Carla's very own swing was now ready for launching by the birthday girl.

He shook away the memories, wondering where the years had gone. His own daughters were a little older than Carla had been then, and Carla was—she was perfect.

Oh, not without her faults, he realized, tapping his fingers against the steering wheel. She still had her problems with speaking before thinking, as his own singed psyche could testify to. It was a fault he shared. But she had turned out exactly as he had hoped she would—all woman, with the mysteries of her femininity and understanding matured deep within her.

I can't wait a whole week to see her, he thought suddenly, as he rounded the first curve that gave him a distant vision of the lights of Chicago, creating a mecca in the winter dark. *I've just discovered her again, and I can't wait until I get that foreign job finished to...*

To make his first move. That's what he really meant. But his thoughts were racing too fast to organize sensibly. He was watching landmarks, remembering the route he had taken to find her apartment, turning off, far out of his way, over to the other highway.

Who had to wait? he thought with confidence.

By ten o'clock on that terrible Monday evening Carla was soaking in the tub, her hair pulled high on her head so she could indulge in hot water almost up to her shoulders. It was a method of relaxing she seldom allowed herself, but at that point she felt she deserved it.

The jarring ring of the telephone, coming just when she had rinsed the final bit of soap from her toes and settled back down into the soothing warmth, was most unwelcome. Carla wanted to stay in that tub for hours. But since only her closest friends and family had her unlisted number, she knew it could be important. Grudgingly she climbed out of the steamy bliss, draped a towel around herself, and padded wetly into her bedroom.

"How did you get my number?" she demanded angrily when she recognized Brigg's voice. Him she didn't need to end her lousy day.

"Copied it down before I left yesterday morning," he admitted calmly. "What are you doing?"

"What do you want, Brigg?" she countered, balancing the phone against her shoulder while she dried off her dripping body.

"You sound as if you're doing calisthenics."

"You were going to tell me why you called."

"I just got back from driving Suzannah to Kansas City. And you were right—your reputation in Shelbyville is shot. That is, if you find being linked with me a disadvantage in your parents' eyes. Like a fool Suzannah told our parents that I spent the night in your motel room."

"I hoped she'd keep that supposition to herself," Carla admitted.

"She thought our dear mother would miss me and

worry about my whereabouts. By the time I reached the farm, Mother had already mailed a letter to your family on her way home from church. She told them she was delighted we were finally getting together and wanted to know why they had not written her the news. She assumes we've been seeing each other in Chicago. So does Suzannah, and she's furious with you for not telling her."

"I don't believe this."

"And Suzannah wants to know where we did spend Saturday night. She called the motel when I didn't show up on time Sunday. I told her it was none of her business."

"Why did you let her think we spent the night together at all?"

"We did spend the night together."

Carla sighed at his forthright logic. "I hope you're making up all this about your mother." She dropped the damp towel on the floor and awkwardly pressed the phone between her shoulder and neck while she reached into her dresser drawer for a clean nightgown. She was beginning to get cold after the relaxing bath, and the gown and robe she had planned to put on were still back by the tub.

"My mother's more perceptive than people give her credit for. She noticed us at her party. She knows exactly what is going on."

"Not 'exactly,' if she thinks there's any love lost between us." Carla tossed the phone on the bed while she pulled the gown on over her head, then slipped between the sheets to get warm.

"What did you say?" she interrupted Brigg's brisk voice.

"Haven't you been listening to anything?"

"I've been doing something else."

"Dammit, Carla! I thought you should know about Mother writing your family. Gossip around Shelbyville doesn't bother me, but I would have stopped that letter if I could have."

The irritation in his voice made it clear that the letter had really been sent. Carla leaned back, feeling a little sick. Her parents believed divorce was immoral and unemployment preventable. This supposed affair with Brigg wouldn't help their concerns about their only daughter's good sense.

"Carla?"

"All I can do at this point is explain to my parents, and forget about what Shelbyville thinks." Her voice sounded hollow.

"What are you doing now?" he asked abruptly.

"None of your business. Is there anything else?"

"I'm hungry."

"Then eat."

"I'm at a truck stop not five minutes from your house. I'll pick you up."

"No!"

"I'd like your company."

"I don't want yours."

There was silence at the other end of the line.

"I mean it, Brigg. Don't show up on my doorstep again. I have other things on my mind tonight, and I simply don't want to cope with you, too."

"Are you this pleasant to everyone who asks you out?" She couldn't tell if he was really hurt. She wished she could see his face to be certain.

"Brigg, please don't." After their talk in her apartment, it wasn't in her to be rude to him anymore. But she was so devitalized after her job loss that she really didn't believe she could manage him in person at the moment. He'd have her blabbing all her troubles, and she knew she had to face them alone, make the necessary hard decisions in her own way.

"All right, Carla, relax. I won't come by." He did not break the connection; she could feel, rather than hear, his breathing. "I'm leaving the country again tomorrow," he finally said pointedly.

"Oh." It was an observation. She couldn't even get out the question "How long?" for she was not certain in her own mind that she wanted to know.

"I'll call you when I get back from France," he promised almost sensuously. "Good-bye, Carla."

"Don't call me," she urged frantically, but it was too late; she could hear him cut the connection.

Please, Brigg. Don't call, she thought in despair, fighting the nostalgic temptation to hope that he would. She didn't need this right now; not Brigg complicating her already shattered life.

Carla was empty for the next several days. There was no better way to describe how she felt. Empty. A shell of a person. Considering herself worthless, wondering if everyone else knew how worthless she was. Unemployed.

Or, rather, almost unemployed. She had contacted the executive for whom she worked in the summers and had been offered a permanent, well-paying post. But it was not how she would prefer to spend her working hours, and so she continued to make it hazily through each teaching day while she indecisively pondered her options.

At least the secretarial offer kept the gnawing fear of financial disaster off her shoulders. She wondered what men and women did when they had no other employment possibilities to fall back on, when they had other people besides themselves to support. How lucky she was that she had continued that summer work, piling up a nest egg for the time when her parents might need some assistance in their waning years, and thus, indirectly, keeping a job open for herself. And she was lucky to be alone. Her terrible feeling of failure was bad enough, and she couldn't fathom how out-of-work heads of families survived emotionally.

No matter that the job loss was not her fault, or that she felt an overwhelming rage with the whole educational system, she couldn't shake that terrible conviction of having messed up somewhere.

It was more than a week before she got everything settled in her mind, and felt at ease with her decision. She wanted to teach. That was paramount. But she realized that if she did not value her own skills highly, no one else would, either. When she went back to her principal to discuss her decision, she explained that conviction.

"So I'll take the reading supervisor job next semester, only if I'm guaranteed full-time status and benefits, including tenure accumulation," she told him. "I know I'm taking a chance that I won't be allowed to teach at all, but I have to establish that I'm not willing to be exploited. I'm a professional."

"You're probably right," he admitted reluctantly, hoping the district would not force his school to lose this capable woman. "The minute I hear anything I'll let you know."

"Don't tell me until you have a definite no, or a firm contract in your hand," she said with shaky humor. "I can't take too many more of these ups and downs."

Later that evening, when Brigg invited her out for a drink, she told him the same thing. Not about her job, of course. She still felt too sensitive about that situation to discuss it with anyone.

"I can't take much more of you popping around in my life" was what she actually said. It struck her as odd coincidence, and very Brigg-like, that he had somehow called first on the day she lost her job, and second on the day she began putting the pieces back together. Again it was late at night and she was in bed, too suggestive a place to be talking to Brigg.

"My plane just got in." He tried to explain away his second invitation, which was tendered at equally as short notice as the first.

How predictable of him, she thought almost sadly. *Come share my wine with me, right now!*

"Do you want to go out for a drink or not?" he persisted.

"Not."

And she had been firm about it. Her uncertain work situation dominated everything else, threatening her independence and judgment. One potential disaster in her life at a time, she continued to remind herself, was enough. Brigg Carlyle was too disturbing, too newly discovered, for her to face.

The matter of facing Brigg, however, was taken out of her hands the very next evening. He showed up on her doorstep about six o'clock, and it was either go out with him to supper or feed him herself, for he made it clear that he was not leaving until one or the other was decided. He wanted to talk to her.

"What did you write to your parents?" he asked once they had been served steaks in a grill not far from Carla's home.

It was a quiet, casual restaurant, a good place to talk, if that was what one wanted to do. Carla was not certain she did.

"I told them about all their old friends I called on, all

the classmates I saw at the reunion, and about your helping me get back to Chicago safely Saturday night because I had car trouble." She raised her head to look at him thoughtfully. "I also said that you were more overbearing than ever and I didn't plan to see you again, but that Suzannah was as nice as always, and your parents looked great." She cut a piece off her steak and began to eat it.

"You omitted a lot." Angrily he carved off a hunk of meat himself.

There was no answer to that, so she didn't make one. Her letter had seemed to satisfy her parents, who had written back immediately with comments about the people she had seen and, mercifully, with no questions about Brigg. Her father had thanked her for the information on Jonathan Bryce Cannon, albeit quite formally. But that could have been because of the intemperance. Her mother had sounded the same as ever, and had urged Carla to come out for the Christmas holidays with them.

"I want you to come down to the farm with me and the girls for Christmas." Brigg seemed to be on the same wave length, at least about the holidays.

"Never."

"Why not? That should shut the town up."

"I'm not going to be concerned about that Shelbyville incident anymore."

"The twins are going to be bored, away from their familiar surroundings, and I'll be torn between them and the folks. How am I going to manage five days at the farm without you along?"

"What do you usually do when you take the girls down?" she asked shakily, alarmed at his sincerity.

"Not stay so long, that's for sure. But Mother seems more sentimental than usual, and I let her and Dad talk me into a long weekend. Why don't you come? They invited you."

"Even if I wanted to be with you, which I don't, it would just complicate things for your mother. She's worried about your single state. Haven't you noticed the signs?"

"Then take her mind off it. Come on down and let her think we're a loving couple."

"Brigg, you have no sense of responsibility."

By his stubborn silence she knew he was as aware as she that a pseudo romance would only hurt his mother more in the long run. But he wouldn't admit it. They plowed through the steak and salad and a half-bottle of wine with almost no other conversation.

"What are you going to do during the holidays?" He asked the question over mugs of coffee after their plates were cleared away. "I'll be leaving late next week for some meetings in Houston, but I'll get home early on the Wednesday before Christmas, the same day the girls get in from school. And I won't be going to Shelbyville until Friday. We could have dinner, just you and I. What about that Wednesday night?"

"You'd go off and leave your daughters when you haven't seen them for more than a month?"

"I haven't seen you, to speak of, for fifteen years, so I'm certainly not asking them along. Carla, you're going to have to start talking to me pretty soon."

"I don't know what you mean."

It was a lie. She did. Something was happening between them. It was as if some destiny that had been misplaced years ago was surfacing, looking for a place to roost. She couldn't deny the reality of the attraction. But she could fight it. She needed Brigg in her life right then about as much as she needed Charles.

"I won't dignify that 'What do you mean?' nonsense

with an explanation," he snapped. "So get back to Christmas. What are you doing over the holiday? I assume your school is off?"

"I'm flying to Colorado to see my parents. It's been a couple of years since I was there, and I need to look in on them."

"Are you going to tell them about us?"

"There's nothing to tell," she snapped, suddenly wanting this whole disturbing situation ended. "Aren't you through yet?"

"I'm never through, until I've won," he warned as he reached for her coat.

Brigg wondered what the problem was. For several days after their meal together he pondered Carla's defensive attitude. It bothered him that she still regarded him with that curiously troubled perception only an adolescent relationship could create: a mixture of unquestioning affection, yet angry rebellion if he approached her feelings too closely. It was different for him. He had been an adult when he had ceased to see much of her, so his attraction to her now was unrelated, he felt, to his fond memories of her when she was a child.

It had only taken him a few hours of being around her to know, irrevocably, that she had matured into all he had long ago envisioned her capable of becoming. A fascinating woman, one he was determined to get to know better.

Yet she seemed to be having trouble separating him from the past. He tried to imagine how she must have regarded some of their last times together. A particular incident came to mind that had his lips tilting in fond amusement. The school Halloween party. Her freshman year. Both she and Suzannah had been in a dither about what to wear, both wanting, in their still childish ways, to go in costume, yet thinking they were too mature to do so and that their friends would all laugh at them. Neither of the girls could drive yet, so Brigg's father had offered to take them both, but when Brigg had unexpectedly arrived home on a break from a foreign assignment, he had been designated for the job.

For what seemed hours Brigg had sat in the kitchen filling up on his mother's cooking and wondering if Suzannah was ever going to get ready. She had tried on three different costumes and one sweater and skirt, and interspersed it all with phone calls to Carla, who apparently was doing the same thing. In the end the girls had tearfully decided they would wear party dresses, and had put on their uncomfortable high heels and teased their hair into the bouffant style that had still been popular then.

Brigg had felt so sorry for them and their traumas on leaving childhood behind in favor of young womanhood that he tucked a surprise up his own sleeve. When they arrived to pick up Carla, and Suzannah had run inside to get her and to conduct last-minute consultations, he had pulled a king-sized sheet out from where he had hidden it under the seat of the car, cut a couple of eye-holes with his pocket knife, and thrown it over his head. It took some hasty improvising with clothesline rope loosely around his neck and waist to keep the thing on, but he had managed. When the two girls finally came tottering out in all their finery, he had stood lounging against the car, wordlessly ghostly.

"Oh, Brigg, you're not! Oh, you absolutely can't! This is horrible!" Suzannah had screeched, totally delighted.

Carla had held a hand over her mouth to hide her giggles and disdainfully remarked that some people never grew up. But her eyes were warm and happy.

Brigg had solemnly escorted them all the way inside to the party, and ignored their loud and sophisticated protestations to their friends that they accepted no responsibility for Suzannah's crazy brother. It hadn't been such a pleasure to find himself the hit of the party, with all their girl friends gathering around, giggling loudly and bemoaning how ridiculous brothers were. But he had managed to make himself remain a few minutes and endure the accolades and insults before warning that he would return.

Given more time to be inventive, he had come back for them as a werewolf. Suzannah's gang had all been waiting for his grand entrance, but he had fooled them and slipped stealthily into a side entrance, then just propped himself against the doorway, waiting to be discovered. He could still remember Carla's ecstatic hoot of laughter and pointed finger when she had been the first to sense his presence.

So what kind of memories did Carla have of that now, he wondered? Maybe still that same troubled mix of happiness and wariness she had had then. He remembered that she had laughingly bubbled all the way home with condescending and sarcastic comments. Yet as she had tumbled out of the car and given fond goodbyes only to Suzannah, she had flashed him one perceptive look, as if she realized he had been trying in his awkward way to kiss her adolescent hurts better; but she was afraid to acknowledge his gift, afraid of its meaning.

And now she doesn't know what to expect from me, the man, he eventually decided with pained insight. He was much more an unknown to her than she was to him. For she had never before seen him with a woman's eyes, whereas he had almost forever seen her through a man's perception.

The idea was troubling, for it meant he would have to slow down. Give her more time. Of which he had very little. The instinctive logic, however, seemed so accurate, that Brigg knew he had to accept it or lose her.

The hardest part for Brigg was to figure how long to wait before reinstituting his get-to-know Carla campaign. His social life was available only in patches—a few days in town here, then maybe free again a couple of weeks later. She apparently assumed that she had scared him off at least until after the Christmas holidays. But he worried that if he waited a whole month to call her, she could have met someone else, had a whirlwind love affair—she could be lost to him again before he even got her back in his life as a friend.

Since he had the Houston business meetings hanging over his head in mid-December, Brigg finally decided he'd give one try at seeing her before he left. But he'd fool her this time. No way would he make it seem like a date. Put her to work, he thought. That had always been their best times together when she was small: Carla following him around, and he indulgently thinking up little tasks for her to do. She might feel comfortable with that, fall right into the old pattern, and then if he were smart he might be able to slip her into the new pattern—Brigg and Carla, man and woman—without her realizing what had happened. Without all the trauma.

It was a job to figure out the proper ruse. He considered taking her to the regional chemical show and asking her to help him pick out equipment, but realized immediately that she would know much less than he about boilers and pumps and turn down his invitation as totally stupid. An emergency need for some typing was another thought, but with six secretaries in his office, he thought that ruse was equally thin. That left only his mother.

"Carla, I need a favor," he lied when he finally screwed up his nerve and called her late one afternoon from his office in downtown Chicago.

From the thumpings in the background and her rather breathless answer, he gathered that she had just come in herself and was dumping her things down after running for the phone.

"What kind of favor, Brigg?" she asked, with less suspicion than he had anticipated, given her past reception of his calls.

"Go microwave shopping with me."

"What?"

"I think that's what I'll give Mother for Christmas. A microwave. Most of the men I know say their wives swear by them, but my housekeeper refuses to have one in the house, so I need help picking one out."

"Your mother might feel the same way your housekeeper does," Carla cautioned.

"The cousins who run the farm for Dad always keep them supplied with freezer beef," Brigg said. "I figure even if she doesn't want to change her cooking habits, it would be handy for thawing out the meat."

"She did seem to have a lot of casseroles in her freezer when I was down there," Carla said contemplatively. "Microwaves are handy for getting them oven-ready fast."

"I'm leaving town in a couple of days and I want to have this present lined up before I leave. Any chance you could go shopping with me tomorrow or the next day?"

"You mean after work?"

"Whenever you say. Most stores are open evenings, and I can break away from the office, just so I plan ahead." He wanted to add that he'd buy her dinner, but was afraid to push his luck.

Misplaced Destiny 81

"Oh, I guess I could. Make it day after tomorrow. Around six-thirty. Where shall I meet you?"

"I can pick you up."

"That would be a waste of your time, Brigg. And I need to do some Christmas shopping myself afterward. Just pick the store, preferably some place close to my area, and I'll be there."

He wasn't really crazy about that plan, but he grudgingly named a large shopping mall near her that had an appliance outlet as well as several department stores.

Brigg was, Carla discovered, a careful shopper. She wished she'd had him along when she was selecting kitchen equipment for her own condominium, for he knew just what questions to ask about the mechanical functioning of everything; he might have prevented some of the expensive maintainence costs she had gotten stuck with. It was all the extras that confused him.

"Maybe she'd like this one with the rotating base and the convection combination," he told Carla, dragging her away from the simple on-off model she was examining to show her the super-deluxe one he had discovered in a far corner.

"Do you really think she's going to use it that much, Brigg?" Carla asked, horrified at the price. People had to be paying, she thought, for the space-age sensor-touch panel and the seven choices of colors.

"Oh, I don't know. Maybe we'd better check one more store."

"Brigg! We've been to three places already. I need to get some shopping done, too."

"So I'll go with you. I need time to think this over." He had her by the elbow and was leading her toward the mall before she could protest. "What kind of shopping do you want to do? I'll help you pick stuff out."

He dropped her arm once they were strolling past the cheerily decorated storefronts.

"I wanted something small for three friends at work. And a gimmicky, inexpensive gift for the kids in my class. But you don't have to help."

"Not pencils," he asserted, again grabbing her arm and steering her into the largest department store. "I always got a new pencil from my teachers and I felt most ungrateful."

"Brat," Carla laughed, freeing her arm, but forgetting that she didn't want his help.

"What about chewing gum? Huge packs, stinky and sticky."

"Oh, you have beautiful ideas. The janitors would love you. Wait a minute—I want to see those pomanders."

The smell which had caught at her senses as she passed the vibrantly colorful display of closet hangings had been marvelous. Carla bent over the small balls strung with colored ribbons from sturdy hooks, testing if the scent had actually come from them, or from the mixture of bakeries and perfume counters on the same floor. They smelled as good close up as from a distance, and the price was perfect. Carla immediately bought three, while Brigg poked around a magazine counter nearby.

"What about comic books?" he suggested helpfully when she joined him with her packages. "Lurid ones about Captain Hero and the space monsters?"

"Space monsters are out. Lovable creatures are in," Carla said negatively, walking on through the store, glancing all around. She hadn't really gotten into the Christmas spirit yet, and the glittering decorations and loud seasonal music seemed luridly excessive.

"Let's get out of here," Brigg suddenly suggested,

apparently as inundated with pseudo cheer as she. "I need a drink before I can face any more microwaves."

"You're not a very good shopper," Carla accused, "if you give up this quickly. You should have bought that one at the first store, as I suggested." She followed him readily, though, anxious herself to be out of the confusion for awhile.

It was almost balmy when they stepped outside, still that unreal weather that had been so intriguing in Shelbyville. And bright. Chicago's lighting cast its own sense of day about the surroundings despite the late hour. Beyond the numerous parked cars and across the street, they could see another string of stores and restaurants, and they automatically began walking in that direction, both seeming to need the space and freshness of the evening to replenish their spirits.

"Actually I hate to shop," Brigg admitted while they picked their way across the curbs and plantings that broke up the openness of the center's parking lot. "Except for work equipment. That makes sense to me, perhaps because most of it is done out of catalogues and through technical reps."

"I didn't think you'd still be making many purchase decisions yourself since your company's gotten so big," Carla remarked.

"My partners and I spot-check almost all decisions of the purchasing department, and I consult on the jobs I'm directly supervising. That way we can keep track of new developments. It's easy to get out of touch when you turn everything over to your employees."

The traffic was heavy, but there was a light at the corner, and soon they were able to cross the six lanes safely. Some of the stores fronting the opposite street were closing early, but Brigg and Carla strolled toward some lighted ones, just in case they would find a quiet restaurant or tavern where they could sit down awhile. Miraculously they located what looked like a neighborhood bar right next to a small appliance center.

"Brigg, would you believe that," Carla said, stopping by the store window featuring all kinds of kitchen equipment. "A little microwave, the simplest kind, and in good old basic black."

"I need a drink, first."

"No. They close at eight. I know your mother would love it. Seriously, she's not going to want to learn all the fancy things she could do with one of those big units. I think you're exactly right. She'll use it for thawing, and to bake potatoes. Your dad loves baked potatoes, as I recall, and it only takes four minutes."

"All right, all right. We'll get that one," he agreed. "Then we'll get my drink."

After they had arranged for Brigg's purchase to be sent to his home, Carla tried to get out of the drink with him, claiming she had to complete her shopping for the children, but Brigg cajoled her into the bar, anyway.

"I'm not going to let you walk back through that parking lot by yourself," he snapped protectively. "But I've been working since five this morning, and I'd like to take a break for a minute. Besides, I've got your students' presents solved."

Carla was seated in a high-backed wooden booth, with a glass of Scotch in her hand, before she could get a word in edgewise. "You play on people's sympathies, you know," she complained, looking at the lines of maturity in his face, knowing that he probably was even more tired than he looked. And hating that.

"How about flashlights?" he countered, offering her a handful of the peanuts he had also ordered.

"What do flashlights have to do with—"

"For your kids. The little penlight kind that clips to your shirt pocket. They can keep them by their bedsides to scare away the bad guys. Read comics after the lights are supposed to be out. Play doctor with them."

"Did you play doctor when you were little?" she asked suspiciously, barely able to keep the contented grin off her face.

"Not by the time you came along. I would have been arrested for child molestation. So what about it? Like the idea?"

"Much as I hate to feed your ego," she said, crunching some of the peanuts as noisily as he, "I love it. If they're not too expensive. We're supposed to keep our treats token things, under a dollar."

"I, dear Carla, just happen to have a gross or more of such marvels left at my office. We buy hundreds of them every year for our technical personnel. They only cost fifty-seven cents apiece, and they come in handy in all sorts of dark factory corners."

"Do they also say Courtesy of Carlyle Construction?" she asked.

"They do not; they're virgin white. Do you want some?"

"If you'll let me pay for them, I'd love thirty of them," she admitted with a huge smile. "They'd be perfect."

"I'll have my secretary send them out to your place tomorrow. Give me seventeen dollars and ten cents." He held out his hand.

She looked down at the huge palm, scrupulously clean, yet scarred with calluses and stained from too many hours of working with too much dirty equipment. "How can you figure that so fast in your head?" she objected, reaching for her purse.

"Rapid multiplication is a gift. I do it instinctively,

but only up to the eights." He grinned as she shoved a wad of bills and coins into his hand. "I thought you'd give me hell for demanding instant payment," he said in some disappointment.

"I know you did. Fooled you." She toyed with her Scotch glass, suddenly feeling relaxed. Brigg was poking over his own drink even more leisurely than she. Sighing, she leaned her head back against the high, private wall of the booth.

"Tired?" he eventually asked.

"Mmm. A little. Drained is more like it. All this Christmas fuss, like we saw at the mall, is getting to the kids already. They want their vacation."

"I suppose stores started the decorating and the hard sell this early in Shelbyville when we were kids," he said, "but I don't really remember thinking much about Christmas until a week or so before the event."

"Me either. Maybe because no one had much money then. I usually made most of my presents."

"Hey, that's right. I'd almost forgotten. You made me a handkerchief one year."

"Which you said looked like a good rag to clean your dipstick with," she said, some of the little-girl hurt actually invading her voice, before she managed an understanding smile. "You were the first teenager in the world with a hand-hemmed sheet for a car tool."

"I gather I was at my usual tactful best that year," Brigg said sullenly, motioning to the waitress for another drink. Carla glanced down at her own empty glass, wondering how much time had gone by, surprised that she had finally managed to finish hers. She was not a large consumer of alcohol. She glanced at her watch and was horrified to find that they had been in the tavern more than an hour.

"I really do have to go," she said. "There's one

more teaching day before the weekend, and I have a little preparation left to do."

"I suppose I should be getting on, too," he said reluctantly, asking the waitress for the check instead. "I'll be flying to Houston tomorrow evening."

"You must spend most of your time in the air," Carla said quietly as they began the long walk back to her car. The air had cooled slightly, and she rolled the soft collar of her knit coat high around her neck, shaking her hair loose so it tumbled outside, adding its own warmth.

"It's the short trips that get me," he admitted. "Most of my work is for weeks or months at a time in one place, and that works fine. It's when I'm jetting back and forth between several cities in as many days that I'm ready to retire."

"Will you, soon? Retire?"

"Now that's insulting. Just because I'm bald I'm not—"

"Oh, quit being so touchy. I mean that lots of men your age who have been so successful retire extremely early and take up something else. I just wondered if you had that in mind."

"Maybe. The idea has crossed my mind quite recently. I'm away from home too much. Of course, with the girls at school, I suppose it doesn't matter, but—"

"Here's my car." Carla interrupted his musings when they almost passed the lane where she had parked.

"I could follow you home," he offered. "It's late and—"

"I do not need protection on the drive home," she scoffed, opening the door to the Cadillac with her key and sliding in. "I've learned to be on my own quite well."

"Look, I—thanks for helping with the microwave. I really appreciate it." He was standing awkwardly by the door, holding it open.

She looked at him in puzzlement. "It was a good idea. For your mother," she reassured him, reaching for the handle.

"Yes," he let the door slide out of his fingers, and stepped away. "It was a very good idea."

Chapter Four

It was amazing how human beings could continue to function under the most adverse of circumstances. Or so Carla thought. Take herself. Up in the air about a job, disturbed by that ghost from her childhood threatening to reenter her life, and yet she made it to work on time every day, kept classroom discipline, and even managed genuinely to teach—right up to the last.

That sense of finality was the worst. Each day she carted home a few of her personal teaching supplies that she could do without, preparing for the end of December when she should have her own things out to make space for the returning teacher. When she finished the unit on Mexico, the fun one where they always made a piñata, she wondered if she ever again would have the pleasure of cracking one open with her students. When she put away the beginning level of second-grade readers and got out supplies for the advanced level, she wondered if she would ever be working with that educational series again.

The list of "lasts" could go on and on. But Carla tried not to dwell on such dismal reactions, tried to convince herself that things always worked out for the best. The indecision was wearing, though.

When she called her parents and confirmed her arrangements for a Christmas visit, she mentioned nothing about her job problem, although she thought it would be wonderful to sob her helpless rage out on her mother's shoulder, just as in the childhood days. Perhaps she would have, had she thought any advice would help. But she had made her offer for staying in the teaching profession, and it seemed to her that there was nothing further anyone could do but wait for action from the school board.

One cheering incident did happen. She got a package from Houston covered with hand-written instructions: Do open before Christmas. Open immediately—not perishable, but IMPORTANT.

It was small and heavy. A rectangular box about the size of her dictionary. The return address was a petroleum company, and for a moment Carla wondered who could have sent it, until she remembered that Brigg had said he would be in Texas. She decided the precise, engineering-type lettering had to be done by him, and almost eagerly she opened it.

When she saw the box with hundreds of pencils, she was puzzled. A note shoved inside said merely. "How's this for a public relations nightmare? Here are some for the whole school, so all the kids can hate you." The public relations bit didn't make sense, and she studied the bright green pencils with their fresh rubber erasers, wondering what he meant. Only gradually did it sink in that the lettering actually read "Carlyle Destruction Company."

"Oh, boy. Oh, boy!" She laughed, throwing back her head in genuine amusement. Destruction—Brigg must have exploded, absolutely hit the roof. She could visualize the way his cold gray eyes would have looked surprised, then disbelieving, then frosted up, while his neck turned slightly red and his chin jutted forward in the telltale way that had always warned her she had better scoot out of his sight for a while.

Carla took the pencils to school the next day, and she felt happy for the first time in weeks whenever she passed on Brigg's story.

It was a couple of nights later that he called. "What's the weather doing up there right now?" he barked into the phone with no preamble.

Carla wrapped a robe around her nightgown, wondering why he always seemed to catch her in the tub or in bed, both of them too suggestive for talking to Brigg. "It's still warm. Indian summer and almost creepy, with Christmas only a week away."

"Damn!"

"What's that supposed to mean?"

"I saw these hand-knit Scandinavian hats and mittens at an import shop here. Not too long ago I sent the girls checks for new winter parkas and I thought those might be good Christmas presents to go with them."

"Well, it certainly won't stay this way long. And they can always use them back at school."

"I guess you're right. I'll get them. But I'd better look for something else, too. It won't seem like Christmas to them if they can't use their presents right away. Bye."

"Brigg!"

"Huh?"

"Is that it?"

"It?"

"Why you called?"

"Yes."

"Oh. Well—well, I want to thank you for the pencils. I've already sent them around to all the classrooms. The teachers got a big kick out of your dilemma. They've used them as an object lesson on the perils of public relations propaganda, and the students all think I'm wonderful!"

"They already arrived, huh? Could you use five thousand more?"

"Are you kidding?"

"I wish I were. Of course, the company I ordered them from is providing replacements, and they make good conversation pieces. But it takes a lot of conversation to pass out five thousand bloopers."

She smiled to herself, loving the sound of his amused voice over long distance. It seemed as if he were right in her apartment, sharing his joke.

"When did you say you'll get home?" she asked.

"This Wednesday. I'm due in several hours before the girls, so I plan to hang around the airport to meet them."

"That's convenient."

"Yes."

The conversation was going absolutely nowhere.

"Well, thanks again," she mumbled. "And, Brigg, don't buy your girls sleds, either."

"Even I can figure out that hinges on cold weather, too," he laughed. "Look, I'd better let you go. Have a good trip to Colorado."

"And you to Shelbyville," she said, knowing she should hang up, yet not doing so.

"Yeah, well—"

"Maybe we'll cross paths after the holidays," she said restlessly, suddenly, irrationally, wanting to see him again, job or no job, nostalgia or no nostalgia.

"We probably will," he agreed quietly. There was another long pause, and this time she did hang up. Reluctantly.

They saw each other sooner than either of them had anticipated. On the Wednesday afternoon before Christmas, Brigg called her from Houston because he had gotten tied up with business and had missed his flight home. There wasn't another seat to Chicago available until late evening, and he seemed frantic that in three hours his little girls would be expecting him to meet their plane at the O'Hare airport.

It occurred to Carla later that she should have had the foresight to refuse to fill in for him. But, foolishly, she had agreed to meet his daughters' plane. Of course, she did have excuses for not thinking logically. She had just gotten in from work when he called. It was the last day before the holiday and the children would have been excited enough even without the classroom Christmas party and her gift of the little flashlights; Carla had never had a wilder or more fun day. There was still the packing to do for her trip to Colorado the next day, and she was riding an emotional high. Her job situation was settled—just that afternoon she had signed a one-and-a-half year contract as a full-time reading supervisor, effective the first of January. It had been exhilarating to learn that the school board had come up with the necessary financing rather than lose her.

She had been tempted to share her good news with Brigg, but sensing his concern that his twins might be stranded in the confusing megaport, she had set aside her own exuberance and agreeably jotted down the flight information without once realizing that it would be better for someone who knew the girls to go for them.

Carla had waited at the correct concourse exit outside the security gate for thirty minutes, expecting a stewardess to bring forth tiny cherubs in winter snow jackets—mini-Nancys, smiling and bubbly. Brigg had said the girls were around eleven years old, immature for their age, and she had believed him. He also said they resembled their mother, which wasn't true either.

She had eventually noticed the two fashionable young women sitting across from her because they looked so much alike. Undoubtedly they were identical twins, although one wore her blond hair much longer than the other. They were attractively sophisticated, their faces skillfully made up, and had they not been so short, Carla would have assumed they were models. With nothing better to do while she waited for the airline to respond to her inquiry about the Carlyle girls, her glance flitted back to them occasionally.

It was almost comical when it suddenly dawned on her that she was looking at two faces exactly like Brigg's. Carla did some mental calculating of her own, and concluded that Brigg's daughters had to be almost sixteen years old, despite what their father thought. She could hardly believe that underneath the false eyelashes must be his two "little girls." They resembled their mother only in their diminutive stature. Their features and prominent bone structure were so like Brigg's that Carla should have been able to pick them out anywhere. Even the way they narrowed their gray eyes, the wry amusement noticeable in the slight tilt of their lips, were Brigg all over again.

He was such a giant, it was understandable that he would not realize that his daughters, who were barely five feet tall, were full-grown women. And he hadn't looked lately if he thought they were immature for their age. They were built like miniature candidates for Miss Universe, dressing accordingly in tight sweaters, slinky ultrasuede skirts and high heeled boots. Their fur jackets were not, she suspected, what their father had envisioned when he had told Carla they would be wearing the new winter parkas he had just sent them money to buy. It must have been an open-ended check.

Identifying the girls, though, proved to be the easiest of Carla's problems. Someone at that exclusive private school they attended in the East had done a good job of warning them about kidnapping scams. When she had finally introduced herself as a friend of their father's, who was to take them to her apartment until he arrived on the next available flight, they had suspiciously refused to go with her. Instead they insisted on calling first his housekeeper, then his secretary, to confirm her story. Unfortunately Brigg had not bothered to notify anyone else of Carla's existence, much less of his change in plans, and it was not until they reached Suzannah in Kansas City that they finally believed her story.

These girls had learned about men and women at that school, too. When Suzannah burst into delighted hysterics on the phone and inadvertently let slip a few innuendos about Carla, they looked at her with new eyes. She knew then she was in for trouble.

Carla could well remember her own shock as an adolescent when it had suddenly dawned on her that her parents still made love. She could imagine what resentment she would have felt if she had suspected her father had a mistress.

It would have been better to have taken them to their home, not to her own apartment. When she parked, Carla knew she was meant to overhear the whispered question: "How much do you suppose this condo is costing Dad?" They wanted her to sense their disdain.

Once inside they sat stiffly on her couch, making conversation impossible by their stilted responses, and sighing to make their boredom evident. Finally, after they refused her offer of soda or food, Carla told them to make themselves at home and went to her bedroom to do her vacation packing. She hoped things would get better if she left them alone.

Preparing for the Colorado trip didn't take long, and when she walked back through her living room, casually suggesting as she went that the girls would be welcome to watch television or listen to her records, they again rebuffed her. It was done so politely that Carla almost admired their skill in the games teenagers like to play with adults. She gathered they were serving notice that Carla might stay in her place as their father's mistress, but the privilege did not extend to any authority over them. It would have been funny to her, had they been anyone else but Brigg's daughters.

Giving up on any kind of a pleasant evening with them, Carla returned to her room and pondered how to pass time until Brigg arrived. She decided to begin a long put off necessity, packaging her knickknacks into boxes suitable for moving. In September, anxious to shed herself completely of Charles' taste, Carla had used her summer job savings as a down payment on a tiny carriage house in the suburbs, and ordered minimal furniture. She intended to move into the house after the first of the year, at which time she would be renting out her condominium fully furnished. So there were all the personal items to ready for transfer.

It felt good to have some work to do, since she was unable to make those confused girls comfortable without their cooperation. For some time she sat cross-legged on the floor before a stack of cardboard boxes, mechanically wrapping little things in newspaper and thinking idly about the twins. Carla had no idea which was Jane and which was Ann, because they had never identified themselves, enjoying the awkwardness of her being unable to call them by name.

"Do you mind if I smoke?"

The twin with the short haircut looked suitably bored as she entered the room. The question was in no way a true request for permission; the cigarette and lighter were in hand, and she was looking around the room for an ashtray.

"Actually, yes," Carla said flatly, not really minding, but not wanting the girl to get away with her presumptuous condescension. "Since I quit smoking, I die for a cigarette every time I smell one." It wasn't exactly untrue. Carla had smoked years ago, and stopping permanently had been a somewhat painful exercise. "Go out on the deck if you want a cigarette."

The offer was hardly tempting if the girl couldn't be inside, annoying Carla.

"It doesn't matter." She tucked the pack and lighter back into the oversize purse hanging over her arm, but remained looking around the bedroom.

"I don't suppose Dad smokes here, then?" she asked, her face curiously vulnerable as she glanced pointedly toward the bedside table, which was void any ashtray.

Carla mentally cursed Brigg. She hadn't realized the girls might actually be hurt that he had suddenly sprung a "kept woman" on them. Denials would never be believed and would probably only make things worse, because the girls would think she was belittling their intelligence.

"He'd better not," Carla settled for saying, not being able to remember whether Brigg smoked at all.

"Your relationship with Dad doesn't sound very cooperative." The other twin joined her sister in Carla's bedroom.

"One thing your father will never accuse me of"— Carla rose to her feet, impatient with their pitiful jabs seeking information—" is being cooperative. In fact I'm feeling most uncooperative right now. I have no idea when he'll be in, and I'm starving. I don't intend to wait for him."

She brushed past the girls, leaving them standing there as she went into her kitchen. She couldn't bear to see them hurting so much.

She made herself a ham sandwich, noisily opened a large bag of potato chips and a can of juice, and left the remains on the counter top. She did not, however, get out the chocolate chip cookies she had hurriedly baked after receiving Brigg's call. They were sitting on the refrigerator, on top of the Monopoly game she had borrowed from a neighbor when she had been looking forward to entertaining Brigg's two *little* children. She almost choked on her sandwich to think of that.

Eventually the girls joined her in the kitchen, but said nothing to her, so she didn't talk to them either. She had offered a meal once, and they had refused; she wasn't going to give them a second chance to play at humiliating her. Instead she picked up the evening paper and buried herself in the financial page. But when they remained standing awkwardly in the doorway, she relented a little.

"Help yourselves if you get hungry," she said with her mouth half-full.

It was a relief when she heard the crackling sounds of the potato chip package being opened, and could smell the sweetness of freshly sliced apple. There was space in the booth for both of them, and Carla didn't even have to slide her paper away when they sat down across from her. She glanced over the top and gestured toward a pile of magazines on a rack in the corner, then went back to reading. They soon followed her example.

The tension between them measurably eased. Eventually she did get out the cookies. And when she began to make a pot of coffee for herself, and the girls asked for some, she made enough for them, too.

They didn't really seem to like the hot brew, for they merely sipped at it while they thumbed through some fashion magazines. But by drinking it they had made their point that they were equals with her, and eventually they included Carla in their stilted comments, which she took to be a slight gesture of acceptance. When she got up and began rinsing off her plate, the long-haired twin surprised her by offering to dry, and the other girl wiped off the table. They both functioned as if they had never done such tasks before. But working together seemed preferable to the uncomfortable silences which had filled the previous two hours, so Carla decided to push her luck. She asked them to help her carry some boxes outside.

"What are you doing with all this stuff?" the long-haired twin named Jane asked when she saw the boxes in the guest bedroom. Carla now knew it was Jane, because the other one had called her by name when they were working on the dishes. Finally!

"Getting ready to move. I have to be out next month."

"You'll never make it."

"I'm not taking the furniture," Carla said, "just little personal things. I'm giving these books to a veterans' second-hand store."

They helped her put the three heavy boxes out in the hall where a pickup driver would be getting them the next day.

"I'd think you'd want to take books with you," the short-haired twin named Ann observed as they walked back to Carla's room.

"I won't have enough shelf space. Since I won't be

teaching this semester, I'll have to bring home all the personal books I had in my classroom, so something had to give. Most of those volumes we took out were my husband's."

"Your husband?" The girls attacked that statement with interest.

"We're divorced, and he's remarried," she said bluntly.

How that hurt, even now. It had taken her a couple of years to adjust after the decision to separate from Charles. But he had not had similar difficulties. Just three months after their divorce, he had remarried. The new wife had her own public relations business and apartment in Detroit, where Charles had a branch store, and she had supported him until he had reluctantly divested himself of several other branches, and the economy picked up enough to put his business back into the black. Now she handled his public relations account for free. Charles kept an apartment in Chicago near his main store, and they maintained an apparently satisfactory commuter marriage.

Occasionally after he was first remarried he had called Carla when he got lonely, so she had changed her unlisted number. Almost groaning, she snapped out of that train of thought.

"I've already given away most of the things he left behind, but I had saved some of my favorites from the books. Oh, well."

It was painful to give up Charles's collection of Russian authors; that was one of the few passions they had shared in common. But she had read them all at least once, and one had to be practical. Her house was quite small.

"I'm surprised you have to move just because you lost your job."

Carla was amused at the way Ann said "lost your job," as if she had been fired and Brigg was withdrawing his support, too.

She hadn't decided just how to respond when Jane asked bluntly, "Are you moving in with us?"

"No, I am not!" Carla turned her back on the girls and pulled out a stack of bubble paper before beginning to wrap one of the music boxes arranged on the shelf by her bed.

"Well, it seemed a logical question," Jane explained belligerently. "Jody doesn't really need the whole downstairs apartment, so I guessed Dad might figure he'd have room..."

"Jody is your housekeeper?"

"Yes, she's raised us since we were babies."

"I assure you Jody is in no danger of having to share her apartment. Nor are you. I have a place of my own."

Carla avoided the issue plaguing the girls. She doubted they'd believe Brigg was not paying for this new place.

"What can we do to help?" It was Ann who sat down beside Carla, her face a little less hostile. So, with an accepting sigh, Carla waved her hand toward the bubble paper.

"I'm packing my music boxes." Her adoration for her collection helped her get her voice back to normal. She admiringly picked up a gold filigree miniature, grimacing self-consciously. "It's silly for someone as mammoth as I am to collect such delicate things, but I love them."

"I can see why." Ann picked up a porcelain dancer standing on an ivory inlaid grand piano. As she pressed the release mechanism the dancer turned to the tune of a Chopin waltz. The music was in perfect pitch, the tone warm and light. Ann watched in awe.

"Ann's an artist. She'll have to examine each one." Jane squatted by the bookshelf and began efficiently wrapping a less delicate box. Her movements were so like Brigg's, even in the way she bent over the packing crate to put in the wrapped item, that Carla almost stared.

"You're not as interested in art?" she asked Jane curiously.

"No. That's one way we're not identical. I have no talent. My drawings always look like blueprints."

"Where *are* you going to live?" Ann had finally torn her eyes away from the dancer and returned to the question that worried her the most. And this time it was incredibly funny. Both girls were looking at her with such undisguised anguish, that she burst out laughing.

"Listen, you two women of the world"—Carla grinned at them almost affectionately—"I happen to prize my independence very much. I am moving—at my own expense, I might add—into a tiny, tiny Victorian carriage house in the suburbs because I prefer a house to an apartment. I have lost my teaching job due to declining enrollment, but I will still be self-supporting. You and your father are nice people, but you are not, I repeat, not, included in my future plans."

"I was only making conversation," Ann stammered, her face seeming to lose ten of its pseudo years of maturity in her confusion.

The air had cleared a bit after Carla's amused declaration, and they had worked together rather well. No one could say they had become friends, but at least they were more comfortable together.

They were having a second cup of coffee when Brigg finally arrived. Jane let him in, but both girls watched him curiously when he approached Carla in the kitchen. She could feel the return of their resentment toward her, and realized they were expecting him to kiss her passionately.

"Some father you are, working so late that you miss your flight." Carla threw down the gauntlet immediately, not even getting up from her place in the corner of the booth. "Your daughters were rightfully suspicious of some strange woman showing up and telling them they were to come home with her."

"We did call Jody and a few other people, Dad," Jane explained sheepishly. "I mean, you always told us not to go with strangers."

"You didn't bother to tell your office or your housekeeper of your change in plans," Carla continued in genuine disgust.

"Why should I have bothered? I asked you to get them."

"No one even knows me, Brigg. The girls were perfectly right to be careful. They finally called Suzannah."

"Oh God!"

"Aunt Suzannah said—"

"I can imagine what she said," Brigg grunted, slouching into the booth beside Ann.

He glared at Carla, then his expression softened as he looked at Ann at his side, and Jane, who had seated herself across from him beside Carla. It was as if he had immediately thrust aside their complaints as irrelevant. He was home and they were no longer to be upset with him. Carla almost hated him for his insensitivity.

"What happened to your hair, sweetie?" He ruffled Ann's short cut.

"Oh Dad, she beat me to it," Jane wailed before her sister could answer. In the awesome presence of her father she amazingly lost the mature aplomb she had been exhibiting all evening. "We decided not to look like each other anymore, and I was thinking of getting mine cut that short."

"I didn't know," Ann protested in equally reverted immaturity, glancing at him fearfully as she ran her hand over her short, soft curls.

Brigg stared first at one, then the other, at a loss for words. Apparently when he couldn't figure his daughters out, he decided their concerns were inconsequential. His eyes fell to the table where he saw the steaming cups in front of him.

"Are you letting them have coffee?" he accused Carla incredulously.

"I am," she said firmly. "Shut up, Brigg, and have some yourself." It would be tragic if he treated his daughters like incompetent babies in front of her. They would never forgive her for witnessing their humiliation.

He was scowling at her and just opening his mouth when Jane popped out of her chair.

"I'll get your coffee, Dad," she said enthusiastically. "I want mine warmed up anyway."

Brigg blinked at that, but upon Carla's harsh kick to his ankle underneath the table, mercifully said nothing in reply. He was too busy trying to interpret Carla's determined glare.

For once he seemed unable to read her thoughts. He drank most of the coffee before shoving his feet in front of him, taking up more than his share of the breakfast nook, and turning his attention back to his daughters.

"What's that you've got on your face, Ann?" he finally asked.

"Makeup," she answered haughtily.

"Did Carla give it to you?"

"She did not," Carla exclaimed in exasperation, climbing over his feet so she could join Jane leaning against the counter. "Ann and Jane know what cosmetics are best for them without any advice from other adults. Isn't it time you three were getting on your way?"

Brigg remained sullenly in the booth, trapping Ann there. But the two girls seemed so anxious to leave that he finally did unwind his form and stand up.

"Here's your hat, what's your hurry?" he grunted to Carla as he strode past her.

"Un—Dad, you might want to get your money clip," Jane's face was flushed. "You know, the one Ann and I had monogrammed for you on your birthday. It's where you left it, in Carla's bedroom."

Carla was startled, not having noticed any money clip in her room. But then she wasn't an ardent duster and could easily have missed it. Her eyes darted to him, but he was already striding unselfconsciously toward Carla's bedroom. She couldn't figure out when he might have laid it in some cranny there, but apparently he remembered exactly where it was.

The implication of how that missing money clip might appear had finally hit Brigg by the time he returned with it in his hand. He began hastily explaining what good friends Carla and Suzannah were, and how it had been such a coincidence to run into Carla again at Suzannah's high school reunion. Then he launched into a ridiculous story of how he had dropped the clip in Carla's car when she had taken him and Suzannah to the reunion, and he had decided to have her pick up the girls so he could get both them and the clip. It was too ludicrous to allow it to continue.

"Your daughters aren't babies, Brigg," she exclaimed. "They know we sleep together. Now, fun as this has been, I wish you three would get on your way because I have an early flight out tomorrow."

She pointedly held the door open, refusing to acknowledge Brigg's flabbergasted fury. The girls, however, were perfectly pleased with Carla's calm reply. They even expressed their thanks for her help and wished her a rather enthusiastic good night.

When she closed the door behind all of them, she leaned wearily against the wall, undecided whether to laugh or cry.

It was after two o'clock when Brigg called Carla. He knew it was too late, but it had taken him that long to get the girls settled at home and Jody placated for all the confusion he had caused by missing his flight. And with Carla's peculiar behavior plaguing him, he was in no mood to be considerate.

"Disturbing me in the middle of the night is a habit I wish you would give up," she grumbled sleepily after he identified himself.

"What did you tell those little girls about us?" he shouted into the phone.

There was silence for a moment, and he almost thought she had hung up until he could hear the soft rustle of fabric and figured out she was burrowing down in her covers. Yellow ones, warm and fluffy, he thought sullenly, if he remembered correctly from his brief study of her bedroom the morning he had left her apartment.

"Why don't you look at them carefully tomorrow," Carla finally said sleepily.

"If I'd known you'd try to upset my little girls, just to get even with me, I would never have asked—"

"You listen to me!" she shouted back, now apparently fully and indignantly awake. "Your little girls happen to be almost sixteen years old if you haven't counted recently, only slightly younger than their mother was when she started sleeping with you. And they have been attending a school full of extremely sophisticated young people. If you think their father can send a strange woman to take charge of them without their drawing some adult conclusions, then you're more stupid than I think. From the minute Suzannah admitted you knew me, they resented your springing me on them that way. They even assumed that you're paying for my apartment."

"They're too young for those ideas."

"And, furthermore," Carla ranted, "you made their suspicions worse by starting that dumb, garbled explanation about how your money clip got in my apartment. They'll never believe anything you say about us after an idiotic move like that!"

"They darned well better believe me. Keeping my hands off you the night I slept there wasn't the easiest thing I've ever forced myself to do."

Her gasp at his lustful confession was audible, and he immediately regretted his impetuous honesty, cursing himself for blowing his efforts to go slowly with her. There was a strained silence. He could hear her shifting restlessly in her bed.

"Carla?"

"Brigg?" They both spoke at once.

"So the girls think that you and I—" He ventured carefully in the tense gap, still finding the idea of his daughters reaching such conclusions utterly incredible.

"They think it," she confirmed gently.

"I never thought picking them up would place you in an awkward position. They probably won't tell any— oh, hell! They've already called Suzannah."

"My reputation is irrelevant at this point; it's the fact

that they're almost sixteen, not six, that you need to be grappling with. Your daughters are short *women,* Brigg! I went to that airport looking for elementary-school children. Instead I find curvaceous, knowledgeable, competent—"

"All right, all right. I get your point. I'll take a good look at them at breakfast."

"And keep your mouth shut. Don't criticize their makeup and don't suggest taking them to a Walt Disney movie for the day."

"Anything else?" he snapped sarcastically.

Carla sighed heavily. "It's none of my business," she admitted. "I—it's time we both got some sleep, Brigg."

"Who can sleep?"

She had no answer for that.

"Why didn't you tell me you've lost your job and you have to move?" he demanded.

"Your girls talk too much." He could tell she was annoyed.

"They said you won't be teaching next semester and that you have to move," he insisted. "How bad is your financial situation?"

"Look, Brigg, I want you to stay out of this. I'm fine. I'm moving by choice and I do have a good new job."

"You haven't changed, Giant Child. Always ready to help others, but rejecting their concern for you."

"I don't want you in my life, Brigg," she said bluntly, almost making him believe it. But not quite.

"You've got me, whether you want me or not."

Chapter Five

Carla enjoyed her long Christmas weekend in Colorado. She had arrived in time to help her parents decorate the tree, but there was little else in the way of work for her to do the rest of the visit. Her mother was an excellent cook and housekeeper, who missed having a daughter to fuss over, so she refused all Carla's offers to help. Most of the days Carla ate as much as she could reasonably tolerate, napped, and took numerous short walks in the mountains with her father. The weather was sunny and the winter snows seemed in a pausing pattern, which made the cold climate bearable for outside activities. Carla did ski one afternoon with a recently divorced doctor who was also visiting family there. And in the evenings numerous neighbors would come over for long conversations before the fire.

All in all the visit set her mind greatly at ease concerning her parents. She could see that they had a satisfactory social life, and the mountain climate still seemed to alleviate her mother's allergies and invigorate her father despite their increasing age. She made a subtle examination of their finances and felt that they were managing fairly well; it was not yet necessary to suggest they accept any help from her. However they didn't object that her Christmas gift to them was a voucher for round-trip airline tickets to Chicago. The fare would have seriously strained their budget, but they had found the two years since last seeing Carla too long, so they readily agreed to her request that they spend spring break with her.

Her mother was excited to hear about the new job as reading supervisor, and despite Carla's honest explanations, she assumed the job change was a long-overdue promotion. Carla helplessly wondered if parents ever got over their blind pride in their children.

Predictably they wanted to hear all about her visit to Shelbyville, and brought up their oldest friends, the Carlyles. Somehow Carla managed to tell stories of the reunion visit without letting her own tenseness reveal itself. And they had appeared satisfied, especially after she reported that Brigg had gotten bald. It was hilarious to her that her father considered her too young and attractive for a bald man, even if that man were Brigg Carlyle, whom he admired very much.

She arrived back in Chicago in midweek, rested and ready to tackle packing up the rest of her personal things for moving. She wanted to get all her knickknacks delivered to the new house before school resumed, leaving only her clothes to transfer at the end of January.

She was in and out of her condominium the remainder of the holidays while she ran errands, hauled boxes, and rearranged things into the shelves and closets of her new location. Most of the necessary repair work and redecorating of the carriage house had already been done. The furniture she had acquired for it still had to be delivered, but the kitchen was equipped, and she kept a cot there, so she even spent the night twice. It had been fun work, because she could always run the few feet to the main house for a break with

Tom and Mattie Howard, the couple who owned the farm on which her house was located. She had met them when their youngest daughter was a student of hers. They had run short of cash that fall and had been pleased to sell the little house and it's half-acre lot to her, both to solve their financial crisis and to guarantee that they would have an agreeable neighbor. One of the nights she stayed over was New Year's Eve—a significant gesture, she decided. She enjoyed a quiet celebration at the Howards' with a few of their friends, and had gone to sleep early the first morning of January rather satisfied with her future prospects.

On the second morning of January, her last day of vacation, she was giving the condominium a thorough cleaning when the Carlyle twins surprised her with a call.

"Carla, Dad thought you might like to do something with us today." The young voice sounded much too casually innocent to Carla's sensitive ears.

"Are you Jane or Ann?"

"This is Jane. Dad thought you might enjoy some company."

"He gave you my number and had you call for him?" That didn't sound like Brigg. He was a man who made his own dates.

"We copied your number when we were in your apartment, in case we ever needed to find Dad." Jane hesitated, seeming to be trying to cover the mouthpiece. "It would just be Ann and I today. And a friend."

It took Carla a moment to react because she was thinking how like Brigg his daughters were, even to the pragmatic idea of copying her unlisted number.

"A friend?" She eventually asked suspiciously.

"The daughter of Dad's French partner is here.

We're entertaining her while the men have a meeting, so of course she would be included."

"I see," Carla said carefully, and she did. Quite well. "What's the matter, Jane, don't you speak French?"

"It isn't that. We really wanted you to do something with us."

"We're both adults. It's all right to level with me."

The girl hesitated, then put aside her conniving. "She's deaf." Jane whispered into the phone.

"The French girl? Then why are you whispering?"

"I don't want to hurt her feelings just because we can't figure out what to do with—oh, she can't hear me anyway, can she?" She mumbled self-consciously.

"How old is this girl? I mean, really. Not what your dad told you."

"He's not too good about ages, is he?" Jane admitted. "She's ten. Since you're a teacher we thought you might—"

"I would think she'd enjoy the same games and toys you played with at that age, if you still have any around. And you can always gesture."

"It's not that easy." Frustration tinged with tears was noticeable in Jane's risingly pitched voice. "Dad's going to be so mad at us if she's not happy."

Carla's heart lurched. How like Brigg to put such personal pressure on people, even unintentionally. Everyone was too eager to please him. She remembered herself at almost that same age, anxious about what a much younger Brigg would think of her.

"What have you three been doing this morning?" Her voice softened perceptibly. She knew now why they had called her for help. Of all the people they knew, her awareness of their inadequacies would matter the least.

"Dad and his partner had to meet some people early,

so they dropped Elise off here. Jody cooked pancakes, then we gave Elise a tour of the house. And now she and Ann are in the living room acting as though they're looking at magazines. It's awful. We can't very well watch television all day, since she can't hear it."

"Have you thought of taking her someplace? The weather's unusually warm, so it should be nice getting out."

"Where? Her father said adults have been taking her to zoos and museums all the time they've been in this country."

"Did your Jody have any suggestions?"

"She's just like Dad. She thinks kids automatically have a good time together. What are we going to do?" Her voice broke. "Dad will be so mad," she repeated bleakly.

Angrily Carla wanted to tell her to forget about what her father thought. But she didn't. "Do you have good bus service from your place to downtown?" she asked instead, having no idea where Brigg lived.

"Sure. We're taking the bus down to meet Dad and his partner at his office at five o'clock."

"I'd enjoy meeting the three of you for lunch, if you'd like to walk around and look at the Christmas decorations in the Loop. They're still up, I assume, and I haven't had a chance to do it yet this season."

"Oh would you? That sounds perfect." Jane sounded so relieved it was pitiful.

"Pick a time and place for me to meet you."

"Why here?" Carla asked curiously of Jane when she arrived at the candy counter at Marshall Field's.

"Dad always meets us here when we come into town."

"It figures," Carla said in amusement, glancing at

the lollipops, jelly beans and chocolate Santas cheerfully displayed all around. It would certainly never occur to Brigg to meet them at the cosmetic counter. She turned her attention to the scrawny, very frightened little girl listlessly hanging behind Ann.

"This is Elise," Ann tugged the child forward and gestured stiltedly to direct her attention toward Carla.

Obediently the girl shifted her eyes, her confusion evident.

Carla moved directly in front of the child and whispered in what she hoped was correct French, *"Bonjour, Elise. Je m'appelle Carla."*

The girl's face was immediately transformed by a bright smile, and she enthusiastically stuck out her hand, repeating a close approximation of *"Enchantée, Carla!"*

"She lip-reads; she understood you," Jane gasped, astounded.

"I wish my French were better." Carla continued to smile back at Elise as they solemnly shook hands. Knowing whispering was frequently easier for deaf people to lip read, she quietly formed the words. "I am a friend of Jane and Ann. *Je suis une amie,* uh—" She made the deaf sign for the English word "friendship," and added Jane and Ann's names. Elise nodded enthusiastically and made the sign back, repeating some guttural French syllables that Carla could not understand, more, she suspected, because of the language difference, than because of Elise's speech difficulties.

Carla explained that her French was not very good. Then she dragged out of her shoulder bag a signing dictionary from one of her courses with handicapped students, which fortunately had been in the final box of books she had yet to transfer to her house.

Thinking it might be best to eat lunch before walking

around the city, she began turning through the pictures of families eating. After watching Carla's hand signs and glancing at the pictures, suddenly Elise enthusiastically said "*Oui, oui, J'ai faim*" and rubbed her tummy. Jane and Ann burst out laughing, certainly understanding that sign.

Once it was decided to have lunch, they still had to make up their minds where and what to eat, so Carla began working through the dictionary again.

As she and Elise continued their rudimentary conversing and gesturing, Ann and Jane were also telling Carla: "Roast beef, I want. No, me for Taco."

"Girls, you really don't have to speak to me in one word sentences," she grinned. "I can hear you."

Just then Elise came up with an excited gesture and a very clear pronunciation of: "Hot dog! Mmmmmm!"

"That's it!" they all laughed together.

Carla chose a small grill which overlooked the avenue along Lake Michigan. "Europeans love their parks, and along almost every river running through their cities they create places to eat and walk," she explained to the twins. "Elise should feel at home looking out over the lake."

And Carla had been right. During lunch Elise had been visibly more relaxed, and the Carlyle girls made use of the deaf dictionary to manage some communication with her themselves.

After their meal they walked past the major stores in the Loop and admired the variety of Christmas displays, many of which were animated. Then they worked their way back to the shoreline to stroll free of crowds and skyscrapers. The wind coming off the lake was chilling, but Elise seemed in no hurry to leave. She was fascinated with the motion of the waves, and watched eagerly any movement out in the distance, occasionally calling the twins' attention to a far-off boat she particularly admired.

"There's nothing wrong with Elise's eyesight," Ann commented as they all recrossed Michigan Avenue, with the vague idea of finding a coffee shop where they could get something to drink. "I should learn from her for my drawing. Maybe if I wore earplugs I could train myself to look better."

"Speaking of looking gives me an idea. We ought to take Elise to the Sears Tower," Carla said. "I'll bet she'd love the view."

Jane was carrying the signing dictionary and she showed Elise a picture of a skyscraper, but Elise just smiled politely, wondering what she was supposed to do.

"Like the Eiffel tower," Ann explained enthusiastically.

"Oui, oui. Allons!"

"Let's go!" Carla laughed.

It was overwarm with all four of them crowded into the cab, and Jane rolled down a window slightly. "It must be terrible not being able to hear," she observed pensively to her sister. "Just think of all the sounds of the city you would miss." They became still at that sobering thought, and the din of fast moving traffic, the occasional honk of a horn, the lonesome noises of the distant lake traffic seemed doubly poignant.

But when they glanced sympathetically at Elise, they were surprised to see her happily looking out the window too. She was lifting her face to the breeze coming from the open window, and as if on cue, they became aware of what she must be absorbing through her other senses. They discovered the contrast of the cool wind on their flushed faces, of the smells of the Italian restaurant they passed, the colors of winter coats, traffic lights, and decorated windows. It was almost anticlimactic to arrive at their destination.

But the trip up the Tower was a huge success, too. At first Elise was frightened by the height, for she was not accustomed to skyscrapers that size in Paris. But once she got to the top and saw the panorama spreading below her, she was enchanted. She babbled in French and signed so enthusiastically, that soon she and the twins were laughing together over everything she pointed out.

Later, in thinking over the day, Carla decided that teenaged girls were decidedly strange. She had certainly had her own irrational moments as an adolescent, and times seemed not to have changed. Now Elise, still only ten, Carla could understand. Elise had become a loyal friend and had bid an affectionate good-bye when Carla left them outside Brigg's office building. But the Carlyle twins, once they realized the end of a successful day was in sight and they would be taking a *happy* Elise back to her father, couldn't get rid of Carla quickly enough. She suspected that they were worried she might go with them to Brigg's office and receive part of the credit for herself.

After getting home she decided she had seen the last of the Carlyles for a while. And as if to punish herself for even hoping otherwise, she washed the city dirt off her windburned skin, pressed soothing lotion over her face, and then shunned putting any makeup back on. She changed into an old pullover sweater and some wool slacks that bagged in the seat from age, and brushed her hair unstylishly back from her face.

Carla didn't fool herself, though. When the doorbell rang later that evening, every reaction in her body hoped it was Brigg. She hated herself for that, and her resulting caution was evident when she opened the door and saw him standing before her.

"What do you want?" she demanded.

He didn't touch her when he first came in. Instead he tossed his coat on a table and stalked restlessly around the living room, obviously not pleased by his reception. Disturbed herself, Carla returned to the chair where she had been mending an old sweater.

"Can't you afford new clothes?" he snapped harshly, looking over her full figure, so ill complemented in the garments she was wearing. She didn't know if he was talking about the things she had on or the sweater she was mending.

"I *like* these clothes," she said honestly.

"Suzannah told me Charles Blake was almost ready to file for bankruptcy when you divorced, and that your pulling out was what saved him. You refused alimony, assumed responsibility for the loans on the condo and his car, and left your sizable investment in his business with no strings attached. When the economy picked up, he should have bought out your half of his business. You were a fool to let him write off your money. Did you get a job for next semester yet?"

It was quite a speech. She sighed. "I've had a job all along. It's just not classroom teaching."

"But not for enough money to keep your apartment or buy a new sweater."

"I'm subleasing this condominium because I want to, not because I have to. I saw the handwriting on the wall when Charles began overexpanding, but he didn't want my advice. So I squirreled away a little savings for myself besides what I put into his firm. Brigg, for heaven's sake, won't you sit down?" Her neck ached from trying to look up at him.

He sprawled on the couch across from her, stretching his long legs out in front of him. She could tell that he didn't believe her assertion of financial independence and was waiting for another explanation. But she stubbornly refused to expand on things.

Brigg was not her keeper. It was none of his business that there had been too little equity in the condo at the time of their divorce to justify selling, so even though she had planned eventually to move into a house, she had kept up the payments as an investment. Now the neighborhood had become so popular that the resale as well as rental potential had skyrocketed. So Carla had taken the savings she had accumulated with her parents in mind, and bought the carriage house. The rental she would get for the condo, furnished, was more than her monthly cost of both properties, and would maintain a future nest egg if her parents should ever need help.

"And where have you been all week? I've been ringing the phone off the wall." He was making a faint scratching sound as he rubbed his hand across his whiskers.

"You need to trim your beard," Carla observed, trying to get his mind off her.

"I may keep it like this until the weather gets hot." He sounded distracted.

Unexpectedly a churning ground deep in her gut as she wondered what it would be like to be kissed by that bearded man. Not the careful, planned show he had forced upon her at the motel. But a genuine kiss, full of caring. Her lips tingled almost hurtfully.

"Ouch!" She had absentmindedly jabbed her finger with the needle.

"What are you doing, woman!" Brigg leaned across and grabbed her hand, examining the little drop of blood oozing from the puncture. It was really nothing. But the pressure from his holding her only forced the drop to swell. Brigg placed her finger to his mouth.

"A pinprick is hardly a snakebite, Brigg," she protested, too much aware of every sensation of the texture of him against her fingertips: the roughness of his tongue sucking away the blood, the way his gray facial hair was more bristling than the dark brown, the warmth of his lips, the hardness of his firm chin. She saw him start to bury his lips in her palm and she pulled her hand out of his grasp.

Angry, he bounded up and again stalked restlessly around the room. "Where have you been? I called your parents and they said you came back in the middle of the week."

"I've been moving stuff to my new place, and I stayed overnight a couple of times." Then she stood up in annoyance, wondering why she gave him an accounting of her whereabouts.

He appeared of no mind to leave, and she questioned what to do about him. She doubted that he had eaten, for the girls had said he would be dropping them off at home before taking Elise and her father to their motel. But she hesitated to share the intimacy of a meal together.

"Why did you come?" she asked instead.

"To thank you for helping out the girls," he grunted grudgingly, standing awkwardly across the room from her. "I realized after we left Elise at the house that they could never handle the situation. But Maurice and I had to get to a meeting and—"

"I hope you didn't tell them that?"

"That I had a meeting?"

"No! That they couldn't handle entertaining Elise. They try too hard to please you as it is."

He shoved his hands into his pockets and glared at her. "Why is it that every time you talk to me about my daughters you start making insulting accusations?"

She threw up her hands. "So I'm thanked for entertaining Elise. Thank the girls, too."

"You can't let it alone, can you? Okay. I'm the world's worst father, I admit it. Does that satisfy you?"

"You know you're not the world's worst father," she said unsympathetically, "or your girls wouldn't love you so much. You're just an ostrich."

"Fine. Am I supposed to be pleased with that?"

"I really don't care if you're pleased or not." She moved toward the kitchen, his puzzled dejection defeating her.

"Have you eaten?" she asked curtly.

"Yes, no. I don't know. Lunch, I guess."

Carla checked to see what she had in the freezer. The past summer one of her neighbors had given her produce from his country garden, and she had made several pots of homemade soup. She thought that maybe, with some crackers and a piece of fruit...

Brigg filled the doorway behind her. "What are you doing?"

"I've already eaten. But I can give you a bowl of vegetable soup."

"I'd like that."

In his presence every sound was dynamic. Carla loosened the frozen soup from its container, and it plopped into the pan with a loud bounce. The blaze of the gas jet whooshed like an explosion. And the crisp paper that was wrapped around the crackers was the worst of all. Her fingers shook as she tried to undo it with a minimum of noise.

"I wish you'd just go sit down in the living room until I have your food ready," she said nervously.

He moved from his position at the door, but toward her instead of away. She dropped the crackers to the counter and stood motionless, her hands fatalistically hanging at her sides. Even before he gently clasped her shoulders, she could feel the warmth of him all along her height. When he drew her against him, it was only a completion of that intense, hot aura that was already engulfing her, tempting her. She tried to fight the pleasure, tried to quell the thought that this was what she had been waiting for. Perhaps all her life. This one moment, to stand with her sensitive back pressed against Brigg Carlyle's body.

She couldn't help the softening, the release of a pent-up sigh. His breath immediately expelled the same emotion and he buried his face in her thick hair.

"This feels so good," he groaned against her neck.

She couldn't deny it. It felt wonderful. His beard tugged at her hair as he nuzzled deeper. She began to think she would die if he didn't kiss her soon. But she was too shy even to lift her mouth. In the end he had to turn her, then raise her face to his.

The kiss hurt. How it hurt! Not the pinpricks of his beard, although there was that sensation, too. But the very lushness of it was agony, pleasure so excruciating she ached. She had never believed pressing her body against a man's and exchanging a simple kiss could bring such intense pain, frustrating and passionate all in the same confused moment.

"Don't," she moaned, easing away from him slightly.

"Why not?" His breath filled her mouth. "Until I met you again, I didn't realize I'd been so lonely." His words were almost too soft to hear. He moistened her lips gently, and she momentarily wet his lips with her tongue before opening her eyes wide in distress.

"Don't," she said more firmly, this time moving out of his arms.

He reached for her, but she slid along the counter

away from him. "I don't think I can handle this, Brigg," she said pleadingly. "You always were almost too much for me. But this, this—"

"It's called desire, Carla." He halted close to her. "Surely you're not thinking of your reputation now," he said almost humorously. "As you pointed out, the girls already believe we're sleeping together."

His reasoning was so surprisingly tempting that her whole body reacted instantaneously. She thought for a moment her breasts would explode with hurtful longing if he didn't touch them soon. Her sob of protest was genuine, and he saw the tears forming in her anguished eyes.

"I always seem to make you cry," he said gruffly. His calloused hand cupped her cheek and he brushed at the moisture with his thumb as he had that other night in her apartment. "I don't mean to," he added quietly.

"About your girls—" she said in an unnaturally high, weak voice.

"Do we have to start that?" He thrust his hands deep into his pockets and walked to her kitchen window, where he rested his head wearily against the frosty pane.

Silently she observed the long line of his body, the virility of him. Curiously his bemused puzzlement as he stared out at the night only heightened his masculinity. He hadn't moved by the time she had his food ready.

"Eat your soup," she said, careful not to touch him as she set his meal in the little booth. After he took a seat, she slid into the seat opposite him and absentmindedly nibbled on crackers she did not want. At least she, too, could contribute to the crunching and slurping noises breaking the eerie silence.

He ate heartily, which, oddly, pleased her. At least he would not go away from her completely unrestored.

"That tasted good," he said in a flat, level voice once he had gotten up and set his dishes in the sink. Then he looked at her solemnly and added almost in the same breath, "We could always get married."

She jumped up in consternation.

"What a stupid idea!" She was certain he was joking.

"You can't even see us as lovers?" There was no teasing in his voice, and the silence grew heavy while he waited for her answer.

"You're Suzannah's brother," she protested irately.

"I'm not exactly suggesting that you sleep with *your* brother." He smiled at her reaction.

"It would feel like making love to family," she said urgently. "You've always been outside my life, untouchable."

"You were always untouchable to me, too." He took her hand and began kissing the finger she had pricked earlier, kissing it again and again between short sentences. "Too young. My kid sister's plaguing buddy. But that didn't stop my interest. I was noticing you even before you started developing breasts. I'd never really faced up to all I'd forced out of my mind, until I saw you again." His eyes moved in satisfaction down her figure before he chuckled and drew her against him. "But you definitely don't feel like family in my arms."

Carla held herself stiffly, fighting the comfort and pleasure his body gave her. "But that's it, Brigg. We're both just caught up in schoolkid nostalgia. It will pass as fast as it hit. I'm lonely, too. I'd feel the same for any old friend I got involved with under similar circumstances."

"You saw numerous old friends at Suzannah's reunion. How many have you felt *this* for?"

While he kissed her he covered her breast with his hand, and she could feel his lips curve in jaded satisfaction when she couldn't control her instant response. The melting while he shaped her fullness through the sweater went all the way to her core.

When she tried to stop him, he caught both her wrists and held them behind her back with one hand, then continued to knead her breast suggestively. "Let whatever's destined between us happen," he urged huskily against her throbbing lips.

"I've been married once to an aggressive businessman like you," she protested brokenly. "I couldn't survive that kind of relationship again."

"I'm not Charles." His lips rasped around the outline of her mouth to imprint his own identity there. "I'm Brigg."

His hand remained lightly against her aching breast, his fingertips hovering just over the nipple. He was punishing her.

Her lips trembled and she tried to escape his touch, but he wouldn't let her. Instinctively her body relaxed then, and her breast engorged even more fully into his addictive palm.

"What's that old saw about taking the girl out of the country but not being able to get the country out of the girl?" she asked earnestly. "I can't see myself with a long-term lover. I suppose I need my man coming home every night for pot roast. Can you honestly see yourself in that role?"

"If we married, instead, you'd have a ready-made family. My daughters need a mother at home, cooking pot roast every evening," he pointed out, perhaps not aware that his response hardly answered her observation.

"That's the last thing in the world they need."

Sighing he suddenly released her. "I suppose you're going to insist on making some point."

"They just need their father, that's all. You've done beautifully raising babies, but they're not babies anymore. Do you realize they don't even have the foggiest notion what you do for a living? Today Ann actually said she thought you were a translator."

Brigg did look startled at that, but he said nothing.

"They'll soon be leaving home themselves, and then it will be too late for the three of you to get acquainted."

He frowned angrily and turned away. "You're obsessed with ruining my precious time with you. Always."

"Oh, go home!" she groaned in disgust. He did slip his coat back on and go to the door. But then he just stood there, waiting.

"Aren't you going to wish me a safe trip home?"

Gradually she realized he had no intention of leaving until she came to him. Knowing that implacability behind the brooding countenance, she walked hesitantly toward him.

He had some pull over her; she couldn't deny it. It wasn't the same as in childhood, when her response had been a mixture of childish rebellion and hero worship that she fought with all her young fiber. This was more subtle. Not exactly dominating, for Carla was too independent for that. More the pull of her own caring, her unwillingness for him to go away hurt.

I should sleep with him just once, Carla thought recklessly as she felt his attraction increase with each step as she came closer. *Just get him out of my system, cope with the nostalgia, and kill it with brutal reality. We'd probably be terrible together in bed.*

"Good-bye, Brigg," she said tonelessly when she was as close to him as she could get without actually touching. "Of course I want you to have a safe drive home."

"I'm picking you up at seven for dinner tomorrow."

"No."

"Yes. Wear that blue dress you wore at the farm."

"Never!" She reacted violently to the suggestion. She would never give him opportunity to humiliate her again. What was he trying to do to her? His vileness even to broach the idea gave her the strength she needed to fight him. "I won't go with you."

"I promise to leave the dress alone. In public. You can wear it closed up to your neck with a dozen pins if it makes you feel good."

"Get out of here."

"Although that would be a shame for the elegant lines of that dress. And you'll be seeing lots of elegant dresses where we're going tomorrow. It's a formal gala."

"I won't wear it," she exclaimed. What was she saying? "I won't even go."

"I want you with me. It's business, I won't deny it—I have to make a presentation. But I want you with me. Haven't I given you enough time to get used to the idea of me as the man in your life? Since Thanksgiving. How much time do you need?"

Carla stared at him. Was that what he had been doing all along? Courting, giving her time? Somehow she had known, but couldn't face the reality of it. "Leave me alone, Brigg," she pleaded, weakening.

"Seven," he reiterated, knowing before she did that he had won. He closed her door as he left.

She was relieved that he was gone, but conversely regretted his loss. He hadn't even kissed her good-bye.

She hadn't yet latched the door and it juggled her shoulder when he reopened it. He didn't draw her to him. Instead, he clasped both hands lightly behind her head and leaned into her lips softly—a warm and moist kiss.

"Good night, Carla," he sighed.

This time he set the latch before again closing the door behind him.

Chapter Six

The best cure for wanting anything harmful, Carla decided as she rummaged through her closet the next afternoon, was to overindulge in it. The treatment might be brutal, but effective in getting the obsession behind you. And what was Brigg Carlyle, if not a harmful, unwelcome obsession?

The day was not only the first one back after holiday, but also her first one in her new supervisory post, and there had been much to organize. Therefore she arrived home especially tired, which didn't help with decision making. The only thing she knew for certain was that she would not wear the blue dress. She was almost certain she would sleep with Brigg when he brought her home, but that would take a little more thought when the time came. Contemplating a one-night stand with Brigg Carlyle just to get him out of her system was one thing. Doing it was another.

Her white evening gown would have been perfect to wear, had his business gala been the previous week. But now she couldn't get by with it on the grounds of the unseasonably warm temperatures, because the weather had changed overnight. Winter had finally arrived and with it the first snowfall. Great white flakes had come down all morning, exciting the schoolchildren to an unmanageable fever pitch, then stopping just in time for the roads to be cleared before the ecstatic students and exhausted teachers could be dismissed.

Carla would have much preferred to save herself the trouble of enduring a social evening, and to stay home dressed in those old sagging slacks Brigg found so offensive. If he wanted her badly enough, she thought sourly, he could rip the things off.

She knew she had a bad attitude before the date even commenced. Nervousness, she supposed. But he had suggested such confusing delights. Brigg and Carla? The linkage was absurd, but deliciously tempting.

She tugged first one garment, then another out of her closet, making a much bigger problem out of the choice than necessary. Finally she decided on the long, mauve cocktail suit. It was nicely cut, the fabric a taffeta that shimmered with several shades as she moved in the light, and the skirt was slashed to mid thigh, giving a provocative contrast to the stern design of the beaded jacket. It was almost as elegant as the blue dress, and had the advantage of being less suggestive.

It occurred to her, with a momentary lack of confidence, that Brigg might not want to make love to her after all, that perhaps his advances had been due to temporary loneliness. But as she prepared for the evening, she still took the necessary precautions against pregnancy, bathed with special care, and made herself as lovely as possible.

Brigg arrived on time, looking unforgivably exciting in a tuxedo tailored to his mammoth proportions. She already had on her coat and he agreeably led her outside without noticing that she had not worn what he requested.

In the car her split skirt fell from her thigh beyond

anything her coat could cover, and his eyes kept roving to her exposed leg, shiny tan in her sheer nylons. He said nothing, but his aggressive male appetite, whenever he glanced at her, was a tangible thing. Carla realized then that his interest the previous night had not been temporary. She would certainly have the opportunity to make love with him that night if she wished.

Although the snow had been removed from the sidewalk, the drifts among plantings near the Field Museum were evidence that winter had definitely come to the city. This snowfall was so recent that the three inches covering the tiny patches of lawn and clinging to branches still looked fresh, unsullied by the city filth. One could almost welcome the beauty of winter, had not temperatures fanned by the breezes off the lake been so cold.

Brigg let Carla off at the front of the museum and suggested she wait inside while he parked in the distant lot. But she had preferred to wait for him on the sidewalk. She was shivering even under the protection of her mink coat, so despite turning the collar up high around her neck and stomping her feet a bit in her delicate shoes, her losing battle with the cold was noticeable when Brigg finally came hurrying toward her. He responded instantly to her breathlessness and rosy cheeks, drawing her companionably to his side. His warmth felt so good that she did not object, until he stopped and kissed her thoroughly, forcing other people to go around them.

"We're too old for this public nonsense," she hissed, almost missing the first of the enormous stone steps.

"Speak for yourself," he teased laughingly.

"Wait! We're not really going here, are we?" She

suddenly halted. "What tricks are you up to? I know the Field Museum doesn't serve—"

"Tricks? Can't you see everyone else is formally dressed too?" he soothed, keeping his arm around her to guide her inside.

She couldn't deny that they appeared to be at the right place. Never in her many visits to the Field Museum, not even at special invitation events, had she seen such an elegantly dressed crowd. Curious, she was quiet when they entered the large foyer where people clustered in line for the cloakroom. Through the noisy crush she could catch random glimpses of the familiar great hall, and was amazed that dozens of round tables laid with china and crystal place settings filled the chamber. She looked up at Brigg wonderingly as he helped her ease out of her coat, his own topcoat already shrugged off and thrown casually over his arm.

"Be patient." He grinned into her questioning eyes. "I'll just check these."

When he rejoined her, he noticed what she was wearing. "That's the strangest shade of blue I've ever seen," he said gruffly, frowning at the high neckline.

"I told you I wouldn't wear that dress," she answered belligerently. But she realized that Brigg had been right; no one there would have thought an open neckline too revealing. She had never seen as many sophisticated women in one place. Most were wearing international designer originals—some backless, others almost frontless, and many so outrageous in color and style that the garment attracted attention merely for being different.

Although the mauve cocktail suit was satisfactory, Carla was vain enough to be grateful that she had added to her attractiveness by piling her hair high in loose curls, and emphasizing her height with dangling diamond earrings and extremely high heels. At least when you paired her with Brigg, they were a striking couple.

"I don't dress to aid men in business," she added even more belligerently, feeling her looks disappointed him.

"I wasn't thinking about business when I asked you to wear that blue thing again. But I've just changed my mind about your wearing it here." He didn't elaborate on that statement as he pulled a card from his pocket, then led her to the grand chamber.

Once inside she was so overwhelmed with the unexpected festiveness of the formal hall that she couldn't continue the argument. A chamber orchestra filled the landing of the grand staircase at the opposite end. Its presentation of Mozart muted the level of conversation while people milled about, helping themselves to glasses of champagne from elaborately decorated serving tables. Soft lights gleamed off the high ceilings while candles flickered among the sumptuous flower displays filling the center of each smaller dining table. In the adjoining major display rooms, the scene seemed to be repeated. Tables were set up with gleaming white linens and place settings, and tuxedoed waiters hovered patiently nearby.

"Your mouth is wide open, little girl," Brigg teased gently, enjoying her awe.

"But this is a party suitable for royalty. I've never known the museum to stage such a function."

"You, my dear Giant Child, are attending the Third International Conference of Construction Engineers, complete with guest diplomats from most major nations of the world. We've booked the museum for the night because engineers are not very polite people. We insist on having something interesting to look at, in case our speakers get boring."

Carla laughed, her mood suddenly light. "But what an extravagant, wonderful gesture, to engage the whole museum."

Pleased at her response, he took her arm and led her toward the reception line formed at one side of the grand hall.

"You'll have to meet the big diplomatic and engineering guys before you can get any champagne," he warned. "And that includes Maurice."

"You mean Elise's father?"

"He's a vice chairman of this conference, but he's begged off staying at the head table and will be sitting with us. Don't look so pleased, or I'll believe you actually enjoyed your day out with our three daughters."

"Of course I enjoyed it. What's so odd about that?" she questioned defensively, then bit back any additional sharp retorts because they were being announced to the first dignitary. In passing along the line with Brigg she could not fail to notice the deference with which he was treated. Few had to be told his name, and all took time to make some personal comments to him and to express appreciation of Carla's attractiveness. Even Maurice, who was apparently surprised that Brigg had brought a woman with him, appeared delighted that they would be spending the evening together. He was a small man, but not at all bothered that Carla towered over him.

"You appear to have made an impression," Brigg observed, once they were free of the formalities.

"And you appear well respected by the powers that be," she countered. "Did I detect deference in their manners?"

"I do business in several countries," he shrugged off her indirect compliment casually. "Since that always includes governmental negotiations, these diplomats like to keep amicable contacts."

"I just heard from Maurice that you've brought a gorgeous woman to relieve our boredom tonight." A silver-haired man laid a hand on Brigg's shoulder. "Why didn't you tell us the good news this afternoon?"

He was John McQuiddy, Brigg's other partner and a confirmed bachelor, so Brigg claimed when he introduced them.

"I'm not so set in my ways that I wouldn't prefer talking to a beautiful woman than my business partner anyday." McQuiddy grinned good-naturedly, handing Carla a glass of champagne.

"I suspect he'll feel free to talk business, anyway." She smiled, secretly pleased to learn that perhaps Brigg had not been as certain of her acquiescence as she had thought.

Their table was in the gem room. When Maurice was eventually free of the reception line duties and could join them, they began their slow progress to that location—slow, because the men kept nibbling at the appetizers conveniently located along the way, and Carla kept seeing some natural history display she wanted to stop and look at.

"Carla, you're gawking," Brigg observed humorously at one point.

"I have the most delicious feeling I'm doing something sinful," she confessed to the three men. "Surely drinking champagne in the Field Museum is as taboo as eating popcorn in a library, or running over the tops of church pews."

The men laughed spontaneously, understanding and enjoying her delight at this rare opportunity to socialize in a heritage location.

"You have never been to a function of this sort, then?" Maurice gallantly presented her with a second glass of champagne once they were at their assigned location.

"Never. But I love it." She answered his unspoken toast by raising her own glass to sip of the delicious wine.

"I wonder if you would be enjoying yourself this much if we had been located in the fossil room," Brigg teased as he seated her. "You might have found it intimidating to have a mastodon hanging over your shoulder."

Just then a string quartet in the corner began to play a sonata, too loudly at first, then adjusting the volume to fit in as background music.

"Brigg must bring you to Paris sometime," Maurice observed when conversation could again be heard. "Occasionally we are able to arrange a little party in one of the châteaus of the Loire. It would be my wife's and my great pleasure to take you both."

Carla lowered her eyes at the assumption that she and Brigg came as a pair. Perhaps it was only logical, but— *You are going to be lovers, you know,* an inner voice assured her, the decision suddenly made. *Lovers for a night.*

She tried to control her blush and realized Brigg was sending messages to her with those ice-gray eyes, promising her depths of pleasures he was willing to share.

Maybe for two nights, she amended honestly, because Brigg was hopelessly charismatic. It might take twice for them to learn they were disaster together. The first time would be too urgent.

"What are you thinking?" he asked quietly.

"Nothing," she lied. "I'm just enjoying this place. And the good company," she added more loudly, bringing Maurice and John back into their circle of attention.

Brigg set down the glass of champagne, and small iridescent bubbles of the wine clung to the hair around his lips. Seeing her eyes settle there, he roguishly licked them off with great relish.

"When are you going to shave that scruffy thing?" John McQuiddy asked. "You look like Captain Ahab."

Carla laughed aloud at that, and in a moment Brigg was explaining Carla's childhood story about his name to his partners. While she listened, the words brought back in vivid instant replay that day she had told him — the deserted cemetery, the uneasiness she had felt but couldn't identify, attributing it to feminine overconcern. She remembered that blinding feeling of rightness, of how perfect the beard and baldness were for Brigg-the-man. And as John continued to banter about the need for him to shave it off, her whole body protested. She wanted to feel that beard against her skin, rubbing every inch of her. Rough, stimulating her body with the reality of all that was Brigg.

She looked away in hot confusion. *Maybe three or four times. Just a week or so of seeing each other.*

The rest of the evening passed quickly in a haze of stimulating conversation and laughter. They drank very little wine with their meal, so Carla could not blame her golden feeling on that. It was the aura of Brigg, the easy respect he shared with his colleagues, and their acceptance of her that felt so right it was frightening.

There were four others at their table. Introductions had been made all around and occasionally conversation was universal, but most of the time she was in the private world of Brigg and his partners.

She scarcely noticed what they ate. There were several courses, served on lovely china that appeared over her shoulder, then was taken away again as if the waiters were part of the ethereal staging. There were speeches, most of them mercifully brief. All guests carried their after-dinner brandy in to the Main Hall for those, and it was there that Brigg made his brief presentation of a fellowship the conference was awarding a young Japanese student. Later, finger desserts and demitasse were set on small tables throughout the hall, chairs were clustered for conversation, and there was more music and dancing. Guests wandered throughout the museum at will.

Although Carla exchanged dances with all three men, it was so enchanting to enjoy the museum at night among a beautifully dressed holiday crowd that she suggested they spend the remainder of the evening browsing through the exhibits.

It was after one o'clock when they said their goodbyes in the chill of the parking lot, halfway between where Brigg and John had left their cars. Departing guests were waiting for transportation in such confusion in front of the museum that Carla had insisted on walking along with the three men, maintaining that she needed the fresh air and exercise. So she found herself included in the last-minute business discussions they had to have before parting.

Brigg planned to take Maurice and Elise to the airport the next morning for their flight back to Paris, but John objected to that. "No need for you and Carla to get up early," he explained, with no insult intended. But she had flushed anyway.

"You will be taking care of the Houston meeting then, Brigg," Maurice intercepted smoothly, sensing Carla's consternation.

"Yes, I'll have to go down late next week," Brigg replied, as unaware of Carla's reaction as was John. "I hope it will just take a few days. Then John and I are going to try to consolidate the construction dates on those three smaller Illinois projects. I'd like to—"

Discretely Carla signaled her goodbyes to the others and moved toward Brigg's car, looking distastefully at the snow piled high at the edges of the lot. In the few short hours they had been inside, it had already begun to accumulate the soot of the city. Restlessly seeking a fresher view, she glanced up at the sky. Few stars were visible in the cluttering light of the immense city. She wondered if more might be noticeable in Shelbyville, perhaps as many as that night she had stood so briefly on the patio with Brigg. The skies had seemed afire when she had shared the view with him.

Brigg's arm was within her coat, his hand warm against the small of her back when he guided her down her hall. Wordlessly she handed him her keys and he followed her inside, systematically bolting the door and putting on the night latch behind him. Carla made no pretense of telling him to leave.

"Do you want a glass of wine or some coffee?" she asked after he lifted the mink off her shoulders.

"Coffee, for now."

She left him to care for the wraps while she went in the kitchen to brew the coffee. By the time she came back, he had made himself comfortable, having removed his jacket, black tie, and shoes, loosened the collar of his ruffled shirt, and elevated his immense length on her couch.

She set the coffee down on the low table beside him, her lips curving slightly. "I think you're about to go to sleep."

"Not until later," Brigg said lightly, watching her retreat to the chair opposite him. Then he swung his feet to the floor and reached for the cup she had brought him. Slowly they savored the special feeling of companionship that seemed inherent in sharing coffee together late on a winter evening. For they had plenty of time. They both knew there was no hurry.

She had bought the coffee beans and ground them in the store only that afternoon. The fresh aroma still lingered in the steam rising from the cups, promising a taste too satisfying to exist in reality. But it was good, its warmth and heartiness revitalizing them.

"There's only one thing needed to make my evening perfect," Brigg said softly when he eventually set his empty cup aside.

"What's that?" Carla asked suspiciously, for she expected him to request steak and eggs, home cooked.

"You. Wearing that blue dress."

She set her own cup down with a clatter, unprepared for his malice.

But he laid a restraining hand on her knee, halting her struggles to get out of the deep chair. "What you're thinking is wrong. I simply want to see you in it."

She tilted her head in confusion. Absentmindedly he stroked her knee left bare by the slit skirt.

"You were right that at the family party I wanted revenge for your contempt," he finally said. "But more than that I wanted to make you aware of me as a man. I was tired of being 'Brig' of the past. I intended to fluster you, then pin the dress back up. But when I saw how beautiful you looked I couldn't resist leaving you open to the waist. I regretted it once everyone else started watching you too."

"You were so possessive. I felt like a thing," she said jerkily.

"Yes, I was possessive. I didn't want anyone else getting ideas about you."

"It was like being used by Charles all over again. My body was a business asset."

They seemed to be discussing different fears simultaneously.

"I thought I could take other men looking at you tonight, just so I could see you in that dress again," Brigg admitted gruffly. "But once I was there, I realized I want you to wear it only for me. Please put it on, Carla."

"You're serious?"

He nodded his head. "I need to see you in it again."

He smiled lopsidedly before drawing her to her feet. "With no pins. And with your hair down."

Carla felt in a daze. He walked beside her to her bedroom, then watched her locate the dress in her closet.

"I think I want you to go back in the other room," she said breathlessly, his presence too overwhelming.

He seemed to intend to refuse, then chuckled. "Maybe I'd better. The way I feel right now you'd never get as far as zipping it. But leave the door open. It's nice to hear you dressing."

She was conscious of every sound she made as she slipped out of all her clothes before dusting her naked breasts lightly with scented powder. She didn't bother to put on any fresh underwear or hose. The sound of the zipper of the blue dress harshly broke into the stillness. In response she heard Brigg get up from the couch, and a terrible feeling of waiting enveloped her. Hurriedly she slipped into high heeled blue sandals, then numbly took down her hair. She reached for lipstick, then changed her mind, seeing in the mirror that her mouth was already swollen and red with restrained passion. Her partially exposed breasts undulated in shadows and light while she brushed her curls until they were flowing free to her shoulders.

Her eager yet vulnerable appearance startled her. She hoped Brigg would not be disappointed.

When she switched off her bedroom light, she could tell he was gradually dimming the lights in her living room. The waiting hush when she joined him was so intense she could hear her own breathing.

He had found some wine in her refrigerator, and stood near the couch, holding two brimming glasses. Carla accepted the one handed her, standing proudly erect, almost as tall as he. His eyes slowly went over every inch of her.

"You're magnificent," he said almost reverently. "You can't know—"

She could hardly force the first sip of wine past the lump in her throat. But the second went down more smoothly, easing her nervousness, warming her. As if she needed any warming. Her body was flushed all over with explosive desire.

"Thank you," Brigg said simply, his voice deep and masculine.

She could tell beyond doubt that he was far from disappointed.

They stood a foot apart, still not touching, going through the motions of sipping their wine. Whenever her hand raised the glass to her lips, Brigg watched how her breasts moved in reaction, lifting slightly, extending the valley between them and casting a new pattern of shadows and light across her skin. Meanwhile she took in every crag of his face, every deep shadow over strong bones. Her eyes moved to his hands. Big hands, tanned. She liked the way his fingers curved against the wineglass. Masculine strength against delicacy.

His hands will look that way against me. The thought excited her and it showed in her darkening eyes.

His glass was empty and he set it down. Carla still

had wine left, but he took her glass, sipping some of its contents himself before holding it to her lips and letting the warmth of his own mouth reach her indirectly. The feeling was erotic. She let him help her drink, tilting her head back until the remainder was gone. When he lifted the rim from her mouth, a last tiny drop fell to her breast and she shuddered at the minute cold shock.

He looked at where the drop glittered iridescently against her skin, then set down her glass, too. Slowly his bronzed finger traced from her moist lips past the shimmering droplet to her waist, probing slightly to shape her navel before trailing back to capture the droplet and raise it to her lips. She ran her tongue over his finger, thinking wine had never been so delicious.

"I wonder if there's any left on your lovely skin," Brigg murmured. She could feel his hands shape lightly against her buttocks to steady her while his mouth followed the line his finger had just traced. Slowly his coarse beard prepared the path, scraping the soft skin, making way for his lips to kiss it in reward for what it had suffered.

She drew in her breath to make room for his mouth within the narrowing fabric at her waist, and for a time he pressed her against him, his lips nuzzling in ever larger circles, forcing the dress to spread wider and wider. She sank her hands to his shoulders, wanting him badly. But the game was no longer satisfying him, either.

Carla felt her zipper move before he knelt and drew her dress low on her hips, giving him the access he needed to caress her belly thoroughly. Later, when he lifted her to the couch, her sandals were her only covering, and he towered over her, looking, looking. Absurdly, humorously, she couldn't resist stretching her long legs into a classic pinup pose, letting them drape temptingly up over the arm of the couch before she sank more comfortably into the pillows. His answering grin accepted her provocative challenge.

He's fun to play with. A man, a boy. Everything! She could hardly bear the waiting while he took off his shirt and cummerbund. She liked what she saw. His shoulders were heavily muscled despite his age, the hair across his chest dark and thick, with some grey adding to the attraction.

Brigg could tell that she was deeply moved; her reaction pleased him so much that he abandoned loosening his trousers and left his suspenders hanging at his waist as he eagerly lowered himself against her.

"I don't think I've ever seen you without a shirt before," she mused, watching him adjust his body to the confines of her couch before his stockinged feet played along her ankles and tickled at the straps of her shoes. She shaped her fingers across his forearms, reaching, but unable to go around the hard muscles.

"Didn't we ever swim together?" he asked against the hollow of her neck before letting his mouth nip lower and lower. "How could I have missed dragging you into my favorite farm pond?"

"You did once, but we both had all our clothes on. I—" She withheld a groan of disappointment when he teased around her breasts and moved away, up toward her arms. "You were angry that I—oh!"

She had wanted him to seek her breasts, but this alternative was amazingly pleasurable, this capturing of her arms to stretch them high above her head, so that he could nuzzle deeply into the smooth caverns beneath them, stroking her with his tongue.

"Oh, Brigg." Finally she had to break her hands loose from his grip and stroke him, run her eager fingers across his head, over the thick neck and shoulders. He shifted more intimately against her, and her moan of desire was uncontrollable when he began to suckle her. She stretched her hands far down his back, trying to touch him as temptingly as he was touching her.

For a long time they moved restlessly against each other, burrowing deep into the enveloping cushions, groaning, sometimes laughing, whispering nonsense and passion in the same breath.

Brigg had a scar low on his left shoulder blade. She discovered it sometime in her increasingly frantic caresses, and eventually she leaned up over him to touch it tenderly, kiss it. He laughed at her compassion and rolled beneath her, having to double up his legs awkwardly to make room for her to lie between them.

"Why are two giants like us trying to make love on a couch?" he grunted. But his response when she lovingly rested atop him denied any dissatisfaction with their location. Urgently he pulled her face toward his and kissed her so completely that she heard ringing in her ears.

She could feel him opening his clothing beneath her, and she impatiently lifted herself slightly away, wishing he would hurry. She wanted to touch all of him. But something was wrong; there was still that ringing in her ears. It was strange to resent any sensation when she was so enraptured, but the sound was intrusive; she kissed him back desperately, hoping to blot it out. Still the noise persisted, stopping Brigg's hands from doing the beautiful things they were doing to her. She groaned at the loss.

"The phone?" he ventured, shifting her to his side against the back of the couch once he finally identified the sound.

Disbelieving, she stifled an almost hysterical giggle.

It took a moment for her vibrating body to adjust to the reality. *The phone?* Wasn't this the rescue fictional virgins always welcomed? Time after time, naked in the arms of their men, weren't they saved from the disaster of their passions by a call or an unexpected visitor? But she was no virgin, and she didn't want rescuing.

"Let it ring," Carla mumbled against his throat, reaching the decision instantaneously. Any possible disasters necessitating a phone call to her could wait. She was no youngster whose passion could be quelled with a few second thoughts.

Nor was Brigg. He was kissing her again, deeply, his mouth practically engulfing hers. And his hands—intoxicating, what they were doing.

"Don't stop."

"That damn phone!" He sat up, shuddering.

Her expression revealed her chagrin that he was unable to ignore her personal calls.

"I told the girls they could reach me here tonight," he explained gruffly, looking toward the obnoxiously noisy instrument resting half a room away. "They might be in trouble."

His reactive father instinct shocked her into reality. It had never occurred to her the call might be for him. She dropped her hand from his bare back, her mind clearing. "Answer it," she suggested tentatively.

"Maybe you'd better. If it's someone else, you might not want my voice—"

Laughing in anguish she struggled to her feet. Thinking of her reputation at a time like this. She wanted to cry.

Unashamed she walked erectly across the room, naked except for the high heeled sandals. Upon hearing the distraught young voice on the phone, though, she immediately lost her aplomb and beckoned Brigg to her side. Something was definitely wrong at home. He must have sensed it.

As Brigg listened to his daughter, his face darkened and he ran his hand distractedly over his balding scalp. She perceived his worry and turned away.

Walking across the room to give him privacy, she could still hear the almost childish tones in frantic, unintelligible explanations, could absorb the calming effect of Brigg's quiet questions in response. He was hunched over the telephone table, his naked shoulders shadowed, his trousers resting low on his hips. It was when he juggled the receiver against his shoulder and began struggling to refasten the zipper and waistband that Carla realized the full implication of the scene.

The overriding sound of his daughter's worried voice set against their own flushed disorder suddenly made her feel dirty, something she had never expected to feel in her life. She held her arms to her breasts as she stumbled over her discarded dress and rushed into her bedroom. While walking toward her closet she caught a glimpse of her naked, peach-toned body in the mirror, saw the long curve of her legs, the seductive thinness of her strap sandals.

Sordid. That was the word hovering in her mind. Her first affair—aborted because the man's children needed him at home. Ashamed she kicked off the frivolous shoes. She had already pulled on a bra and heavy knit shirt when he entered her bedroom.

"I have to go," he said in controlled, clipped tones. He was hastily sliding his arms into his shirt.

She nodded, scurrying to her dresser to get fresh panties, since she couldn't find where she had tossed her own clothing when she had changed. Her face reddened because he was watching her struggle into them.

"Jody fainted." He broke his absorbed fascination with her derriere and began fastening the cuffs of his shirt. "The girls were upstairs and heard her fall. She's regained consciousness and says she's fine, but the kids are scared to death."

She watched him trying to stuff his open shirt into his pants. "You'd better button that first."

"You aren't going outside dressed like that, I hope," he countered huskily, still stuffing at the unbuttoned shirt. "I like the view, but you won't look so lovely with a frostbitten bottom."

"Outside?"

"I need you to come with me. I may have to take Jody to a doctor, but the twins are so rattled I shouldn't leave them alone. Jody has been the only mother they've ever known."

Carla watched him go back to the living room for the rest of his clothes. She didn't want to accompany him home. She couldn't take much more, she thought. But still she struggled into warm slacks and boots and hurried out to find Brigg lacing his shoes. He had on his tux jacket, but the ruffled shirt was still hanging open and his tie and cummerbund were abandoned on her couch.

"Ready?" He got their wraps from her closet.

"You have to button that shirt," she insisted, moving to do it for him when he shrugged off her suggestion as unnecessary. The girls could think what they wanted, but she was not going to be blatant about what their phone call had interrupted.

It was pain to brush against his heated chest. He also felt the sensation and tensed, forcing her fingers to fumble in her hasty job. When he helped her into her coat, his sigh of regret said it all for both of them.

Chapter Seven

Brigg reached home in twenty minutes. He should have been arrested.

There was a parking space directly in front of the narrow row house, and as they jumped out and hurried inside, Carla gained no satisfaction in observing that he looked little better than she felt. They both needed more time for their suffering bodies to adjust to the deprivation of lovemaking.

However, the girls did not pay close attention to either of them, because they were anxious to have Jody cared for.

"I just smashed my thumb, that's all," the elderly woman ranted after Jane and Ann noisily ushered Brigg through the first floor to her bedroom at the back. But when Jody held out her hand to demonstrate the problem, her wizened face crinkled in pain despite her attempts to hide it. Brigg turned up the light before examining the extended thumb.

Standing at the bedroom doorway Carla was unable to tell how bad the injury was, so she studied Jody herself. The woman was not at all what she had visualized. Expecting a hefty, healthy grandmother type, she saw instead a tiny cronelike creature wearing a red flannel nightgown and filling only a slight portion of the big bed in which she was lying. Her hands and wrists bore the marks of arthritis, which was not unlikely if her age were anywhere near what it appeared to be. Her thinning white hair was tightly wadded into pin curls, giving her a metallic, balding look. But her eyes sparked belligerent fire as she looked at Carla.

"Who's she?" the woman demanded.

"That's Carla." Brigg snapped, carefully taking her wrist to turn the hand so he could see better. "Did you fall on this thumb when you fainted?"

"No. I'd dozed in my chair watching the late movie, so I was groggy when I got ready for bed. I closed a drawer on it. It didn't hurt at first. I could hear the girls still rattling around up there, and I had walked to the stairs to tell them to get to sleep, when the numbness wore off. I just blacked out for a minute. I kept telling them that." She glared at the twins, trying to intimidate them.

"We heard the thud all the way upstairs, even with the stereo on." Jane objected nervously. "She was out like a light, Dad. She probably has a concussion or—"

Brigg took a look at the slight bump on Jody's head.

"Okay, Miss Jody, girl. You're going to see a doctor." He put his arm around her thin shoulders, lifting her from her determined hole in the pillows.

"I don't need a doctor." She tried to reach around him to point out a cup resting on her nearby table. "I've been putting my thumb in ice. It will be fine if I keep doing that. And I don't have any concussion."

He gently helped her sit on the side of the bed, and motioned for the twins to get her coat. "The girls will feel better if you have this looked at, Jody," he whispered to her. "You're frightening them."

Her lips thinned in preparation for another protest, but when she saw the twins rushing tearfully toward their father with armloads of winter gear, her eyes softened. It was obvious they were near panic.

Grudgingly Jody allowed them to lift her coat sleeve carefully over the injured hand. Brigg went to use the telephone, and Carla stayed out of everyone's way, feeling extremely unnecessary.

"Your doctor's arranged for one of the residents to meet us at the hospital emergency room," Brigg explained when he returned. "That will hurry things up. We'll have a few X rays, and I doubt they'll keep you very long. Now, don't look so angry. I'll be there with you."

"You can't leave these girls alone half the night," Jody sputtered, her further protest cut off when she tried to stand up, and bumped her thumb. Her face turned white and she swayed a little before Brigg swept her up in his arms.

"Carla's here to stay with them."

The housekeeper wasn't satisfied with that and raised her eyebrows questioningly toward Ann and Jane.

"It's all right, Jody." They both fluttered to her side. "She's Dad's girl friend. You know, we told you about her."

"Ah, her," Jody grunted, looking over Brigg's shoulder to examine Carla.

They all followed along to the car, carefully picking their way across the remaining wind-blown snow. Carla had grabbed up an afghan she saw on a couch in Jody's apartment, and she leaned inside the open car door to tuck it around the old woman's knees, while the twins waited anxiously on the sidewalk and Brigg rushed behind the steering wheel.

"Get the girls to bed, Carla." His voice was almost drowned out by the starting of the engine. "I've had all the dramatics I can stand for one evening."

"So I noticed," Jody snorted weakly, looking pointedly at his shirt front. His topcoat and tux jacket were hanging open, and Carla realized in dismay that she had closed his shirt crookedly. The collar was two buttons off.

Jody seemed to find the fact enormously amusing. "I'm going to be ashamed to go in the hospital with you," she said wryly.

Brigg glanced down at his chest to see what both women found so interesting. His glare at the grinning Jody was livid as he drove off.

She can't be hurt too seriously, Carla thought while following the twins back into the house. Not and still harrass Brigg like that.

Jane and Ann, of course, didn't agree. They were almost hysterical despite Carla's assurances, and she realized immediately that bed was out of the question. Somehow they felt they were to blame for the accident. For a while Carla kept them busy making up Jody's bed again and getting fresh ice ready for a new pack.

Then she ran out of ideas of useful things to do. And giving up on reassurances, she instead listened with feigned interest to them repeat over and over their babbling story of Jody's accident. Talking about it seemed to give them the greatest relief from worry. They admitted they shouldn't have been staying up so late—if they had been asleep Jody might have gone on to bed after hurting her thumb and never fainted. Their guilty suppositions were endless.

It took Brigg's finally bringing Jody home to convince them that everything would be all right.

His expression to Carla upon finding Ann and Jane still up was murderous. But he managed to hold his temper under control while he and Jody explained that although she had a broken finger, she was concussion-free and would be fine once she had gotten some sleep. Only when the girls started once again on their guilt-ridden apologies did Brigg bark his displeasure so forcefully that they scurried upstairs to the family apartment. That left him and Carla to settle a very weary Jody for the night.

She had been given a pain-killing tranquilizer, so there was little to do but help her out of her coat and shoes, get her into bed and arrange her splinted finger on a pillow on top of the covers. Jody didn't give up her long-standing authority easily, though, and issued numerous hazy instructions to them both for a few groggy minutes before falling asleep.

When Carla and Brigg eventually came upstairs, they found the girls still scurrying around. Sighing his annoyance, Brigg led Carla down the long hall on the side of the house to the front living room. Motioning her to a chair, he was just turning back to corral his daughters when they burst in, carrying two steaming cups of very strong coffee, and proudly announced that they had put clean sheets on Brigg's double bed.

"For you and Carla to sleep in," Jane explained in a high voice. When she saw her father's darkening glare she hurriedly added, "And we set out cereal for tomorrow, and—"

"Go to bed!" Brigg roared.

They tearfully set down the cups on a small table and retreated toward their rooms.

"You didn't have to scare them to death. They're upset; they think Jody's accident is their fault," Carla objected, tilting her head to better hear Jane and Ann's progress down the hall.

"Damn!" Brigg muttered. Even he could not ignore

the sobs coming from the rear of the house. "You wait here," he ordered belligerently before following his daughters.

He was gone about ten minutes. Carla walked restlessly around the large room, only half looking at the ornate Victorian furnishings, and vaguely observing how the heavy rose and green tones dominated everything. She could hear Brigg's voice, gentle now, comforting. And before long the sobbing ceased.

When he returned, they both settled awkwardly on formal chairs, waiting in uncomfortable silence for the scattered noises of running water and rushing footsteps to lessen and for the house to settle into quiet.

Neither of them wanted the coffee, so Brigg took it back to the kitchen and dumped it out. By the time he returned, Carla had moved to the couch.

He glanced at his watch. "It's almost five o'clock. I feel a hundred years old."

There were a pillow and an afghan on this couch, too, just as downstairs. Carla guessed the frail Jody rested here when she was upstairs cleaning for the family. She kicked off her boots and drew the afghan up over her feet before stretching out. "Go to bed, Brigg," she suggested, closing her eyes.

"Come with me."

"No." She didn't even open her eyes.

"I want to hold you." He stood above her.

"No." There was pain in making the refusal, but, paradoxically, she knew she would not change her mind.

His temper was rising. She could feel the heat from him when he thumped to the floor beside her and grasped her shoulders, forcing her to look at him.

"There was no question before," he barked, trying to lift her up.

She swung her feet to the floor to face him equally.

"That was different."

"I want to go to sleep with you warm beside me. The girls have our bed all made up. You saw that they don't care."

"I care. It's not right. I won't share your bed in your own house with your two daughters in the next room."

"Dammit, Carla!"

"Leave me alone," she moaned, drawing the afghan protectively up around her, her eyes fiery. He knew that upset, stubborn look. He could overpower her, but it wouldn't win him the affectionate response he wanted.

"You'd better not wait too long to decide on marriage," he warned stormily, rising to his feet. "I can't take much more of this."

He bypassed the room the girls had prepared for them and stomped up a narrow flight of stairs that led to the third floor. Carla lay trembling on the couch, trying to force herself to relax and not be bothered by the restless sounds she heard from overhead. But it was hard to ignore the scratch of a heavy desk chair being pulled around the floor, the rustle of paper, sliding of desk drawers. Gradually the faint smell of pipe smoke drifted down to her. She could picture him up there, hurting. She sighed, her own body also knotted in painful longing.

Lovers with Brigg? Impossible. He had even more power to destroy her than had Charles. Her life had been tied up with one-sided caring for Brigg too long.

She arranged her heavy coat over her feet to keep out the advancing chill before sinking deeper under the afghan. With strange fatalism a name bounced over and over in her thoughts. *Carla Carlyle. Carla Carlyle.*

Terrible. It sounded like some night club stripper. It was a joke of a name.

She didn't know what awakened her. Perhaps the light from the double windows alerted her that she was in a strange room. Maybe it was the unfamiliar sounds of urban traffic on the narrow street below. Whatever the cause, she stirred from under the afghan, trying to decide what she was doing in that awful, overdecorated monstrosity of a Victorian room. Lazily she looked at her wrist, but she was not wearing a watch. She was stretching tentatively, aware that she must have overslept, since the room was filled with daylight, when the lateness of the hour finally came through to her.

Scrambling off the couch, she could see no clock in the room, and she rushed down the long hall past a small dining room, then paused at the kitchen.

"Nine thirty!" She couldn't believe it. She was already an hour late for school. Although she hadn't yet started accepting regular reading students in her new job, she had testing conferences with numerous youngsters scheduled throughout the day, and she was horrified that she had notified no one she would be late.

The rest of the house was deadly still, and it took her a couple of minutes hunting on her own to eliminate the kitchen and living room as possible locations for a telephone. She saw one, finally, on a table in the bedroom that was apparently Brigg's. A double bed with rosebud sheets carefully turned back and unslept in was along one wall of the pink flowered room. Slowly she moved inside, distastefully stepping on the pink roses of the rug, cringing from the pink roses on the walls, and gingerly picking up the—yes—the pink telephone.

Nancy must have been in a Victorian flower garden syndrome when she decorated this house. Carla hurriedly dialed the suburban number, her thoughts distracted. The principal himself answered.

"What's happened to you?" he asked almost frantically.

"Would you believe I overslept?" Carla wondered why she hadn't thought up some excuse before she placed the call.

"Well, at least you're not sick," he grunted heavily. "We have three teachers, including your new replacement, out with the flu, and the substitutes are ill, too. My secretary is filling in for one classroom and a couple of mothers have volunteered to stay over for the other classes until we get someone. But from the sound of things in the halls, discipline is already out of hand. I need to pull you off the reading conferences today and get you back with your old students. They're pulling this mother's leg. How soon can you get here?"

"In a half hour, I—" Carla glanced down at her slacks and knit shirt. She couldn't show up wearing those. "Make that an—oh, look, I'll just get there as soon as I can, okay?"

Her voice must have been louder than she thought, because Brigg had apparently been awakened by her call, and as she hung up he stumbled into the room, his eyes heavy with sleep. He was wearing only his shorts.

"What time is it?" he moaned.

"I have to get to work! Find your shoes." She ran past him back to the living room, thinking distractedly that Brigg would look ridiculous running out of the house in only his underwear and shoes. She hoped he didn't try to tease her with that ploy. She could visualize him insisting that he was just doing what she ordered. Hurriedly she got her boots on, then threw her purse and coat over her arm, thinking all the time that the house was remaining too silent.

Carla soon discovered why. Brigg had fallen sound asleep in the middle of the flowered bed.

The first thing Brigg was aware of was the prodding on his shoulder. Dimly he seemed to hear some words, too, but he burrowed deeper into the softness surrounding him; involuntarily his muscles tightened to protect himself from the cold air he felt against his exposed skin. He tried to shut out the insistent voice, wanting only to sleep, to let his beleaguered body, too abruptly startled from its restless limbo, sink back into forgetfulness. He had had a terrible night, and the morning didn't bode much better. He groaned and buried his face deeper into the pillow.

"Brigg, wake up!" The poking got rougher. He swatted at the offender. "I need you to drive me home so I can change for work and get my car. Brigg!"

He was doing a pretty good job of ignoring the female voice until its owner scrambled onto the bed and began genuinely shaking him. Fighting the inertia in both his muscles and brain, he rolled slowly over and focused on the face hovering above him. Carla! He stared, a slow smile starting, before he remembered the night before. *Lord, what a night.*

"Jody's okay. And the girls don't have to leave for school until tomorrow," he moaned groggily, grasping Carla's wrists.

"I'm already at school. Wake up!"

That statement didn't make sense. From his angle Brigg could see Carla's marvelous hair draping around her face, her breasts disturbing the flatness of that knitted thing she was wearing. She looked very on-the-spot to him.

"You're not at school. You're attacking me in my bed." He tugged her down on top of him and threw both arms heavily around her shoulders.

"No! I need to teach—"

The minute her body touched his he was fully awake

and remembered everything. He felt an instant arousal and began kissing her. But because he remembered everything, especially her own embarrassed distress, he was careful to keep his lips light and teasing. Self-control was possible simply to have the pleasure of briefly caressing her.

Carla was in no mood for games, though, and tried to bite his lips, which was a mistake. She should have remembered that her angry reactions to his taunts always made him worse. Lazily he threw his legs around hers to quiet her, and kissed her in earnest.

"Brigg, stop it!" she protested. She tried to avoid his seeking mouth and to wriggle out of his arms.

Enjoying her genuine resistance, he abandoned the kissing tactics and went to work on her clothes. Despite her struggles he had managed to pull off her knit shirt, and was just releasing her bra fastener when he heard the noise in the hall. The girls. How could he have forgotten they were home? Stupid! They were no longer tiny things in cribs, unable to get out until someone came for them. His hands felt helpless on Carla's warm back, and it was too late for him to keep her bra from slipping apart as his daughters walked into the room. They hadn't slowed down their eager entry with any measure of polite caution.

"How's Jody?" the two young voices chorused eagerly. "We heard—oh!"

Damn! Brigg thought fatalistically, sensing Carla's shock all the way to his toes. He jerked to a sitting position, still with a disheveled Carla trapped protestingly against his chest. He studied his daughters' expressions with interest. They were too surprised at his apparently ardent behavior to even back out of the room. Their eyes wandered over his big form, clad only in shorts. Then over Carla in her heavy winter slacks, serviceable boots, and bare back. She was modestly covered by his chest and surrounding arms, but her bra straps were slipping ludicrously off her shoulders. Instinctively his arms tightened even more protectively to shield her.

Both twins were wide-eyed; for all their claims of sophistication, they still obviously had never thought that adults as ancient as their father would behave so uninhibitedly.

Ann recovered first. "Dad, I'm sorry. I mean, you left the door open and—"

Suddenly the irony of it struck him. He had spent a lonely, frustrating night alone to placate Carla's sense of propriety, and here she was, caught in an even more compromising situation. Brigg couldn't help himself; he burst out laughing.

"Dad?"

The poetic justice of it pleased him so much that he couldn't stop the chuckling. He could almost feel Carla's fury heating up beneath his hands. Finally it was to her that the girls looked for an explanation.

"Carla, are you all right?" they demanded, sounding almost protective of her. Brigg loved it and laughed louder.

Carla managed to preserve her modesty while tugging an arm loose from where it was trapped against his heaving chest. "Your father thinks he's funny," she said in a strangled squeak, while she waved vaguely toward the door. "Why don't you go check on Jody? I'll be there in a minute."

The girls gratefully retreated, and as they thundered down the stairs, he collapsed against the pillows, dragging Carla down with him. When she started sputtering and ranting at him, he couldn't resist tugging her bra completely off and threatening her with public ravishment. He knew there was no danger of the girls walking in on them for a while, and it was a ploy he simply couldn't resist. She looked so wonderful when she got angry.

"Brigg, let me go!" She was flat on her back, her magnificent breasts pouting up at him while she struggled, but definitely in no mood to let him pursue the obvious.

"Oh, darling, you deserved it"—he smiled against her mouth—"after the night you put me through." He rested lightly against her, kissing her, trying unsuccessfully to gentle her. But Carla found nothing humorous or acceptable in the situation.

Brigg let her pull free of his teasing arms; then he leaned back against the bed contentedly, enjoying every minute of her furious struggling to get back into her clothes. She cast him a withering look as she flounced out to find his daughters, but he was unchastened.

He was still grinning and telling her it served her right when he dropped her off at her apartment.

"I won't have an affair with Brigg!" Carla kept telling herself that the rest of the day while she struggled with the fractious youngsters in her substitute classroom. She told herself that during the ensuing long night alone in her bed, and the next day and night. And the more she repeated it the more she missed Brigg and wished the twins' anxious phone call had been an hour later. Just an hour. Or maybe two. So they could have made love, once, and destroyed their attraction.

She was in pain with missing him. And her feelings were hurt. She knew the Carlyle twins were to return to school the day after her debacle in Brigg's bedroom, and she had halfway hoped to hear from them before they left. Or at least from Brigg. But she hadn't.

Another day went by, and she was into another long evening at home, alone, convincing herself that the fickle Brigg Carlyle hadn't meant any of it, not about being lovers, certainly not about getting married, when a phone call turned her whole turbulent world around again.

"Where are you?" she shouted into the receiver when she recognized Brigg's voice. She felt that she had to do something to make herself heard above the roaring and chattering noises in the background.

"At the Houston airport. I just got off the plane from Chicago."

"You sound as though you're right on the concourse."

Actually he sounded wonderful. *So much for wanting you out of my life.*

"I am. I grabbed the first phone I found. Look, Carla, it's been a mess at our house and at work, too. I started to call you a dozen times, but something would come up, and I wanted us to have time to—"

"It's all right. How's Jody doing?" The harried guilt in his voice worried her. At the pace Brigg worked, he didn't need guilt dragging on his health.

"Weak. Her cousin's going to look in on her for a few days. The girls were frantic trying to help around the house, but they don't know how to do a thing. And Jody's been barking orders to all of us."

"I'm glad I wasn't there," Carla laughed softly.

"Look, Carla, I'll only be down here a week. When I get back, we—"

"I will *not* have an affair with you," Carla interrupted staunchly, her preconditioned negativism erupting as if one cue.

"Darling, we're *already* having an affair." He breathed the words so gently, she felt as if he were pointing out the obvious in a sex education course. "It's marriage you're going to have to start thinking about. Whether you can take on me and the girls and Jody."

"Brigg, stop that!" she moaned, really hurting. "I wish you'd be serious."

"Carla, you can't possibly not have known, from the minute we saw each other again, that we're right for each other. I've been a widower fifteen years and have never even considered remarriage. I know this is happening fast for you, but I need you; why waste any more precious time?"

"I don't need you!"

"I don't believe that. You just have a bunch of childish hang-ups from the past."

"I have a bunch of grown-up hang-ups from the present," Carla snapped irately. "I broke up the marriage I had fully intended to honor forever, because my husband was never home. Do you honestly think I'd be insane enough to get myself into an identical situation?"

"Your fool Charles was never home because he didn't have the sense to recognize how lucky he was. He put his work first. There's a big difference in what I place first. I'm already feeling out changes in my business that would give me more time with you."

"Brigg, I can't handle this now," she almost shrieked. His ardent voice confused her, and with her whole body aching so badly for him, she was ready to agree to anything he suggested. Stupid, stupid, stupid!

"Darling, tell me about your day, everything you did."

His abrupt change of subject startled her. Carla stifled her panic and obediently parroted: "I'm still substituting in my old classroom. The new teacher, and several others are out with flu." One part of her brain looked upon the words spilling from her mouth with disdain. Why didn't she hang up? He was just placating her. He didn't really care.

"So you haven't started your new job yet?"

The warning part of the brain lost its vitality; the part of her that loved teaching surfaced, the part that remembered the little bit she had already told him, that wanted to tell more and more. And so she talked. And Brigg listened. With the noise of takeoffs and landings in the background, the laughter of children, squawks of equipment, he listened. And asked questions.

Finally she ran down. "What are you going to be doing in Houston?" she asked guiltily.

He told her of the distillation units his company was replacing in a huge oil refinery and of the time pressure and of practical problems involved. Carla concentrated carefully, wanting to piece together some understanding of his skills, of what made him tick. Eventually, when he got into talking about Houston, the climate, how he lived there, she quit concentrating on meaning and simply let the warmth and masculinity of his voice wash over her. It healed so many hurts.

But she did understand his parting remark. His tone vibrated deeply when he murmured, "Darling, don't think so hard. Just remember I miss you."

Carla sat for a long time afterward with her trembling fingers pressed against her flushed face.

He called each successive evening he was in Texas. And despite her best efforts not to, she looked forward to the conversations, came to expect them.

Frequently he would give her a hasty summary of his workday, and Carla gradually garnered a superficial understanding of his responsibilities in updating the outmoded oil refinery. She found his work fascinating and could easily have eaten up all his long distance time listening, but he also wanted to hear about her activities. He shared her fascination with her new challenge, since the regular teachers were all back and Carla was inaugurating her new reading program.

While she talked, it would occur to her that Charles had never asked about the travails of her job, and the comparison almost frightened her. She didn't want to see Brigg in such a favorable light.

Carla wondered if those hasty calls, substituting for real time together, didn't prove Brigg was actually no different from Charles? She kept reminding herself that she had been almost destroyed by one workaholic husband to whom she meant nothing significant. There was no way she would go through that again.

But the tenderness in Brigg's voice each night he spoke with her, his apparent interest in her work, his obvious pleasure in simply talking with her—these emotions had never been displayed by Charles.

Although, in all those subsequent phone conversations, Brigg never again brought up the question of an affair or marriage, Carla almost felt loved. It was terrifying, for she had believed herself loved once before.

Chapter Eight

They began dating. It seemed incredible to Carla—dating! Like two junior high schoolers: chaste little outings in which Brigg called ahead, showed up at her door exactly on time, with his fringe of hair brushed smooth and his teeth shiny fresh, and deposited her back at home at a decent hour, with a peck of a kiss to send her inside alone.

And for almost two weeks he never once brought up love or marriage. He was driving her crazy.

Of course the places they went weren't exactly what she had endured in high school. No soc hops at the school gym, no hanging over the innards of an old car so that the boyfriend in question could show off his mechanical expertise to the doting girl. The first evening Brigg was free after returning from Houston, he took her to the Palmer House for dinner. A few evenings later it was to his club, for a wine and cheese tasting extravaganza staged to raise money for charity. He even gave her a grand-scale opportunity to dote over his mechanical expertise by having her meet him downtown for lunch on a Saturday, then taking her through his office. She was introduced to the few secretaries and engineers who were doing catch-up work that weekend; she dutifully looked at the complex drawings

Brigg spread out on his lighted blueprint table so that he could explain the proceedings at the Houston oil refinery; she even waited patiently on a couch in his private office while he took care of two business calls from Europe.

To say that she was impressed with his professional ability was an understatement, but unlike in her high school days, she certainly had the good sense to refrain from telling him so.

If she wanted to plague herself with the hopelessness of the whole situation, Carla pondered the realization that on a long-term basis, Brigg would probably be able to devote even less time to a relationship with her than had Charles. Brigg and his partners operated a multimillion dollar business, providing key construction services to major chemical corporations throughout the world. Numerous livelihoods besides their own depended on the smooth operation of their company. Brigg himself was planning three projects within Illinois, while still keeping tabs long-distance on the Houston work and consulting on some European contracts. His schedule was unquestionably backbreaking. When she was willing to let herself be depressed, that was what she thought about.

But when she wanted to look on the bright side, she pondered, with meltingly awed appreciation, how amazing it was that he found any time to be with her at all. Perhaps, she thought, there was something to his claim that whom he placed first in his life, presumably that "who" being herself and his daughters, made all the difference.

Since Brigg didn't bring up marriage during these ridiculously formal dates, Carla began to wonder if his proposal had been merely for the show of things, a gesture to make her feel more comfortable with eventually letting him tumble into her bed whenever he could fit her into his work schedule.

That idea became increasingly funny to her. Who, after all, needed convincing to sleep with Brigg? She had certainly lost her own determination to refuse the honor; she was becoming so frustrated with his pecking good night kisses that she knew it was just a matter of which one of them could hold out longer in this silly game he was playing, before they'd test out their attraction. Carla was still uncomfortable with the idea of a long-term affair; marriage seemed out of the question, since she feared that she could never adjust to having him gone so much, yet she feared a one- or two-night stand would never get him out of her system. This man could take her months to tire of.

Therefore she was determined not to be the first to give in. She had had years of learning to withstand Brigg's teasing, and she figured that since she hadn't told him about owning the carriage house, if she could just hold out until the end of January when she would begin living there, she would almost disappear from his reach, for a while at least. And that would give her time to gain perspective on the whole situation, to know what might really work for them.

But how she wanted him. She endured each platonic date with a smile on her face and rage in her heart. It was especially bad the evening in mid-January when they went to a play at the University of Chicago theater. Carla was weary, yet interested, because she had spent the day working with the students from her old classroom, helping them get ready for their own annual school show, which was to be the next evening. The new teacher had graciously asked Carla to continue the preparations she had begun in December, and so she saw the college performance with part of her worrying about her own students, and how they would do with their show. Brigg had realized that she was distracted, although not knowing why, so he had made it worse by draping his arm over her shoulders and snuggling her close to him throughout the performance.

His old-fashioned flirting had her wanting him so much by the time he took her home that she had been hopeful that he was ready to call his little war with her a draw. But he had given her that hated peck of a kiss at her door and turned to leave, just as always.

"Brigg!" she snapped at his back.

"Hmm?" He turned around to look at her, his expression inscrutable.

"Would you want to come in for a cup of coffee?" she hedged, not willing to capitulate completely.

"Not unless you're planning to attack me."

She studied his eyes, hoping for a clue. His mouth was quirking a little. But only a little. He was, she thought with desperation, going to hold out for her complete defeat.

"Get lost," she puffed, with no dignity at all. He laughed all the way to the elevator.

She spent a particularly lonely and restless night, and arrived at school the day of the play, emotionally depleted.

It annoyed Brigg that Carla was working in a classroom when he phoned the school shortly before noon that same day. He had counted on her being immediately available in her own office. But he asked that she be told to return his call, not realizing that she wouldn't pick up the message until the afternoon break.

He found the waiting intolerable and ran through all sorts of explanations in his mind. She was fed up with his platonic treatment and didn't intend to call. She hadn't gotten the message at all. She was going to wait to phone until she got home. But that would be too late.

He was looking up the number of her school again, determined to be more insistent, when she rang in. "Next time I'll tell that school it's an emergency," he barked.

"Is someone hurt? What's wrong?"

He liked the way her voice broke, then strengthened bravely, ready to tackle anything. "Nothing's wrong." He was immediately calmed, no longer ready for a fight. *Amazing what her voice can do to me.*

"Brigg?"

"I have to catch a plane to Houston at six thirty this evening. A problem cropped up on the site early this morning." The following silence was as weighted as his heart felt. He could visualize the way her gorgeous body was tensing and her eyes were trying to mask her feelings, as they always did when she was hurting. How he hated to leave her! "Are you still there, Carla?"

"Why did you call?" Her voice was flat.

She probably thinks I don't know how much I'm hurting her. That I'm not torturing myself, too. What a mess. "I need to see you before I go," he said urgently. "Could you meet me at O'Hare as soon as you finish there? I could get to the airport by five, and we'd have almost an hour for a drink together."

"Meet you at the airport?" He thought she sounded tempted, and his spirits lifted. But she crashed them immediately. "No, I can't do that. I have to work."

"Work? Your school gets out at—"

"I feel like telling you to go to hell." She paused a long moment after the impulsive admission. "Forget that last remark, Brigg. I'm not being difficult—tonight is the school's winter show for parents. All teachers are staying over to get things ready. We couldn't use the auditorium earlier, so we'll have scenery, displays, everything, to set up."

"What are you going to do for a meal?" he barked in concern, believing her.

"A meal?" she asked, it apparently being the furthest thing from her mind at the moment.

"You must eat. I won't have you staying at that school until late tonight without even a meal."

"We're having a sandwich supper catered," she answered weakly, his worry confusing her.

"Why do they make you and your kids do this show?" he asked angrily.

"We want to do it," Carla corrected, not allowing him to bait her. "The students have been working hard, so their families can see what they've learned. They're going to be great."

"Can't they do their thing without you?"

"Thanks a lot."

"I didn't mean—"

"They're already getting along without me in the classroom," she interrupted coldly. "It's a matter of pride to me that I don't ask them to do so for this play, too."

Brigg hadn't meant to imply that her work wasn't valuable. But he needed that time with her so badly, he hadn't considered that anything else would be more important. *Except your own work,* he chided himself with sudden insight.

He juggled the phone awkwardly, wondering how to apologize without making things worse. No answer came easily for he knew Carla's way of thinking. She would reason that if he wanted to see her badly enough he would arrange time to do so. Making it possible shouldn't all be on her back. But how? This three-million-dollar project in Texas was in jeopardy because of a labor dispute, and if he wasn't in Houston by daybreak to intervene, a lot of people could find themselves out of work.

"There's no way you could slip away for a few minutes?" He couldn't stop himself from asking again.

"The program starts at seven. I wouldn't have time to get out to the airport and back, much less talk."

She sounded disappointed. That helped him accept her decision, even if he didn't understand it. "What are your students doing for this show?" he asked curiously, wondering about her commitment to them.

"They're reciting some stories they've written themselves. And singing with the other second graders. The songs are jazz-action. Quite complicated." She sounded defensive, like a mother hen protecting her brood. "What did you need to talk about? Perhaps I can help you now?"

His lips tightened at her detachment. This was going to be difficult. Did a man dare set a wedding date over the phone? Perhaps, with some women. But not Carla.

He couldn't tell her over the phone that he wanted them to marry immediately, but he could only allow a long weekend within a business trip for a honeymoon. She would be sensitive about that. After what she had gone through with her first marriage, she wouldn't believe he was trying to rearrange his work to have more time eventually with her. She needed kisses and caresses, deserved lots of time to look into his eyes and absorb how very much he loved her. Telling her wouldn't convince her.

"Brigg, I have to leave in just a moment. My kids are already coming back into the classroom. What do you want?"

"You. Look, good luck at the program tonight. I'm sorry." There wasn't much else to say, but he held the receiver regretfully long after she murmured her own good-byes.

Later the regret was still hanging over him like an albatross as he wandered around the airport. Carla was so stubbornly loyal to that school. What were they doing, letting a teacher like her go when she gave them such loyalty? he wondered angrily. He thought about what she would be doing at that performance, of how she'd be watching over her students. But who would be watching over her? That audience of parents had better love her part in that show. They'd better tell her so.

He cleared security and strode the long concourse to his gate before his need and disappointment built into uncontrollable levels. There had to be a way.

Not an easy man to defeat once he made up his mind, Brigg grabbed an airport phone and set to work. Within ten minutes he had wrangled space on a midnight flight to Houston, canceled his previous reservations, talked John McQuiddy into coming to the airport at eleven thirty to take Carla home, then instructed valet parking to bring around the car he had left with them only a scant hour earlier.

After Brigg's call, Carla returned to her classroom with a dead feeling. This most recent demand, that she drop everything if she wanted the pleasure of his company for a few minutes, told her conclusively what she meant to him. Nothing much. He had said he would probably be in Houston three weeks. By his return she would be settled in her new house, and she would be a fool to let him into her life again. If only giving him up before she even had him didn't hurt so!

As she automatically worked the remainder of that

afternoon she kept trying to tell herself that she had built a fulfilling role for herself since her divorce and that she could continue to do it. She tried not to think about the fact that she would no longer have her love of teaching to sustain her and that her new job was an untested alternative challenge.

Troubled, she approached the program that evening with a detached concentration most unusual for her. One part of her did all the routine things necessary: assisting the art teachers in setting up the children's scenery, bringing out samples of her students' work to be posted with others around the auditorium, helping the new teacher straighten the classroom for a visit by parents. But all the time she thought of Brigg, missing him so deeply that she felt ill. *Surely it's better to go through life alone than to face the agony of telling him good-bye over and over again.*

Carla felt exhausted by the time all the teachers took a break for their box dinners. Joining the noisy excitement in the faculty lounge and putting her feet up while munching a dry roast beef sandwich did little to energize her.

Even greeting the excited children, freshly scrubbed and proud in their shiny shoes and neat clothes, didn't boost her spirits. She met her students in her classroom and mechanically did the right things to reassure them, but she had trouble separating herself from her own personal ache. She gave herself an angry lecture, realizing sensitively that before long her detachment would affect the children's performance. And that simply wasn't fair. They had worked so hard, accomplished so much.

Once the children were lined up in the hall, ready for the program, she looked curiously into the auditorium and discovered that it was packed. One thing Carla could say for the parents at this school; they were supportive of their youngsters. Even many grandparents, brothers, sisters, and friends had filed dutifully into the cavernous room to hear the little ones.

Carla eventually settled into her seat in the row of teachers lined up in front and tried to let the usual excitement of such events flow over her.

The second graders were to perform early in the program, but the room was already becoming warm with the crowding when Carla's students joined the other classes of their grade and began their songs. The catchy rhythms of the group music went well. After that Carla's class remained on stage to perform individually. But by then the heat was noticeably beginning to bother some of the youngsters. Sensitive to the cause of the children's uncomfortable wriggles and drooping expressions as they prepared for their part of the program, Carla slipped quietly from her seat and went through the hall. Quickly she opened three windows behind the curtains for ventilation and turned on a small circulating fan which kept air moving gently above the children's heads. The relief seemed almost instantaneous—her students relaxed, their smiles full once again. Carla then remained backstage, not wanting to create any commotion by returning to her seat. But that was a mistake.

Every time any child stammered momentarily, his eyes swung behind him, looking for her to mouth the words they couldn't remember. Carla wilted with almost motherly relief when each faltering child recovered himself and proudly continued his recitation, but she regretted that she had not returned out front where her assistance would have been less noticeable.

Later in the evening the principal announced that, as a group, her students had scored the highest marks in the nation on a battery of tests covering reading skills. Professionally Carla was pleased to hear those results. But she was appalled when he continued in a dramatic fashion to announce that her services had not been lost to the district, that she would be continuing on as full-time reading supervisor. Surprisingly, the audience burst into a standing ovation. In embarrassment she came on the stage, as requested, to acknowledge the applause, but she couldn't help thinking that if the district had really valued her as a teacher they would have kept her on in that capacity. She wished people would not go through this method of trying to make it up to her.

Things were incredibly confusing after the performance. The children tumbled back to the classroom like monkeys, dragging their indulgent families along. Carla offered congratulations, answered questions, and helped numerous youngsters find where their favorite work was displayed, so they could show it off to their families. Once everyone moved to the cafeteria for refreshments the confusion became even worse. Carla accepted the compliments of many other parents with that depressing detachment she had been fighting all evening. She slowly drank the too-sweet punch served by the parents' organization, nibbled politely on the cookies various children generously shared with her, and felt terrible.

The final shattering blow came when she accepted a cookie from one little girl who was a particular favorite of hers. At the start of the year the child couldn't learn, and Carla had stretched all her professional imagination and skill to bring her out of her difficulties. But when Carla leaned down to tell the child how proud she was of her, the little girl had not even paused to listen, running instead to hug her mother and hear her words of praise.

I don't even have anyone of my own to be happy for, Carla realized with brutal clarity. She had no right to share the triumphs of these children. She had just been doing her job. The realization was shattering. For three years she had built her life around teaching, but now it didn't even matter if that sublimation were being taken from her, for no longer would it be enough. She, too, needed someone of her own to care about. *I'm so alone! And nobody even realizes, or cares.*

The enormous chasm she was visualizing in her life was stunning. And suddenly she had to get away. Pinning a meaningless smile on her face, she began to work through the crowd.

It was agony. In that crazy, excited mass of happy people she felt isolated. Then she started seeing things. Brigg. There, walking toward her, smiling at her with affection. She wondered if people really went crazy instantly.

"Carla, what's wrong?" The mirage man was reaching toward her, his expression concerned. But his touch felt real enough.

"Brigg?" She halted, entranced.

Oh, Brigg. Mine!

"Are you all right?" His arm was around her, his stance protective.

Someone of my own to love. Brigg!

"Carla, I didn't intend to throw you into shock."

"How, why—?"

"I changed to the midnight flight. Your kids did the best, but just because you were there supporting them. Everybody could tell that." He was possessively stroking her arms, unmindful of those around him, ranting proudly. "You shouldn't have been so modest, ducking your head and scurrying away after that ovation. I've been in the back row all the time, hearing people say how great you are. But it's taken me forever to find you. Say, did you know these parents are passing around a petition to get you—"

"I think I'm going to cry," she confessed, grabbing his hand helplessly.

He was puzzled, but reacted instantly. "Let's get you out of here."

He accomplished it quickly. Her coat and things were collected, her office locked, and she was in his car within minutes.

"Kiss me," she demanded weakly.

"I thought teachers were not allowed to neck on school premises," he teased gruffly, obligingly leaning over to comply with her request. But she couldn't even let the kiss complete itself. She broke down completely, crying and sobbing so heavily that he awkwardly slid from behind the wheel and took her into his arms as fully as the cramped quarters of the car would allow.

"You should be happy with how things went," he mumbled in distress against her hair. "Suzannah will bust when I tell her about your ovation tonight. I don't understand—"

She fumbled her hand up to his lips, stilling him. Automatically he kissed her fingertips.

"What is it?" he asked anxiously. "Are you hurt because you won't be teaching anymore?" His body hardened. "Damn them for doing this to you!" His arms tightened protectively and he launched into violent cursing. He attacked the principal, progressed to the school board, and was starting in on the taxpayers when Carla got control of herself.

"It's not what you think," she said unevenly, straightening in his arms and sliding her hand to his bearded cheek. She adored the feel of him against her palm. "I just felt so alone," she soothed.

"You should have told me about your job sooner, let me help fight your battles with the administration."

"No, no! It's not—kiss me." Then she was laughing and crying and compulsively spreading kisses all over his face. Only a loud thump against Brigg's car stopped her ardent display.

"What the—" Brigg was angry at the interruption. When Carla saw a grinning sixth-grade boy laughingly shaming his finger at them, she grabbed Brigg's hand before he could scramble out after him.

"You were right. Necking isn't allowed in school parking lots," she said between the laughter and tears. "Oh, darling, let's get out of here."

They started to drive off, then remembered Carla's car and her need to have it for work the next day, so had to come back for it. Brigg drove behind her to her apartment parking lot, then tucked her in beside him in his own car and rushed to the airport.

There were so many things to be said in the short time he had left. "Carla, I've been trying to straighten out things at work so our marriage would have a fighting chance," he stunned her by explaining as he threaded his way through the nighttime traffic. "By getting these three Illinois projects scheduled at once, I can justify supervising their construction myself, so it would mean I could be with you almost every weekend for at least six months. It's not ideal, but better than the long separations we've been having."

"Much better," she agreed, staring thoughtfully ahead.

"The Illinois work will begin in three weeks, and I thought with me coming in and out so regularly it would allow us to get used to each other, but something else has happened. I hadn't planned on it."

He could feel her body tightening, and he rushed on. "I wanted us to have a few months together before tackling the girls. But things have been going on at school—"

"What's happened to them?" she asked in alarm.

"Recently they slipped out of their dorm with a bunch of friends and went to a party at a stranger's house. When they realized drugs were being used there, they got scared. They made it to some phone booth nearby and called me collect in Houston. It was the middle of the night, they had no more money, and I'm hundreds of miles away."

Carla trembled, feeling his horror.

"I reached the police up there and they got the girls back to the school safely. Then, after I could break loose from Houston, I flew up to talk it over with them. And I learned a lot. They admitted to having slipped out to drinking parties before. It appears that most of the kids there are doing it, and they wanted to be like everyone else. So far they've just been observing all the goings on." His voice trailed off in worry.

"You've made me realize they're young adults now, and they deserve some guidance from me," he eventually continued. "I can't let them believe the high-flying life-style is acceptable for them. After they finish out the semester in three weeks, I'm bringing them home. There's a good private high school near the house, and Jody and I are just going to have to find a way to cope."

He had pulled up at the airport as he finished his jerky explanation, and nothing more could be said while they were leaving the car with the valet and making their way through security. But once they found chairs off to themselves near his departure gate, he continued almost painfully.

"I didn't want to rush you into marriage. I wanted you to be as certain as I am that this is right for us. But if we're going to have any private time at all together, we're going to have to get married this weekend, even though I'm still involved in this Houston work. I got the license and had my blood tests done today. And you could get your tests tomorrow."

"Get married...right away?" she asked weakly, her thoughts spinning in confusion.

"It's not the best time for us," he admitted. "I'll only be able to break away for a day or two. But I could fly up from Houston for a ceremony Friday morning, and take you back with me for as long as you could get off work."

"What do the girls think about us getting married?"

"How would I know? They're so furious at being taken out of that school it isn't the time to discuss my private life with them." He stopped suddenly, gauging how this all must sound. "I'm not offering you much, am I? A part-time husband. Two resentful daughters underfoot. A difficult but definitely permanent housekeeper. It wasn't what I had in mind when I first asked you to marry me."

Carla looked down at her hands. She had to agree with him. It wasn't at all what she would pick if she were planning wisely. "Brigg, I'm so scared." She felt desperate. People were lining up to board the aircraft, and John McQuiddy was hovering discreetly nearby, prepared to see her home.

"Scared of me?" Brigg asked urgently, taking her hand.

"Of failing at marriage a second time. I don't think I could survive it, Brigg."

"I want this to be forever."

"I know. So do I. But I thought the same thing with Charles."

"Forget Charles! Get your blood tests tomorrow."

They were announcing his flight. Reluctantly he let go of her hand, unable to delay his departure any longer.

"Brigg!"

"I'll call you tomorrow night," he promised before rushing toward the frantically beckoning flight official. Then suddenly he lurched back to kiss her one last time. "I'm yours, darling. I need you."

He had to go then. In seconds the big metal doors of the flight ramp were closed behind him and Carla was staring at the bleakness of the nearly empty departure lounge. John still remained at a tactful distance, giving her time.

Marriage again? The very thought was terrifying. But Brigg had said the one thing that could have convinced her. Those innocent words: "I'm yours."

Charles had never been hers. He couldn't give himself to anyone. But Brigg? *Mine!* She knew it was true. He might not be around much for the rest of her life, but he would be hers to love, irrevocably. It would have to be enough.

"I'm ready to go, John." She walked over to the silver-haired man who was patiently waiting for her. She started to tell him she was marrying Brigg, then stopped. Brigg would want to be the first to know. From the anguish in his look as he slipped from her arms she knew he had not been certain of her at all.

Chapter Nine

"You got married today? You're both crazy; the name will never do." Suzannah hooted her pleasure into the phone. "Carla Carlyle sounds like a jingle. No, better yet, like something out of Edgar Allen Poe. Let's see—" Her voice grew dramatic:

> "My lady drifts without a smile,
> Carla Carlyle, Carla Carlyle
> Ethereal, wispy, down the aisle,
> Carla Carlyle, Carla Carlyle."

"I'm going to hang up!" Carla threatened seriously.

"I'm going to ban you from our house, Suzannah," Brigg roared into the extension. "That kind of garbage is the very reason we didn't invite anyone to the wedding."

"Have you told Mother and Dad yet?" Suzannah asked cheerfully, unrepentant.

"Yes. And Carla's parents and the twins. This summer we'll invite everyone up for a celebration party."

"You didn't even have the girls to the wedding?"

"We most especially did not have the girls. Carla and I need a little time alone. Besides, they'll be home for good when the semester ends in two weeks."

"For good? Well hooray for Carla—she finally got you to take them out of that sophisticated school. I never thought it was right for them. Where are you going on your wedding trip, by the way?"

"None of your business."

"Galveston. We're there now."

Brigg and Carla spoke simultaneously.

"Galveston?" his sister protested, paying attention only to Carla's response. "Brigg, you're not working? Carla, I'll bet money you've already had to sit out a business meeting in Houston on your wedding day. Now you must—"

Brigg came storming into the bedroom from their sitting room, where he had been using an extension. Carla lifted her shoulders in apology, holding the receiver slightly away from her ear to let Suzannah's free advice flow out unheeded. She should have thought before she revealed they were in the Houston area. Suzannah was too quick to figure things out.

Carla pressed the phone back to her ear in time to hear Suzannah say "And if you don't get him under control right now—"

"We have to go, Suzannah," she interrupted firmly. "We're taking a walk on the beach before it gets dark. Give your kids a hug for us."

"We should have sent her a telegram instead," she joked tentatively after hanging up, hoping to lighten Brigg's disturbed expression. He had already apologized for rushing Carla into a chartered airplane the minute the wedding ceremony was over, then leaving her alone in a rickety trailer-office for three hours while he inspected his Houston construction site and signed some necessary papers. She knew he felt guilty enough without his sister on his back. Carla could have done without Suzannah's comments herself, for she was trying to overcome her own qualms as to whether she would be able to accept the requirements of Brigg's work year after year.

"Although Suzannah gave me some very good advice which I intend to take," she added mockingly, wishing Brigg's frown would go away. "*After* my honeymoon."

"Some honeymoon," he grunted. "Lasts one weekend and starts off with me working."

"It starts off with us together. I'll settle for that."

He turned at her quiet words, trying to read her expression. Then he reached for her hand. "It won't always be this way."

Carla stiffened slightly, not wanting to hear promises he would never be able to keep. She had made her decision and she would learn to live with whatever came. "I was serious about walking on the beach." She withdrew her hand, feeling awkward. "Since you brought me here to see the gulf, let's go before it gets dark."

Brigg looked as harried as she felt and seemed to be of the opinion that nothing could salvage this first day of their married life, but he agreed to her suggestion.

They hadn't even unpacked before making the necessary family calls, so Carla had to spread open her suitcase on the luggage rack and rummage for the tennis shoes Brigg had suggested she bring. It felt strange to be doing something so personal as changing shoes in front of him. Slipping into a sexy nightgown might have been easy. But old shoes seemed shockingly more intimate. She glanced shyly toward Brigg and noticed how his broad shoulders strained against the soft fabric of his shirt, while he tossed away his loafers and tied his sneakers. He had hung up the suit coat he had worn all day, but hadn't even loosened the tie.

"We don't look very suitable for the beach," she

scoffed self-consciously, starting to remove the jacket of her now-rumpled traveling outfit.

Apparently not hearing her observation, Brigg walked out on their balcony overlooking the gulf. "Don't take that off," he advised, coming inside to put his coat back on. "We'd better wear Windbreakers too. It's going to be cold and wet out there." He frowned angrily. "I should have taken you to the Caribbean."

It didn't help her own bridal nervousness for him to be so upset about how their wedding day was working out. Angry at the lump in her throat and the strange knotting deep within her, she pulled her all-weather coat out of her luggage and shrugged into it before he could move to help her. She thought almost desperately that if he touched her at that moment, she might fall apart before his eyes.

For more than an hour they strolled silently along the ever-darkening beach. Since most of the beach houses and resort motels were closed for the season, they walked in relative isolation along the narrow strip of sand between the lapping water and the seawall. Brigg seemed lost in thoughts of his own, and Carla appreciated the emotional space his preoccupation gave her. His very presence was almost too overwhelming. He was such a disturbing mystery, this friend of her childhood and object of her womanly desire. She felt on the brink of the unknown, not knowing how to take the next step, and fearful of where it would lead her.

The gulf breezes became chillier once the sun went down completely, but Carla buttoned her coat higher and welcomed the feel of the mist whipping at her face. She needed that distraction. The insistent rhythm of the surf grinding against the packed sand fascinated yet disturbed her with its intimation of leashed power.

"Do you get down here to the gulf much?" she finally asked contemplatively.

"No. There never seems to be time." Brigg glanced at her, so close to his side, and seemed to be aware for the first time of the increasing cold. Casually he drew her within his arm. "Occasionally I can drive to Galveston on a weekend evening to eat. I like fresh crab."

"Crab?" She was surprised. "That seems so tasteless to me. Little shreds of pink stuff from a can."

This was ridiculous, being so uptight that all she could talk about was eating. Carla wished she had slept with him when the opportunity had occurred so naturally, wished that she didn't have to endure this formal waiting, wondering. *Will we be terrible together?*

"It's not tasteless when it's fresh. You'd love crab legs steamed, with lots of butter."

"It's just occurred to me," she forced herself to look into his face. "I don't have the slightest idea about your taste in food. What do you like?"

"You see my size and dare ask that?"

"You mean Jody and I can offer you anything?" That was the wrong thing to say. His face hardened distressfully when he realized she expected his housekeeper to have as much influence in their home as she. "Don't look like that," she objected impulsively, smoothing his brows with her fingers, then withdrawing hastily from the contact with his cool skin. She wasn't ready for that complication to her jumbled emotions.

His expression remained troubled while they walked back to their motel. Since the moon was often hidden by clouds that evening, they frequently sloshed through small pools left by the receding tide, getting their shoes wet and Brigg's pants soaked with moisture almost to the knees.

"I want to take you out for some good seafood," he said stiffly, stopping just within their door to pull off his dripping shoes. "But I'm going to have to clean up first."

"You use the bathroom." Carla left her own tennis shoes on a paper beside his. "If this place we're going isn't too fancy, I'll just change."

Once Brigg's shower water was running, Carla restlessly pulled off her suit. There was a sink and vanity table in the alcove adjoining the bathroom, and she freshened herself quickly, trying to ignore the splashing noises Brigg was making in the room beyond. She could visualize him standing naked under the steaming spray, rubbing himself clean. Her stomach knotted again, making her feel more than ever like a schoolgirl.

I wish we'd already made love. The regretful thought kept recurring. Approaching a bridal night at her age seemed so unnatural. She had slept with no man but Charles, and it had been years since their lovemaking had meant anything to her other than satisfying a basic adult need. *I'll probably disappoint Brigg,* she fretted. This whole wedding night—the big moment—was becoming too consumingly important.

Once again Carla tried to shut out her misgivings, concentrating instead on the simple act of dressing for dinner. He had indicated that they would go to a casual place, so she pulled on a pair of nice slacks and a warm, well-fitting sweater. Then she returned to the mirror to brush her hair. It surprised her that Brigg was still indulging himself in the shower, singing occasionally, almost absent-mindedly, as if so in the habit that he was not aware. Even in the vague sound mixed with the noise of the water she realized he could sing well. He tapered off one song, then eventually as he compulsively launched into another his voice rose to match its rhythm. She recognized the folk tune and found herself humming along.

Then suddenly she stopped. "It has to be the one with dirty words," she thought, remembering the song Brigg used to start singing in front of Suzannah's friends, threateningly, whenever they pestered him too much. In those days only Suzannah knew what words were coming next, and she would rush everyone away before he could finish, shrieking for her mother as she went.

Carla grinned and walked to the bathroom door, raising her hand to pound on it. She had always wanted to know the end of that nasty little limerick.

But just then the shower turned off and she could hear Brigg stepping out. He had stopped singing, and her body could almost feel him moving around naked in the still-steaming room, reaching for a towel, sopping the dampness off his hairy chest, drying his waist. The sound of the fabric rubbing across his skin reached her before his sigh of satisfaction at the sheer refreshing pleasure of being clean and warm. Her palms were sweating as her hand fell to her side. This was definitely not the time to bring up a childhood incident.

She waited for him in their sitting room. There was a window overlooking the boulevard and the seawall beyond, and she turned out all the lamps so she could watch the undulating water. There was a shimmering light some distance out, but Carla couldn't decide whether it was a boat or a marker. Her eyes turned shoreward, noticing that no one seemed to be walking on the beach anymore. She and Brigg had encountered only a few hardy souls when they had been out, and now the brisk winds seemed to have discouraged everyone. Of course it was off-season on Galveston Island, but the isolation surprised her, anyway. She stood up and leaned against the glass, wondering if there might be people walking along the seawall, out of reach of the cold, lapping water.

"Can you see very far?" Brigg asked easily, clicking off the light in the bedroom and joining her at the window. The shower seemed to have revived him. It startled her to smell after-shave lotion, until she remembered he did not wear a mustache.

"Not very. The moon keeps slipping behind clouds. Can you tell what that distant light is?" She took a step back from the window and stole a look at him, noticing that his upper lip was shaved smooth and his beard neatly trimmed. Her skin tingled, knowing why he had gone to that trouble.

"Don't ever shave your beard off," she blurted, again having that curious desire to feel it against every inch of her body.

"What?"

"I like your beard."

"You're funny." He grinned, laying a hand almost companionably on her shoulder before looking back at the light she had pointed out earlier. "I'd guess you're actually seeing quite far, and your light is probably a mass of lights on an oil rig. The refinery I'm working with has some offshore production within sight of Galveston." His gaze moved back inland, and he could see the wind stirring up scraps of discarded paper along the boulevard lining the seawall. "It's a good thing the restaurant we're going to is just a half-block down the street. It's going to be raw out there tonight."

Her eyes followed his. "I don't mind. I'm used to winds."

The sitting room was dark, and Carla wished she had left a lamp on. This seemed so contrived, as if she were trying to get Brigg in the mood for what was to come after dinner. She wished it were morning. They were going to be terrible together, she just knew it. No lovemaking could live up to this intense waiting. Lord, they had been waiting for each other for years.

His hand was warm and heavy on her shoulder. She forced herself to remain still, fighting nervous trembles.

From the corner of her eye she could see moisture glistening on the top of his head. He must have concentrated on drying his fringe of hair and beard, forgetting his tanned skin. She clenched her fingers to keep herself from reaching up to dry him off.

Apparently unaware of her musings Brigg was looking intently at a darkened mound of earth slightly back from the seawall, just beyond where it made a broad curve away from the motel.

"What do you see?" she asked, grateful for anything to break the pace of her thinking.

"I'm not certain," he answered thoughtfully. "I'd guess it must be an old gun emplacement."

"You're kidding?" Carla stared at the area, her attention fully caught.

"No, it's possible. Dad was stationed down here for a few months during the war. He's told me about their observation posts all over, guarding the shipping channel into Galveston and Houston harbors. There would have been big guns too."

"You mean in World War II?"

He focused on her face. "There have been a few wars since then, haven't there?" he observed almost sadly.

She looked back at the mound of earth. It assumed sinister proportions to her and she shuddered.

Brigg put his arm around her, worried by her reaction. "Are you all right?"

She trembled against him as she recalled what her father had told of his own wartime experiences. And her mother's stories of waiting, hoping, being afraid. *Could it ever happen to us?* She drew a shuddering breath.

"I can't imagine what it would be like," she ventured weakly, grasping his hand and holding it tight, "having your man leave for war and not knowing if you'd ever see him again. Oh, Brigg—" Her arms slid around his waist and she hugged him to her compulsively, everything else but how much she loved him driven from her mind.

"Hey, you silly Giant Child," he comforted tenderly, letting her press him close against her body, yet amused by her frightened reaction to the gun emplacements. "That's one of the advantages of marrying an old man. I won't be drafted until—"

"Don't say that," she commanded, standing on tiptoe so she could reach his face. Even the remote possibility of his going into danger horrified her. "Don't," she repeated brokenly, laying her cheek against his.

He felt so dear. Carla stretched to hold him tighter, urgently needing his strength. Dissatisfied, she leaned into him until she could feel his chest against hers, his hips, his thighs. She even moved her feet closer to touch against his shoes. Then she shifted her arms to shape more completely against his back.

Brigg had put on a heavy sweater. The roughness of the wool rubbed against her fingers and wrists. There was something reassuring about the texture. So real. Like Brigg himself, definitely there with her at that moment. It was all she could count on.

"I don't believe I could bear losing you," she murmured candidly, dropping to her heels, but still remaining close against him, while resting her head on his shoulder. "You've been so long coming back into my life."

"Honey, you're too suggestible," Brigg breathed against her ear, aware that her anguish was genuine, but uncertain how to reassure her. He couldn't go through the motions of claiming that he would live to be a hundred. He, better than most, knew that you had no guarantees in life. Soothingly he stroked her hair.

Still shaken, Carla turned her head slightly, letting her lips slide against his beard. The whiskers scratched, but there was relief in the slight pain. She needed to reassure herself with every texture, every aspect of him. Burying her mouth against his neck, she blindly absorbed his fresh smell: clean, yet so unmistakably masculine.

There was airy music coming from outside. At first it was distant, quiet, a comforting sensation. Carla remained against Brigg, letting his vibrancy blend with that of the music to heal her. But then the sound gradually grew louder, becoming jarring and disturbing when it finally peaked raucously. Then almost immediately it began to fade again. The Doppler effect, she thought in vague fascination—like a train approaching from a distance and passing on into the night. But it was a tinkling noise instead, the kind that would appeal to children.

"An ice cream truck?" She broke away, looking up at Brigg incredulously, suddenly not trembling any longer. Surely not an ice cream truck on a winter evening. The incongruity of it, coming so close upon her gruesome contemplations, made her laugh spontaneously.

Brigg roared with laughter himself, grabbing her up and twirling her around and around in his arms. "Life has to go on." He grinningly shrugged the explanation when he set her down and framed her face with his hands.

She stopped laughing immediately. The sensation of his touching her was marvelous. How she adored him! Her breath caught in awe at the hungry love she saw returned in his ardent expression.

"Carla," he moaned, sliding his hands behind her head and pulling her to his lips.

His caresses were almost frantic, as if his love, once released, was uncontrollable. But Carla didn't care about the roughness. She was too eager for him herself. She didn't care about anything, except that he get rid of the cumbersome garments that were keeping them apart.

Somehow they reached the bedroom, leaving little heaps of clothing at intervals along the way. Then they were lying in bed together with no barriers, the most natural, inevitable happening in the world.

"Brigg, I love you so much." He had drawn her almost on top of him, and she said it into his shoulder, letting the words fade to nothing as her seeking mouth slid along his arm, savoring the feel of corded muscles. He was playing a game with her hair, running his hands through it, letting it cling around his fingers while he watched it entrap him. She smiled at his fascination before moving slightly so that she could match her body to his as completely as she had when she had been so frightened. It was much more satisfying lying down. She could feel him chuckling against her breasts, amused at her own little game.

Since he seemed inclined to indulge her, she impulsively twisted on her side so that her back was pressed against his chest and she could bring his arms up around her naked breasts, and his hands to her lips. It was as if he were holding her, only better, for she could lie deeply against him while luxuriantly kissing each of his fingertips, memorizing through her eager mouth the taste and feel of those wonderful, capable hands.

Before long, though, he became impatient with her current obsession. When she felt him moving, she tried to hold his wrists, craving more of the taste of his fingers, but he easily dragged her hands along with his until he reached his goal of her breasts.

"Oh, no, you don't"—he shifted slightly, bracing himself to withstand her tuggings at his wrists—"I get my fun too." Then she could feel his chuckles against her back as he cupped her soft fullness and began to sensuously outline her shape. She let go of his wrists and stretched her arms above her head, enthralled at how outrageously exciting he was making it to share herself with him. He laughed aloud at her wonder, a pleased laugh which moved warmly along her neck and down her back as he slid lower, tucking his legs hard against hers and drawing her into his own curve. He kissed her as he went, his beard rasping lightly, and the gentle abrasion on her skin felt as delicious as she had imagined it would. Then she also laughed aloud, heartily. This was so fun, so marvelous!

"Darling!" Responsively she turned in his arms and kissed him greedily. She almost pulled away when he lifted her enough so that his thigh could slip between her legs, for the intense pleasure of his intruding touch was sweeter than she believed she could bear. But he prevented her escape, his hands coaxingly firm on her bottom and his breath soft against her temple, while he murmured reassurances.

It was then that she let herself relax against him completely, throwing aside all the teasing and holding nothing back. Carla could feel her body rotate smoothly against his leg, unaware that her own undulating hips were creating the motion in response to his mouth covering her breasts. She was moaning softly, grabbing at his shoulders, and her uninhibited response flung him over the brink.

"Oh, honey, I can't—"

He rolled her to her back, his need too urgent to wait longer. He did take care to enter her gently, but she was so soft and ready for him that he slowed only briefly, sighing against her lips as if he had finally found his home, before beginning his hungry thrusts deep within her. With frantic abandon they kissed each other, clinging, reeling with the growing tension.

Brigg tried to slow their ardor, knowing all the rules of love said that to find the fullest pleasure a man and a woman must take time. But rules were made to be broken, and their bodies were feverish with their unsated passion—there was no slowing them down.

They moved as part of each other with a familiarity that astounded them both, bringing their culmination into matched frenzy so completely that they almost immediately fell over the edge of ecstasy together, shuddering in the cycling release of love as one, their waves of pleasure passing back and forth within each other, over and over again.

Gradually, magically, the long tremors subsided.

Flushed with the enervating heat of too-long-repressed ardor, they collapsed against each other, totally fulfilled, totally exhausted. And totally in awe of what they had discovered together.

Brigg only dozed, never quite falling deeply asleep. He harbored on the edge of a never-world, dominated by the nearby presence of the soft, feminine body that was now forever and irrevocably a part of him. At some point in the night he had shifted carefully to his side, carrying Carla with him to a comfortable resting place within his arms, and that contented him.

He could see her well. Although they had drawn the heavy drapes across the windows of their bedroom when they were changing for dinner, fantasy moonlight, rippling in rhythm with the water it bathed, filtered in from the picture window of the sitting room beyond. Privacy in the alcoved recesses of their own suite, yet kinship with the gulf. The combination was explosively suggestive.

But even had he not been able to see, he would have known that her lashes were long against her cheeks and her lips slightly curved in a tentative smile. She slept, he thought whimsically, as she lived: prepared to make the best of what life handed her. The night that she had stayed on his couch he had tiptoed down once to check on her; earlier—that first time in her apartment—he had slipped into her bedroom and set aside the money-clip he had been absentmindedly fingering, because he had felt compelled to stealthily kiss her a secret good-bye. Both times she had been lovely.

He liked watching her sleep. The broad, angular bones of her face vulnerably softened in her relaxation; the power normally behind her steady gaze became hooded, giving her a look of helplessness that she seldom allowed anyone to glimpse. It touched him deeply.

This marriage, Brigg determined, would give her the love and peace she needed. He would make it happen. He had to.

She was so delicate, his Carla. A giant of a voluptuous woman, but delicate nonetheless. Fragile, needing to be protected. She offered herself so willingly to the greedy world that careless people had great power to hurt her.

His body tensed and he regretted more pointedly

than ever that he could not have made this wedding trip of theirs something less hurried, more pleasant and memorable. She deserved that.

He eased his position slightly to restore circulation to his arm on which she slept, but still he remained by her side. He couldn't bear to move far away. For a long time he rested against her, making vague plans for their future, plans which gave them all the time and privacy in the world, precious time to sustain each other, to cherish each other.

Carla awoke gradually, stirring slowly against him at first, as if her body were trying to acquaint her puzzled brain with the strange presence it sensed next to her. Anxiously he watched her eyes flutter open; he wondered what her expression would be when she realized it was he, Brigg Carlyle, her husband, sharing her nakedness and her bed.

"Mmm. Mine!" The possessive words were almost unintelligible coming from her passion-swollen lips. But her look of trusting love was so complete that it struck at his heart, firing his hunger for her yet again. Almost reverently he touched her hair, then ran his hand lightly over her face, tracing its bold outline. As he moved on, memorizing little favorite shapes and textures, her accepting body asked nothing from him, yet softened in readiness to give him whatever he chose to take. His initial foray completed, with trembling hands he drew her into his arms.

This time, he determined, he'd take it slowly, offer her everything that could make it better for her.

But when she began to stroke his face, and to whisper her words of wonder, he forgot about techniques, time, foreplay, all the perks so-called experts talked about as necessary in romance. He fell into the trap of a man totally in love with his wife. He offered her only himself, naturally and with no reservations.

Waking gradually, discovering Brigg beside her, Carla thought she could study her husband's face forever and not become bored. She seemed to uncover so much new in his expression, now that she was truly Carla Carlyle. She wondered if the difference was in her own increased sensitivity.

"I've never seen your eyes such a dark gray," she murmured wonderingly, lifting a bare arm to trace her fingertips across his brows, then around to his jaw.

"You've never seen me after we've made love," he teased tenderly. "It's probably your fault."

"I'm not going to apologize," she teased back quietly, her smile sending the inward radiance she felt flushing across her skin as she tilted her face to accept his kiss. His mouth touched hers longingly, shaped over it, his beard adjusting to her softness; then his breath blended with her sigh of contentment.

She tasted him, smiled, tasted again, and sighed more deeply. She felt so at one with him that it seemed impossible to initiate anything; their loving seemed just to happen. Almost in unison they shifted slightly, adjusting their bodies to each other, urging closer, melding better. This time Brigg sighed in contentment. And Carla, sinking deeper into the self-perpetuating oblivion, held him as best she could in her growing weakness. The warmth and texture of his back, rising and falling with his breathing, cast ever-changing impressions against her bare arms and hovering fingertips. He was so strong and wonderful—and hers. She knew that they were just two human beings, naked together and expressing the time-proven rites of marriage as every couple had always done. And yet for her, making love with her husband was so much more than that.

Poetic! That was it. Loving her practical, huge, horribly irreverent, and disrespectful Brigg was ridiculously, memorably, poetic. Soon, she vowed, she would tell him so. If she were ever able to speak again.

Carla felt unreal. Somewhat like a marble statue of a nude beauty ensconced in an ethereal garden. Her body seemed trapped in time, sculpted at its most attractive moment of existence, and transplanted into its own unique setting—Brigg's arms.

"Do you know how beautiful you are?" His words were lost in the movements of his mouth around her flowing hair. She smiled into the hollow of his throat.

"You've made me feel that I'm the loveliest creature on earth. A priceless marble statue," she admitted.

"Never marble," he protested, running his hands over her shoulders and along her back. His shifting adjusted his hardness against her inner thigh, and she clamped her legs against him, instinctively welcoming the new plane to which they were moving.

Life seemed to be returning to her hands, and Carla ran her fingers feverishly over him, feeling a need for haste to learn every new and intriguing facet of him—of how his shoulders broadened to accommodate the joining with his muscular arms; of how his back muscles flattened and roped around his torso; of the slight indentation, then jutting out of that scar on the shoulder blade. Involuntarily she stretched to reach her hand around him, up to her lips, so she could send a soothing kiss down to that scar, spreading her moist affection all over it.

Brigg's answering indulgent chuckle brushed his chest against her throbbing breasts, and she almost flinched with the sudden pain of missing him. Immediately he turned her with him to their sides, and gave her the relief she needed. She did the same for him, and they touched and kissed and loved and became bathed in their own desire.

When they finally shifted together to seek finality, and he hovered over her, she framed his face with her hands and held him there so she could see his deep, dark, very, very dark gray eyes.

"Loving you is poetry," she breathed hesitantly, needing to tell him and hoping desperately he would not laugh at her.

"For me, too," he responded vibrantly. She thought for a moment he looked sheepish and vulnerable at his instant admission. But as she gazed back affectionately, his eyes darkened even more.

The moment lengthened and they looked at each other, both grinning ecstatically, both radiant, blending their souls every second that they slowly allowed their aching bodies to become one. For a brief moment then, Brigg rested heavily against her as if the mere act of entering her had completed some basic need of his.

Then they showed each other what very magnificent poetry they were able to create together.

Their remaining three days in Galveston were sheer bliss. It was absurd for two adults to be so childishly happy, and they laughed about it. Savored it. Reveled in it.

But it was over all too soon. The pain of parting was in Carla's eyes when Brigg saw her to her departure gate at the Houston airport.

"I wish I didn't have this Houston contract to finish up. I wish you didn't have that new job to get back to," he stormed, not for the first time.

Carla smiled lovingly at him through moist lashes. A

marriage couldn't be poetry all the time. She smiled even more. But absurd how even his angry impatience was wonderful to her.

The impersonal confusion of the concourse was a blessing, for they could sit together in the noisy, plastic world of travelers, and feel alone. Carla's throat tightened as she felt the slight rumbling under her feet that indicated the approach of a plane to their gate. Reaching instinctively, she took Brigg's hand into her lap. It was such a big hand, dwarfing her own rather sizable one. She turned it over, palm down, and began tracing the long lines of the bones spreading down to his wrists, imprinting them on her senses.

"Honey, I'll be back in two weeks," he said brokenly. "I'll have this thing finished up for good here and then we'll—"

Carla leaned over and kissed him. She didn't want to think about the future. The parting might have been different if she were assured that they would have time together later, but she knew that, in reality, she would probably never be able to have the time with him she would prefer. Better to face the adjustments as they came.

They called her flight and Brigg sprang to his feet, lifting her with him. She regretted the desperate loneliness in his eyes, but in determination to spare him more pain, she smiled broadly and kept the tears from flowing.

I have to make this marriage work, Carla thought as he gathered her in his arms for one last kiss.

"I love you," he murmured hoarsely, holding her face in his hands.

She pulled out of his arms after one final, light peck of a kiss. There was nothing more to be said, and knowing she was loved would have to be enough to sustain her

Chapter Ten

Carla was grateful that there was so much to do in getting her things settled into Brigg's house. It kept her busy for the two weeks before he would return and before the girls would be in Chicago permanently. And it helped prepare her for the cycle she knew she would have to adjust to: brief joy when Brigg was home, then long days of painful loneliness, loneliness despite the presence of the twins and Jody, for she did not expect them to consider her a significant part of their lives.

She discovered that Brigg's row house was five big rooms deep on each floor, with a stairwell and closets along one entire side. There were eight feet between each home in the neighborhood, and Brigg had utilized his share of that space to add a fire escape with a letdown ladder that could not be reached from the street. Its accessibility to each sleeping room gave Carla, who had always lived on ground floors and was thus uneasy about fire, a great deal of confidence.

Jody had dutifully given Carla a brief tour of her own first floor apartment and had seemed pitifully relieved when Carla showed no interest in taking over what had always been Jody's quarters. Apparently mollified, she had then given a more detailed explanation of the second floor, which housed three bedrooms and two baths, a kitchen-dining combination, and the front living room.

They took only a cursory look at the third floor. The rear included numerous storage closets and the girls' old playroom. But the walls in the entire front half had been knocked out to make a huge workroom for Brigg. The light from the dormer windows was excellent, and he had installed his desk and drawing boards, along with several bookcases and filing cabinets. There was even a bath with shower, and an extra-long single-bed couch. Jody said Brigg frequently slept up there in preference to the feminine bedroom that was officially his.

Carla considered it significant that he had created a place of work as his escape. But she tried not to think about its meaning relative to her. In all fairness she could see why Brigg might not be comfortable in the bedroom decorated for him and Nancy. She detested it herself, for it made her feel like a horse, not the cute little ponies that might have been tethered in Victorian yards—more like a Percheron. Definitely out of place. But she thought that once Brigg was back she could overlook the pink flowers, the ruffles, even the rose-covered carpet. Nothing else should matter except his warmth next to her. She was not going to insist on redecorating, for she felt his family would have enough adjustments to make, getting used to her, without having the home they had always known changed also.

The drive from the house to work was one of her most pleasant discoveries during the two weeks she was settling in. The forty-five minute trip was like a journey through America. For three square blocks she was in a microcosm of the elegant past. The lovely row homes, symbolic of upper-middle-class success seventy years earlier, had been faithfully renovated by a coterie of Brigg's friends from the University of Chicago, and many of his friends still lived there. Since the section was surrounded on all sides by ethnic neighborhoods that held stubbornly to their identity, a massive urban area remained stable and preserved. Carla marveled that one could still walk these city streets safely, garden in the postage stamp backyards without concern, and let young children play in the neighborhood mini-parks.

As Carla drove through the ethnic areas each morning she would see elderly housewives walking to the neighborhood produce markets with their shopping bags, that habit of daily shopping from the days of no refrigeration hard to break. Farther on were the shopping centers preferred by the younger generations, but not yet crowded with people by the time Carla passed them to catch the interstate highway south to her suburban school.

There was a brief easterly swing in the highway to avoid an industrial section, and it was then that the morning sun glared in her eyes; but soon the route again swung south, gradually easing from the congested high-rise apartments and offices into the suburbs, with their single-story homes and small yards overflowing with swing sets and children.

It amused Carla that just beyond the cloverleaf where she exited for her school, one farmer tenaciously clung to his truck garden acreage despite the encroachment of housing all around him. Carla could see one of his hillside fields as she turned off. In the fall it had been orange with ripe pumpkins, but now it was covered with snow.

Once the farmer's field was behind her, there was a five minute drive through the congested business district of the large suburb where she taught, and that was the hardest part of her trip. She was always grateful to reach her classroom a few minutes early so that she could relax after the wearing concentration.

In the flurry of getting married and transferring her things to Brigg's home, Carla had worried about what to do with the little house she had once planned to live in. Luckily just four days after she was back at work she learned of a young couple wanting a furnished place and upon meeting them and finding them agreeable to Tom and Mattie Howard, Carla had immediately leased the house to them. It gave her great satisfaction to set up a savings account in which the rental profits from both the house and condominium would go, for she knew that her parents might need financial help in the future, and she did not want that burden to be on Brigg's shoulders.

In fact she decided to postpone telling Brigg that she was responsible for the maintenance of two rental properties in addition to the demands of her job and his own household, because she knew he would be concerned that she was doing too much.

She was astounded at how protective of her he had become. During those agonizingly long two weeks after their honeymoon in Galveston, he called daily, giving her stern advice on taking care of herself. Despite the distance between them, he made her feel thoroughly loved.

And there was that gorgeous evening when he finally came home from Houston. Poetry, indeed! Every moment together was spent getting acquainted all over again with the magic of their marriage. During that long night she had never felt more cherished.

But as she had known, even poetry had its ups and downs, and the next morning Jane and Ann arrived home for good.

Brigg was able to remain in town for several days

and the new phase of married life began: becoming a family. It was one Carla had expected and welcomed, but there were many days when she found it difficult not to envy young married couples who could start their lives together with only the minor problem of getting used to each other.

Brigg and Carla, and even Jody, had to adjust to being around busy teenagers on a regular basis, and the girls did not make it particularly easy, for they were periodically resentful about being taken out of their school, plus uncertain about how they would be affected by their father's new wife. Strangely they took it out on Brigg, not Carla.

Once Brigg started the Illinois projects, he tried to come home most weekends, at first arriving late on Fridays, but gradually doing well to make it home by Saturday afternoon, then leaving before dawn on Monday. Still struggling with all their own adolescent adjustments, Jane and Ann would either begin chattering to him the minute he got in and continue to hang around talking for hours, or they would decide that they had nothing to say to their father for the whole weekend. Carla shared Brigg's frustration with the situation, but urged him to be patient, thinking that his daughters would work out their resentments and confusions eventually.

During each week, when he was away at work, life settled into a reasonably comfortable routine for the four women. From long years in that role, Jody was automatically the disciplinarian; so Carla, while always pleasant and receptive to Jane and Ann, left them alone as much as possible. She believed that any gesture toward mothering would drive them into sullen rebellion. When Brigg was home, he took over as disciplinarian, but Jody kept her hand in with plenty of free advice.

Getting along with Jody was a problem unto itself. She seemed to be working herself into exhaustion to discourage Carla from taking over any of her duties, but Carla didn't dare give any reassurances or offers of help for fear of being misunderstood. However, she worried about the frail old woman.

Jody's thumb was healing nicely, but she was severely handicapped by her arthritis, a fact Brigg and the girls seemed unaware of. Each morning she painfully pulled herself up the stairs quite early in order to have a large breakfast ready for the family, and Carla knew she must have been up for hours to get her stiff joints limber enough to function.

One Saturday morning, though, after they had all been together more than a month, Carla did decide to speak her mind. She had wakened early, restless because Brigg would not be able to make it home at all that weekend, and had wandered into the kitchen to have a cup of coffee. She discovered Jody there with hands on hips, staring dejectedly at dirty dishes apparently left from a midnight snack fixed by the twins.

"Jody, do you have to clean up this kind of mess often?" Carla was shocked, wondering how she could not have heard the girls creating that kind of chaos.

"Maybe I've made a mistake, never teaching these girls to pick up after themselves," Jody indirectly answered the question with the admission, for she rarely criticized her beloved twins.

But this was hard for even doting Jody to accept. The milk glasses were still half full. A greasy popcorn pan sat unwashed on the stove. They had obviously ruined the first batch, for another pan crusted with burned kernels was abandoned on the counter top. Cookie crumbs and crumpled napkins littered the floor and dining table; worst of all, plates were left full of uneaten meat sandwiches.

"This has to stop," Carla said firmly. "We should be encouraging you to take it a little easier in the morning, instead of having you mop up after four perfectly capable adults. From now on you're going to let me help clean up the kitchen after every meal. You can tell me what you want me to do."

"I never wanted my babies working as hard as I did when I was growing up." Jody ventured the rationalization to herself, distastefully picking up one of the popcorn pans to see how badly damaged it was by their neglect.

But apparently she changed her mind as the day progressed, and she observed the girls' slovenly habits with new eyes. Things came to a head that noon when Jane spilled her tomato juice. She grabbed a clean dish towel and swiped halfheartedly at the spill, dripping much of it on the floor.

"That's no way to clean up a mess, Jane," Jody admonished her disapprovingly.

"What's the matter with it?" Jane was unconcerned as she tossed the soiled towel in a heap on the counter.

"Everything's wrong with it." Jody's Germanic passion for cleanliness was affronted. She then raised an eyebrow at Ann who was smirking at her sister's plight. "And as for you, young lady, what do you mean by leaving your dirty clothes under the bed? When I went in to mop yesterday, I found several days' worth of filthy laundry on the floor."

"I forgot to put them in the hamper," Ann explained cheerfully, not taking the reprimand any more seriously than had Jane. They both knew Jody never stayed mad at them for long.

"People ought to want a clean house," Jody snapped. "I can see it's time I taught you girls to take care of things properly."

"Oh, not that!" They both objected in dismay. "Carla already has lectured us about cleaning up after we have snacks."

"It's time you learned to keep house," Jody insisted with finality. And that was that.

Once convinced, Jody had gone about her new goal with a passion. Her girls were going to be good housekeepers whether they liked it or not. She had them dusting and vacuuming most of the afternoon, then led them to the laundry room on the first floor to start them on the dirty clothes. That evening the girls tumbled into Carla's room, exhausted and complaining. Carla listened politely, but refused to override Jody, grateful that it was the housekeeper who had adopted the procedure and not herself, because the girls would never have forgiven her. Jody, they decided, had merely become senile, and they grudgingly followed her directions out of love.

Carla had trouble getting to sleep that night. She could take little comfort in the fact that Jane and Ann had sought her out because they were temporarily angry with Jody; that was not the kind of companionship she wanted to encourage. And she missed Brigg terribly. Her bedroom seemed eerily silent without him there.

There was a strange ache inside her, as if some part of her were misplaced. She wondered if the pain would ever go away. Or would it become even worse as the years rolled on and she continued to fail at adjusting to the long times of loneliness with Brigg and his family. She felt so isolated; yet it was different from the sense of failure she had had with Charles.

She tried making a cup of hot tea and reading a boring book to make her sleepy, but she was more restless than ever. The pink flowered bedroom seemed a virtual prison, no place for a Giant Child. Suddenly she felt a strange compulsion. With conviction she hastily tied her robe around her and tiptoed barefoot upstairs to Brigg's haven.

There was light enough coming in from the windows so that she did not even need a lamp; she could find her way to his desk easily. A couple of reference books were still spread open on the surface, and a drawing board nearby contained his latest project.

Gingerly Carla sat down in the immense custom-made desk chair, her feet pulling slightly off the ground as they used to when she was a small child sitting with the grownups at the dining table. She loved the sensation. Surely no chair but one made for Brigg could make her feel small. Smilingly she leaned back, letting her eyes rove about.

It was a sparsely furnished room. In addition to the work equipment there was only one straight-backed chair and the long single bed.

Curiously she touched the objects on his desk—a mini calendar in a silver case, a digital clock, the black desk phone with its switch for the two incoming lines, the old fashioned inkwell, a rare thing to see anymore. It had been a gift from an elderly client, and Carla knew Brigg kept it mainly out of sentiment. It called to mind an advertisement she had seen recently in *The Wall Street Journal*: a little place in outstate Missouri was taking orders for turkey-quill pens for Christmas gifts. They were primarily designed as promotion gimmicks for firms, but perhaps she could talk them into selling her a half dozen for Brigg. He would get a kick out of being able to use the inkwell in the proper manner.

Christmas. She wondered where Brigg would be then. The projects in Illinois would be finished by fall, and she knew the firm had won two bids on foreign projects scheduled to begin shortly thereafter.

Her heart felt heavy as she walked over to the bed, her hands stroking the soft covers. Every week Carla put fresh linens on the bed, to Brigg's amusement. But since he occasionally brought work home for the weekend, she did anything she could to encourage him to take a break and rest. She thought clean sheets always looked inviting.

How impressions could change! Carla sat on the edge of the narrow bed. She used to think Brigg neglected his daughters, but now she wondered how he had managed to maintain as close a place in their affections as he had, given his tremendous work responsibilities. His decisions not only affected many employees and clients, but also the public, because shoddy construction of a chemical plant could mean disaster for a wide area.

She yawned as a strange peace began to flow over her. Just being in Brigg's office seemed to bring him close to her and to transmit contentment. On impulse she spread back the covers and slipped between the sheets of his bed, thinking to test if it were really large enough for him to be comfortable. Once she snuggled down, she noted that the mattress was plenty long; she had a good ten inches beyond her toes. It was a bit narrower than a single bed, but if you were tired enough...

Lazy warmth spread throughout her. Groggily she pulled a soft blanket over her shoulders. It surely couldn't have been very long before the phone rang. She was able to arouse and answer it before the second ring.

"Carla, honey?" caressed the voice she loved above all others. "Don't tell me you were still awake? I didn't see any lights on."

"Brigg, where are you?"

"In a tavern down the street."

"Down the street?" she squawked, flushing with excitement.

"I didn't think anyone was up, and I was afraid that if I came in unannounced you'd think you were being burglarized. Jody might even take after me with a butcher knife." He was chuckling softly, seeming strangely exhilarated.

"You mean you're home?"

"That's right. I got so lonely that I shuffled all my paper work and came on home for Saturday and Sunday."

"It's Sunday morning already, you fool," she corrected, glancing at the luminous clock on his desk. "Get right here. Have you eaten?"

"Woman, I believe you'll ask that on my deathbed. You'll want to send me of to the unknown with a full tummy."

"Get up here!" Carla was feeling exhilarated herself, a girl again. Her lover was home!

The belt of her robe had tugged off when she jumped out of Brigg's bed and she didn't bother to look for it as she ran barefoot down the stairs. She'd fix him a toasted cheese sandwich. No, two or three. And maybe something hot to drink.

She was slicing the cheese when he quietly climbed the stairs. Her stomach jumped excitedly, but she didn't run to him as every nerve urged her to do. *I'll just finish this work, stay calm.*

That was a ludicrous thought, because *he* came to her. And calmness fled. She felt his breath warming her temple just before he slipped his arms around her to shape her against his vibrant body.

"I'm getting your supper," she protested weakly, abandoning the knife on the counter top with a clatter before groaning and turning in his arms to burrow against his chest. He chuckled in contentment and poured light kisses over her hair while she pressed him close, her hands trying to make even smaller the little world in which they enclosed each other.

"Brigg, you're wet," she noticed, drawing back a little to look at the raindrops nestled in his beard. "You need a hot comb on that thing." She laughed, touching the wiry tangle.

"Maybe I should just shave it off."

"Don't you dare!" She put her hand against his smiling lips. "You'll look like an ordinary Brigg again."

"With one g or two?" he teased against her fingertips.

Carla was feeling dangerously reckless. But she tried to put some sanity back into the situation by turning out of his arms. "I'll bet you were still working in that office at your plant through the supper hour." She began hacking away at the cheese again.

"You'll have enough there to feed the whole family," he commented, one hand stroking her hair.

"Go away, I'm working. Is it raining now? Why don't you get dry?"

"Bossy, bossy," he grinned agreeably, leaning around to plant a final kiss against her parted lips before leaving the kitchen.

Carla felt so full of happiness she could have burst. Brigg was home! She heard him take his briefcase up to his office, then later come down and go into their bedroom. When he began to run the shower, the house was as still and as expectant as she.

There were some begonias blooming in the kitchen window, and Carla impulsively clipped the stalk of the fullest one, then rummaged around in the storage cabinet for a small vase. Her movements were quick and almost like an assembly line, so much did she want to have everything lovely before Brigg returned. *Turn off the broiler so you don't burn the sandwiches. Wait, check first to see if the tomatoes you added on top are done. Yes, they're okay.*

She got out a crystal bowl for his cold fruit salad. And a glass for beer, then put it back. Wine with cheese sandwiches? she wondered. Why not? She got down two goblets so that she could drink with him. And cloth napkins.

"Are we having a party?"

Brigg wore his bathrobe and warm slippers, and his skin had a flushed look, as if he had indulged in a very hot shower. She smiled at him, pleased. It wouldn't matter that she had forgotten to make the coffee to warm him up.

"Wine?" She gestured for him to pour, the whispered words barely breaking the silence.

He stared at her, observing how her face so candidly reflected her love. She was breathtakingly open, giving away her whole soul with none of the self-protective facades many women seemed to need. It stirred him deeply.

"I have the strangest feeling that I'm getting into the cookie jar in the middle of the night, and if I make one little noise someone is going to stop me," he said suggestively, looking at her as if she were something good to eat.

"I doubt you'll waken the girls or Jody," she ventured shyly. "They've been on a housecleaning kick today and are so exhausted it would take a cannon to faze them."

"Now that opens lots of possibilities," he responded huskily. He poured two glasses, then walked to her side, fitting himself against her in the most suggestive of ways, slipping his arms around her so that both glasses were held loosely at her waist.

She gurgled only a mild protest, so much was she enjoying how his aroused body felt against her hips. "You're distracting me. I'm trying to feed you."

"Hmm." He stepped away to set the wine on the table, allowing her to remove the hot pan from the oven and place it on the stove top. However, once she had prepared his plate, his arms went around her again, and he filled his large hands with her breasts.

The potential eroticism of the moment was broken by a loud gurgle from his stomach and she laughingly led him to the table.

"Now you know you'd better eat. Your stomach is going to waken everyone."

She softened her words with a deep kiss, which he responded to lushly, enjoying all the attention he was receiving. She was so amused by his appreciative reactions, that she didn't even pull away when he slipped his hand inside her gown to fondle her.

"Now this is the way to eat a midnight snack," he approved, turning her gently into his lap, one hand still warm and suggestive against her breast.

By the time he finally let her leave his lap to take a chair across from him, her robe and gown were hanging open and her lips were swollen from frequent, teasing kisses.

"Please eat. I worry about you," she said huskily.

He shook his head as if food were the last thing on his mind, but he did make it through the sandwiches in short order. Then he eagerly drew her back into his lap while they finished off the wine.

"I can't believe the girls haven't awakened," he said against the warm, scented valley between her breasts. "Let's go to bed."

"I forgot! We *must* do these dishes."

"What?" He jerked his head up.

She laughed at his annoyed confusion.

"Darling, we have to do these dishes." She ran her hands around his neck and into the thick fringe of hair, holding his head so that she could kiss him yet again. "Jody and I had a big scene with the girls over messy kitchens this morning. I have to set a good example."

"You're kidding." He moved his hand slowly up her thigh, watching her eyes darken as his touch grew more inquisitive.

"Do you want to have Jody lecturing us, too?" she asked breathlessly.

"Stay there," he ordered suddenly, rearranging her gown to a more modest level. "And quit distracting me." She wasn't even tempted to help him. Instead she sat straight and obediently in the chair, exactly where he had placed her, her body melting inside with the waiting.

He was a quick, if not thorough, dishwasher. It was scarcely minutes before he took her hand, drew her to her feet, and turned off the kitchen light.

"Where are we going?" she whispered in bewilderment when he led her past their bedroom door.

"Shh."

She followed him to the stairwell, and he drew her inside, locking the door behind him before leading her up the stairs. "I think a little Goldilocks has been sleeping in my bed," he said, dangling the belt to her robe from his own pocket. "She's going to have to pay for that."

"Brigg?" The word was wispy.

He locked the second door, then drew her with him to his bed and spun her into his lap. "Now where was I?" Seriously he studied her before spreading open her robe and gown, then drawing up the skirt almost to her waist. "Ah, that's right." Then he leaned over to kiss her breasts as his hand began to stroke her thighs.

Carla thought she might not be able to bear the excitement of it. His lips were all over her. Exploring, tasting. She clenched her hands around his muscular arms, moaned against his skin, lifted herself any way he needed to give them both more pleasure. Before long he had the gown and robe thrown on the floor with his own clothing, and they were lying together against the rumpled sheets she had so hastily pulled up just an hour earlier.

"It was beautiful, coming up here exhausted, then finding that sterile bed warm from your sleep." He had drawn back from her, deliberately slowing their lovemaking, looking her up and down with satisfaction. His hand idly traced the path his eyes had just traveled, while he burrowed his face against her hair. "Do you know how good you smell? Womanly, fresh. Mmmm."

She giggled at his sniffing against her neck. "I'm so glad you got home! I felt empty without you."

"I can take care of that," Brigg said suggestively, leering at her.

This time she laughed aloud.

"You stay there," he ordered, suddenly serious. "Don't move, I'll be right back."

In bewilderment she watched him shrug into his robe, then grin at her in almost boyish chagrin when they both saw his revealing profile. She heard him unlocking both doors, then the silence for moments, before he repeated the process and returned quietly to her side.

"No fair," he said huskily, pulling back the sheet she had drawn over her, before he again tossed aside his robe. She looked up at him hungrily, thinking how magnificent he was. Would he ever age? His body was so firm, so well formed. She reached for him.

"Wait."

She felt his hands on her ankles, then the pressure against her toes.

"What?" Awkwardly she sat up, to discover him fastening her high heeled blue sandals on her feet. He stepped back naked, observing her with satisfaction.

"There! My beautiful lady. As I recall, I had you like this once before, but we were interrupted." He began kissing her toes, moving quickly past the straps to her ankles. His hands reached ahead, stroking her.

Carla wanted to cry, she felt so lovely, so cherished. He had known! That night in her apartment when their lovemaking had turned sordid in her mind...

"I love you," she sobbed, urging him high against her, unable to bear his distance longer. She wanted to touch him, as she had longed to that night, wanted to have her chance to explore and love his body. She turned him on his back and began.

"How I missed you this week," he groaned under her searching kisses. He let her raise his hands above his head to give her better access to the totality of him.

They were beyond thought when he gathered her on top of him and they melted together, ready for the ecstasy they could only find with each other.

She still had the shoes on when they awakened the first time.

"This is ridiculous," she murmured, running her hands over his hairy chest before tasting where she had touched. "Going to sleep with shoes on, on this tiny bed."

"I like this bed. I think I'll patent it for honeymooners." He lifted her face from his chest and guided her toward his mouth. They turned awkwardly to their sides, never breaking their kiss. When they finally parted to draw breath he smoothed back her hair. "Goldilocks can't be too choosy."

She laughed and pecked another kiss on his grinning mouth. "How did you manage to get home?" She nestled deeper within his arms.

"Just shoved everything aside. I'll have to make it up as soon as I get back." Slowly he sat up, sliding his hands across her hips, down her long legs to her ankles. "If you're going to keep wiggling your toes against me, I'm going to take these off."

She smiled. It was a habit she had, keeping at least some part of her body against him at all times.

"I suppose we should go back downstairs."

"Wrong. You've worn me out, Goldilocks." After dropping her shoes to the floor he lay back down beside her and took her into his arms. "Now you've got to help me regain my strength."

It was an assignment she took seriously. And thoroughly enjoyed.

After that, Brigg managed to make it home by Friday and remain the whole weekend twice in a row. And the girls, perhaps tired from their unaccustomed household duties under Jody's tutelage, began to take his presence in calm stride. They greeted him amiably, chatting with their usual excitement, but not in the compulsive streaks as before. And even when his schedule tightened and the visits home had to become shorter and less frequent, they no longer talked him to death or, conversely, sank into their belligerent silences. They were making friends in their new school, and Brigg began to think the worst was over.

But there was one thing that annoyed him. Jane and Ann began to ask to go places with friends who drove cars. Usually he refused to allow it. But one Saturday in April, when they asked to go to a movie with the children of a good friend of his, he reluctantly gave his permission.

"That's quite a case," Brigg mused after they left. Carla had some of her reading plans spread out on the couch, and he was lounging in his favorite chair, finishing his coffee while he watched her.

"Quite a case," he repeated, "when a man rushes home to be with his kids, and then all they can say is, 'Can we leave now?'"

"I do believe your feelings are hurt." Carla looked up in surprise. "Don't you want them to have friends?"

"You told me I don't spend enough time with them."

"Not exactly. I told you you weren't here with them enough. There's a difference."

"I'll be darned if I can see it. How can I be here with them if they're not here?"

"They'll be home soon, Brigg," she laughed. "You told them to be back by ten, didn't you?"

"Yes, that's late enough when an eighteen-year-old kid is driving. Are you certain that boy knows what he is doing?"

"No."

"Of course, since he's Bill Mead's son, he's been well taught, but—"

"Bill Mead's one of your best friends," she pointed out, knowing the man was an environmental specialist who frequently worked on Brigg's projects. "The boy should be nice. And, besides, his sister will be going, too. What trouble could he give them with his sister along?"

"I just can't get used to my girls being old enough to go out with friends in cars."

"You'd better. They're old enough to drive themselves. You should be enrolling them in driver's ed."

"What? Not so soon."

"Brigg, they're sixteen. They're going to find a way to drive on their own if you don't help them."

Carla smiled as she thought how fascinated the girls already were with cars, especially flashy ones. Jane was ecstatic to have a chance to ride in the Mead boy's Trans Am. A yellow Trans Am at that.

"Forget driving," he said suddenly. "I haven't taken you out for a long time. Why don't you put that stuff away and let's go get a drink? There's a neighborhood tavern near here where everyone wants to meet you."

"Me? Why?"

"I used to drop in there frequently when I was alone. That time I went there to call you, they said to bring you by so they can check you out."

It was one of their nicest evenings together. Brigg had been right that many of his acquaintances in the neighborhood gathering place were curious about her, and it was a surprise to see how he reacted to their interest. He almost blushed, and introduced her around proudly. They stayed only long enough to have a drink and meet everyone, but Carla loved it, and promised to have Brigg bring her back soon.

They were home before ten o'clock. Jody apparently was already in bed, but the girls were not yet home.

"Shouldn't they be in by now?" Brigg glanced at his watch when they settled down to watch the nightly news on television.

"Sometimes traffic can hold you up," Carla reminded him.

He wasn't pleased with that possible explanation and fidgeted restlessly throughout the broadcast. Carla didn't worry much about the girls' lateness the first ten minutes or so, but as twenty, then twenty-five minutes went by, she too began to feel uneasy.

And then it happened—the quick inset into the scheduled broadcast—the terse, jerky announcement that there had been a bad wreck on the interstate highway in the central city. A tractor trailer had jackknifed and caught a car against a guard rail, sending it instantly into flames. The truck driver and all four passengers in the car were killed. Names were being withheld until next of kin could be notified. The only thing known from witnesses was that the car was a recent model yellow Trans Am carrying teenagers.

Brigg whirled toward Carla in shock. He remembered as well as she how thrilled Jane had been about the boy's yellow Trans Am. How many of those cars would be out that night with exactly four teenaged passengers?

They didn't know what to do next. Call the hospitals? The television station, the police? Brigg decided to do all of them, and raced up to his office to start the gruesome task on his private business line while Carla kept the family phone open to receive calls.

He had been up there fifteen minutes before the phone in their bedroom finally rang. Carla's hands were so sweaty and shaking she could hardly hold the receiver. When the voice on the phone finally registered in her mind, she ran shouting to the stairwell.

"They're all right! Brigg!" She could hear him push back his chair violently. "Ann's calling! They've had car trouble and want—"

"Car trouble? *Car trouble!*" Brigg was thundering down the stairs toward her, his tortured face white. "When I get my hands on that boy—"

Carla ran to interpose herself between her husband and the phone.

"They're safe, Brigg. They haven't been in a wreck. It's just car trouble. Brigg!"

He was struggling with her for the phone, amazed at her strength and determination, but gradually the wildness went from his eyes and he drew several deep breaths.

"Darling, they probably don't even know about that accident," she said pleadingly as she slowly relinquished the receiver. "Don't scare them."

He glared at her, but his voice was deceptively calm when he answered. Carla drew a shuddering breath and walked back into the living room where she collapsed in a chair. The girls were all right. She was too stunned and relieved even to cry.

Shortly afterward Brigg appeared at the doorway, wearing his carcoat and angrily clutching his car keys.

"Bill wasn't home so they finally decided to ask me to help start the thing. When I get my hands on that boy..."

"I'm coming with you." Carla bounded up, alarmed at his repeated threat.

"I'm not going to hurt that stupid—"

"Now I know I'm coming with you," she insisted as she wrenched a coat, any coat, out of the hall closet. "You'll ruin their whole evening."

"Ruin *their* evening. They were supposed to be home at ten."

"Shut up, Brigg, just shut up!" she shrieked, pushing ahead of him down the stairs.

He was stormily silent for most of the drive to where

the car was stalled. Then suddenly he surprised her by breaking out into reluctant chuckles.

Carla twisted her head quickly to watch him in amazement. "What?"

"After your battle over that phone, I didn't shout at Ann or anything, just listened. Do you know what my daughter had the nerve to say to me?"

Wordlessly Carla raised her eyebrows.

"First I had to listen to a scrambled story about what happened. From what I could piece together, when the car stalled they thought they were out of gas and walked a couple of blocks to a service station. The attendant didn't have a carry-can, so they drank two Cokes apiece, rinsed out the bottles with water, and slopped gasoline into them. That station guy must have been a kid himself to have allowed it. And, of course, gas wasn't the problem at all."

"What did Ann say?" Carla interrupted impatiently.

He grunted a muffled expletive. "She figures they've had a great adventure, and its even greater that I can start the car, so the Mead boy won't have to pay a towing fee. She said it was very handy I was in town."

"Handy?" Carla sputtered. She was surprised Brigg hadn't exploded on the phone then and there. Her respect for his unexpected self-control knew no bounds.

"Handy!" He began to shake his head, his laughter a roughened mixture of amusement and tortured relief. "Their father is a handy convenience to have around."

"I could have told her that." Carla's shaky voice began to reflect the same mixture of confused emotions.

Then they were both laughing hilariously. At the moment when Brigg swung an arm around her and drew her close to his side, she felt as fulfilled as if they had just made love.

Chapter Eleven

Carla was fighting morbid reflections. She was thinking that despite the many beautiful moments in her new life, there was too much emptiness. *I can't live with this situation at home. I believed I could, but I can't. I'm too greedy.*

Meanwhile two young students were bent studiously over a table in her office, their absorption giving her time for saddened thoughts. She missed Brigg so much. She wondered how some women with traveling husbands seemed to manage their marriages so well.

It wasn't just the loneliness. It was the whole package of isolation, of only feeling fully alive those few hours Brigg was home, and the guilt because she knew he was paying the price for their being together. He was the one who doubled his work load to take the time off; the one who made the drives back and forth.

She was greedy for his sake as well as her own. How long could his health hold up to such a grind? *Soon he'll tire of the effort. It might not be worth it to him.*

Frowning, Carla wondered, not for the first time, if their marriage had been a mistake. She knew Brigg loved her. But was that enough? Perhaps the demands of their life-styles were incompatible. She didn't know if she could ever adjust to seeing him only a few days for months at a time once he returned to the foreign construction projects that were his speciality.

Perhaps she could survive if she could become a real part of his family, contributing to the happiness of those others he loved. But...

Sighing, she glanced down at her fingers. Her narrow gold wedding band gleamed in the morning sunlight. She remembered when Brigg had slipped it on and whispered, "Forever, darling." *Is it possible?*

"This is a dumb clue. I'll never find where she hid the candy." The boy at the table loudly broke into Carla's troubled thoughts, his liquid eyes breathing fire as he waved a slip of paper in the air. "Rosa cheated."

"I did not, Jeff," his curly-headed companion squawked indignantly. "The clue I have to guess is just as hard."

Carla forced her startled attention back to the work at hand. The middle of a vocabulary enrichment session was not the time for mulling personal problems.

"All right, you two, let's take a look together," she soothed. Each child had been given a piece of candy to hide for the other, then Carla had supervised their writing a clue describing the hiding place. "What's the problem?"

"I already figured out the first hard word. But I don't think you ought to make us have two new words. I can't understand this: 'Take twenty-seven steps *lateral* to the front door,'" Jeff said.

"What do you do when you don't know a word?"

"Not the dictionary!" he moaned. When his dramatics got no results, he sighed and turned to the huge book on a stand.

"And what's your problem, Rosa?" Carla sat beside the girl.

Rosa was eyeing Jeff with glee before she whispered,

"You'd think he'd remember a lateral pass from football."

"Did you, before I had you look the word up?"

Rosa flushed and held out her own clue. "Mine's really hard. I'll bet he had to look up lots of words before he could write this clue."

"Read it aloud."

"'On the a-n-t-e-r-i-o-r part of Mrs. Smith's desk—'"

"Anterior?"

"Anterior," she agreed, remembering that her teacher required them to pronounce correctly all new words. "'—of Mrs. Smith's desk is an o-b-e-l-i-s-k.' Uh, obelisk. So what does that mean?"

"What does it?" Carla said unsympathetically, pointing to another dictionary. "Try anterior first."

Rosa had just opened her book when Jeff slammed shut his dictionary and ran toward the door.

"Wait a minute, Jeff," Carla called out firmly. "What is your word?"

"'Lateral,'" he said impatiently, still sidling toward the door, the taste of chocolate already tempting his mind.

"And it means?" Carla insisted, smiling. The children all knew her rules.

"To the side. Can I go and look?"

"Yes, but hurry back. And don't eat it until Rosa finds hers."

"Dummy Rosa!" Jeff couldn't resist the taunt to his partner before he dashed out.

"Brat," Rosa retaliated while her finger ran hurriedly down the page. "'Anterior: Situated before or toward the front.' You mean it's just on the front of her desk?" She looked up disbelievingly. "Why didn't you say so?"

"That *does* say so."

"It's the hard way around," she grumbled, beginning to thumb for the o's. "'Obelisk: An upright four-sided pillar that gradually tapers as it rises and ends in a pyramid.' That doesn't make sense."

"Do you know what a pyramid is?"

"Of course."

"Why don't you go to Mrs. Smith's office and ask if you can look on her desk for a pyramid that tapers?"

Rosa picked up her clue and shuffled off, not at all convinced that she would be successful in her quest.

Carla returned to her desk, wondering wryly if she would get any complaints that week from health-minded parents who felt that bribery through the small bits of candy was detrimental to the whole educational process. But the children seemed to look forward to these hunts and would stretch their minds seeking words to use on each other, so Carla stubbornly maintained that the activity should be used.

"Hey, an obelisk is the Washington Monument!" Rosa returned, excitedly waving a wrapped miniature chocolate mint.

"You mean the Washington Monument is an obelisk," Carla corrected.

Rosa thought about that a minute before agreeing. "Anyway, Mrs. Smith had a Washington Monument paperweight, with drawers on the bottom. The candy was in there."

Just then an equally excited Jeff came in, also triumphantly waving his piece of candy. They ate their prizes and talked excitedly for a few more minutes before returning to their classroom. Once alone Carla leaned back, absorbing the silence. It was her lunch break, but she felt too blue to join other members of the staff in the crowded faculty lounge.

She was lecturing herself on how lucky she was to have Brigg and his family at all, when Betty Saunders, her best friend among the teaching staff, stuck her head in the door. "Are you buying or bringing?" she asked in the same way the children asked each other.

"Buying." Carla managed a grin. "I'm late."

"I brown-bagged it today, but I'll grab a cup of coffee with you if you're coming now."

It took longer than usual to get a lunch tray filled, and when Carla eventually entered the faculty lounge, only Betty was left. "I'm sorry to be so late. Do you have to get back, too?"

"Nope, I have a student teacher this week," Betty leaned back as if she could spend all day.

"Crafty planning."

"Oh, I won't leave her alone long." She sipped her coffee before asking casually, "Is Brigg still working in Houston?"

"No, they finished that job. He's supervising the construction of three chemical plants in outstate Illinois now, so he just gets home a day or two most weekends." She couldn't keep the sadness from her voice.

"I remember when my husband used to have that kind of schedule," Betty recalled. "He sold textbooks during the gas shortage and had a territory covering five states. He'd have to headquarter in an area, then conduct many of his initial contacts by phone. He did well to get home one day a month. I hated it."

"I don't blame you."

"One day I got so fed up"—she laughed—"that I loaded the three kids in the car and joined him at his motel."

"He didn't expect you?"

"No way. I knew he'd have been so worried about me driving the kids by myself that he'd have said not to come. But I was determined to be with him."

"He must have been in shock." Carla laughed, imagining what chaos it would have been to have the expense and confusion of his whole family in his motel room while he was trying to get work done.

"Actually, it was fun. When he had to work in the room, I kept the kids busy taking walks and swimming in the motel pool. By early evening the kids were ready to eat fast food hamburgers and fall into bed. Then we'd have a nice supper sent up for ourselves, eat out on our balcony, and just talk. It was so pleasant that he had me stay a second week."

Carla fell silent.

"Are you all right?" Betty eventually asked in concern, noting Carla's pensive expression.

"Hm? Oh, I'm fine. You've just given me the most outrageous idea."

It was a beautiful early May afternoon. Driving along the flat Illinois highway, Brigg could think of dozens of things he would rather be doing than making his second visit of the day to this construction site—such as being able to drive to Chicago. But that was out. He had been in New York most of the week, and the paperwork on the Illinois jobs had piled sky high, delaying his trip home until the next afternoon. Still he felt a certain satisfaction in seeing that the great hulking distillation tower of the liquid fertilizer plant was finally taking shape. Approaching from three miles back, Brigg noted with satisfaction that the painting of a huge storage tank had also been completed. Its whiteness, necessary to withstand the coming heat of the summer, stood out against the greening landscape. *At least one thing is going on schedule.*

This time when he pulled in off the country road, there were no environmentalists picketing at the construction gate. He drove through unchallenged, relieved that his explanations concerning future landscaping plans had apparently pacified the sleepy-eyed group which had been lying in wait for him at dawn.

In his business he expected at least one complaint from citizens on any job, and it was not always as easy to convince them that their worries were unfounded.

At the second plant site, fifty miles south, construction was still hung up by a court injunction. A nearby city's water supply had gone bad within weeks after Brigg had installed bulk chemical tanks, and some citizens had gone to court, claiming that pollutants from the storage areas were leaking into the ground water. Brigg's own testing and that of the EPA indicated that the pollutants were not the same chemicals as those stored in the tanks, but angry citizens were hauling in water, picketing, and threatening to sue. Situations such as these, while not unexpected, bothered him. He felt deep childhood ties to the farmland, and it insulted him that anyone would think that he was not committed to protecting the environment.

Brigg had called in Bill Mead, who discovered that a porous layer of sandstone running shallowly underground in a dip for miles south of the town was geologically ideal for carrying water soluble pollutants. He was currently checking out all old toxic waste dumps in the county, trying to trace a source of matching pollution.

I hope he finds the problem soon. Brigg shook his head as he parked his car. Hearings over the injunction were taking too much of his time from work on the third construction project seventy miles to the south. It was a problem he didn't need right then.

The spitting sounds of welding brought his thoughts back to the job at hand, and he walked into the construction trailer office to pick up a hard hat. They had run into some problems piping the east wing earlier in the day, hence his stopping back here the second time to check it out.

He had just come outside when Charlie, the project foreman, shouted at him from a truck nearby. "Hey, Brigg, your wife's been trying to track you down. Dorothy left a message on your desk."

Iciness tore at Brigg's guts as he ran back inside and looked for the message note pad. When he finally found it among the scrambled drawings on his desk, he stared at it in puzzlement.

> Your wife glad you found extra motel space. She and girls will be here about seven. Said eat if you're hungry.   Dorothy

The project secretary had already left for home, so Brigg called his motel to see what was meant about finding space. He was astounded when the manager apologized for overlooking Brigg's request for reservations, and explained that his family would have the room adjoining his for the weekend.

What's going on? he wondered, mentally chasing a vague recollection of Carla's commenting that his drives to Chicago were becoming too hard on him. He tried to remember what he had said in reply. Not much, probably. At work he was too accustomed to keeping his plans to himself until they were finalized and probably hadn't bothered to explain. He probably hadn't even told her that he was much better off coming home than remaining in the pitiful accommodations at the construction site.

He had just hung up from trying unsuccessfully to

reach his home in Chicago, when the phone rang. His bark of greeting made only minimal allowances for the possibility that the call could be business.

"Dad?" It was either Ann or Jane. But she seemed to be whispering and he could hardly hear above the clanking of construction equipment near the trailer.

"Where are you?" he shouted.

"Dad, did you want us to come down there this weekend?" the voice asked, again in a whisper.

"Who is this?" he hedged.

"Jane. I've got to hurry. Carla stopped for gas and she doesn't know I'm phoning. She said you wanted us all to come for the weekend, but Ann and I don't believe her. I mean, you've never wanted us with you before. We think she's going to make you mad."

What did she mean, saying he'd never wanted his own daughters with him? he wondered angrily.

"You get your"—he controlled his language with difficulty—"since when did I not want you girls with me? It's just been too difficult before. You and your sister rush back to that car and get down here!"

"Well all right, Dad." Jane's voice rose in surprised indignation. "You don't have to shout. We just thought—"

"You get down here!"

There was a fierce expression on his face when once again he slapped on the white hard hat and strode out of the trailer.

"It seemed a good idea at the time," Carla hissed softly when she and Brigg lay side by side in the darkness. The light flickering from under the adjoining door indicated that the girls were still up watching the late movie. "When I brought up our coming, you absolutely refused to discuss it, so I had to make a decision on my own."

"I didn't know what you were trying to discuss. You don't usually take such an oblique way to get to the point."

"I was trying to feel you out." Through the thin walls of the motel she could hear the tense background music of the television film heralding the approach of the murder scene. Since only the slimmest of wallboard separated their rooms, making all three beds literally back to back, Carla could almost feel the movement of the girls as they shifted about apprehensively. She had had no idea Brigg's accommodations were so minimal. The mattress was lumpy, the blankets thin and faded. She was almost afraid to walk barefoot on the threadbare carpet, although Brigg assured her solemnly that the maid sprayed for bugs and swept thoroughly once a week, whether the room needed it or not.

"I should have been sending you down some food," she whispered, recalling her dinner of chicken dumplings floating in grease served at the shack restaurant across the road. "We could buy a little refrigerator for you to keep in your room. Send down our microwave..."

"Carla, stay on the subject." Brigg balanced on his side to look at her. "What gave you the idea that it was wearing me out to come home on weekends?"

"You always look so tired."

"I'd be much more tired if I stayed around the job all the time. I've told you how much I need that break at home."

"I thought you were just being stoic."

He looked at her in amazement, then flopped back down, literally shaking his head.

"I should have listened to the girls," she murmured apologetically. "They said we'd just be in the way. We'll go back first thing tomorrow morning."

His touch on her shoulder was warm against her chilled skin.

"I never realized they had the impression that I didn't want them with me," Brigg began thoughtfully almost to himself. "It was just that I've always worked in such out-of-the way places. These accommodations here are luxurious compared to many spots I've lived in for months on end. Chemical plants aren't constructed in the middle of lush urban areas. And that's what my girls have been used to."

"By your choice," Carla pointed out.

"I always assumed that was best for them. But maybe it's important that they see their father's work as it really is."

"I didn't mean to interfere, Brigg. I realize that your work has to be the first consideration. I just couldn't bear seeing you look so tired."

"I've been less tired on this job than ever before. Doctors tell me I have an iron constitution. Now, are you trying to talk me out of keeping the girls here?"

"I don't know what I'm trying to do," Carla admitted, hovering above him to smooth down his ruffled fringe of hair. It had become a little ritual she did each night they were together, something she was unaware of.

But Brigg knew. And he obligingly allowed her hands to roam lovingly over him. "I'll tell you what"—he planted little kisses close to her mouth while he talked—"tomorrow we'll run out by one of the chemical plants. Luckily the one nearest to completion is also the closest. I could have somebody in the weekend crew show you three around while I finish my paperwork. Jane might enjoy it. I've noticed her physics papers this semester; she has the makings of an engineer. And maybe Ann could find something to sketch. Of course, they both might be bored and complain, but—"

"Now, Brigg, are you going to be short tempered with them? If so, I—"

"I'm just not going to put up with complaints. That won't hurt them. You got them down here; now let me handle this my way from here on out." His kisses had moved to her eyelids.

"Yes, sir," she agreed meekly, before reaching her arms around him to hold him close. The delicious hug was her favorite treat before going to sleep. The strength of his muscles against the sensitive softness of her body felt so good.

They were both tired, and were burrowing their own spots in the lumpy mattress when the first scream came, a piercing, hysterical noise from one of the girls. Brigg was bounding out of bed even as loud thumps and shouts began next door. He charged into the twins' room in his shorts, a fearsome defender for any attacker to face.

"Daddy, help!"

Carla was scampering close behind him, when she stopped in midstride, astounded.

Instead of confronting one or more intruders, she saw Ann hopping around on one foot, shrieking wildly while trying to avoid a large cockroach that was scurrying across the threadbare carpet. Jane was shouting, too, and attacking a second roach with her shoe.

Color began to return to Brigg's face.

"Get it," Jane squawked as the roach escaped her. Brigg automatically crushed it with his bare foot.

"Oh, yukk!" Ann groaned dramatically, forgetting about the roach near her.

Mumbling under his breath, Brigg grabbed Jane's shoe out of her hand to take care of the other offending bug. Carla watched him dispose of his catch, then clean up in the girls' bathroom. When he returned, she expected an eruption of lecturing, but he said nothing while he walked calmly toward her, his face smug.

"You've got to get us a can of bug spray tomorrow," Jane announced firmly to her father.

"I will," Brigg promised meekly, still with that incredible, amused smugness. He was enjoying Ann and Jane's initiation into his working life-style. Carla suspected that he might even be planning the grubbiest, most uncomfortable parts of his construction site as the route of their tour the next day. She glared at him when he grinningly slipped his arm around her waist and guided her toward their room.

"Carla, you've got to do something about Daddy," Ann called after them, flouncing back into bed. "His ideas of family togetherness are ridiculous."

Chapter Twelve

There was no question in Brigg's mind as he drove down the familiar Illinois highway that Carla would be home. She had told him on the phone only that morning that she would be staying in, cleaning out drawers or something. And with Jody gone to her cousin's, and the girls staying over at the Meads', they would have the house to themselves all night.

Brigg knew just how he would start presenting his news to her. He'd been working it out in his mind ever since hearing of the legal finalization of the new contract and deciding to tell Carla in person. He'd be surprising her, of course, simply by walking in the door, for she didn't expect him until the next afternoon.

So he wouldn't talk at first. There'd be the welcoming kissing to enjoy instead. He'd allow plenty of time for that, but not let himself get sidetracked into bed. He'd have to be strong-willed, for Carla's welcome could be potent when she was surprised and excited.

Once he'd had his share of loving greeting, he'd say, "I have a great new idea for family togetherness."

It was a perfect way to start telling the news. He'd say it seriously, of course. And she would probably flush with that insulted expression she sometimes couldn't hide, and mumble "Very funny." For she was still sensitive about her trip the previous weekend to his plants.

There was really no reason for her to be so sensitive. He thought that, under the circumstances, the visit hadn't gone too badly. There had been the excitement of being there when Bill Mead had pinpointed a toxic waste dump as the source of the pollution near the one plant, and when the court injunction had been lifted. The girls had enjoyed seeing Brigg interviewed by the press about that, and they had appeared reasonably interested in their tour of the construction sites. Of course their complaints about the food and accommodations were something else, but the visit could have been worse.

Still, Carla was embarrassed about springing them all on him, so while he could tease her a bit about it, he shouldn't dwell too long on the family togetherness approach.

While he was turning off the interstate onto the highway that led to his neighborhood, he mulled what he would say next. Probably he'd best get straight to the point, say: "I need to be home more, so I've sold the business." That should throw her.

He grinned in delight. Yes, that was what he'd do. Just sock it to her point blank. He was certain she had no idea that what he had been so hectically fitting into his working schedule, almost since they met again at that reunion, was negotiations with a French consortium to buy the construction company. He hadn't been free to discuss it until it was finalized.

An initial offer had been presented almost two years earlier, and Maurice had wanted them to take their profits and get out then. But neither he nor John had been ready to give up the work they found so fulfilling. Later, though, he had fallen in love with Carla, and about that time Bill Mead began feeling them out on entering a venture with him—a small new company to produce equipment for pollution control. It would be slow, innovative, and not a big money maker at first. But with the sale of the construction company they would have plenty of financing behind them, and there would be the challenge of initiating both research and production.

Brigg began humming to himself as he eventually approached his house. Carla would express disbelief first. Then astonishment. What he would be waiting for with such eagerness, though, would be the delight which would come next. The new business with Bill and John McQuiddy would be just twenty minutes from his house. He could be home almost every evening, and she could also come down to be with him while he worked. He could make a lounge off his office, put in a desk for her to do her school work. It would be hard getting the new company established, and there would be occasional times of separation, but...

He knew she'd be ecstatic. She'd fall into his arms and probably cry all over him for a while, before holding him close and pressing against him as she did when she was upset. And then he would take over. They'd have the house to themselves.

He felt the familiar, hot stirring in his loins, just thinking about it. Finally he knew he could truly make her lastingly happy, not just with his physical love, but by offering her himself—his companionship, his time—sharing her interests.

I should have installed a hot tub. That would have been a great place to celebrate the founding of a new home life and a new business, he thought. They could have had champagne and toasted their own love as well as the joining of Brigg and John's practical expertise with Bill Mead's theoretical knowledge and Maurice's European marketing skill. It would have to be a long toast.

Brigg decided that the shower would have to do. He and Carla had never had the privacy before to take a shower together in his house, and he coveted that sharing. The champagne could come later. Much later.

Although he arrived in early evening, it was already dark and he didn't want to frighten her, so he made plenty of noise entering the house. He called out, "I'm home," loudly and frequently enough to make all the neighbors aware of that happy event. But she didn't answer. Disappointed that Carla hadn't come dashing out to greet him, Brigg went to their bedroom first, where the lights were on. Terrible place, he thought, as he approached it. He'd have to suggest that she redecorate. As he entered he could see that she had definitely been working on the drawers, for clothing was stacked neatly on top of the dresser, and a few items were even tumbled across the bed, as if she had left them there in haste. *She's probably in the bathroom.*

"I'm home, honey. I got a chance to get away early," he shouted at the closed door.

When she did not answer, he knocked loudly, then slowly swung the door open. The bathroom was empty. Puzzled, he threw his coat and briefcase on the bed atop the rumpled clothing and went to look for her.

It took him fifteen minutes of searching the house from top to bottom to realize she wasn't there at all. Their garages were completely separated, so he hadn't noticed whether her car was gone. He stalked outside in his shirt sleeves and was little comforted to find her garage closed but empty.

He'd been home almost a half hour. Wouldn't that

have been time enough for her to have completed any errand important enough to do at night and get back? The stores would be closing soon. He went into the kitchen to see if she'd left a note on the message board.

When he couldn't find one, he absentmindedly began making a pot of coffee, thinking vaguely that he'd give her another thirty minutes. If she wasn't home by then, he'd check Jody's cousin's house. She might have gone over there with Jody. And he could try the Meads'. Carla had said the girls were spending the night at their house so they all could start their drive to the family's Michigan cabin about four in the morning. Jane or Ann might know where Carla was.

The coffee water gradually boiled away while Brigg restlessly paced around the house, continuously checking the front and back windows. When he discovered the empty pot, he scowlingly turned the heat off and reached for his phone directory.

Something about the way some of that clothing had been thrown carelessly across the bed worried him. She had left in a big hurry.

Carla was eating bagels. And laughing.

"This is the most unusual ethnic dinner I've ever had," she said between bites. "Frijoles, bagels, ratatouille and saki. We're going to be sick."

"I guess we lady plumbers can't be picky," Mattie Howard agreed, getting up off the living room floor in Carla's carriage house to look in the brown paper bag they had had Mattie's cousin deliver. "But next time I'll know not to tell him to pick us out a surprise. How about a brownie for dessert?"

."How do you suppose it goes with saki?" Carla laughed again. "Oh, well, who cares? I'd love one."

"I wish you'd change your mind and spend the

night," Mattie said, sitting down in front of the coffee table, which had been their dining place. "It's almost eleven o'clock. That's kind of late to be entering an empty house alone. And I'll be by myself, with Tom out of town."

"Thanks, but I'd better get back. There's always a chance Jody or the girls might have some problems and call for help early tomorrow."

"Then they'd be worried about you."

"No, I'm certain they'd just figure I was sleeping through the phone. No one worries about me." A pensive look crept over her face momentarily before she smiled again. "But I ought to be there if they need anything. At least we got the water turned off and the mess in the kitchen cleaned up. I'll try to get a plumber out tomorrow, if one will come on a Saturday."

"I'm sorry I had to call you. But when I was on the front porch and heard water running in your kitchen, I knew something was wrong. Your renters have been on vacation for three days, and I didn't notice any water noise when I picked up their mail yesterday."

"I'm relieved that you called!" Carla assured her. "If we hadn't discovered that cracked pipe joint soon, the whole house would have been flooded. And you didn't interrupt anything; I was just cleaning out drawers. I'm going to leave a spare key with you from now on, though, so there'll be a way people can get in if we have another emergency when my renters aren't home."

"Maybe your husband can go over all the plumbing in this house. We had no idea it was in such bad shape."

"He probably can—oh!" It occurred to Carla that she had better tell Brigg about owning the house. Even though she wouldn't be asking his help to fix the plumbing, she had put off too long going over her business affairs with him. She sighed heavily.

Mattie misinterpreted Carla's reaction. "Even if any other pipe joints are bad, you shouldn't have any more problems as long as we keep the water to the house turned off. It's lucky your renters are going to be away another week. That will give a plumber or your husband time to go over everything."

Carla thanked Mattie for her help and began gathering together her equipment. For some reason just thinking about Brigg made her anxious to get home, close to the familiar things that made the place his. She might even sleep up in his office all night.

Wearily she loaded the heavy scrubbing mop and the bucket full of wet rags in the car. The pipe that had broken was underneath the kitchen sink on an outside wall. Most of the vinyl floor and several of the under-counter cabinets were well soaked by the time she had arrived. She would have to come back after everything dried out and assess how bad the damage was.

Undoubtedly the pipe joint had been oozing for days, she thought, before finally cracking enough to let a steady flow through. Since it was under the sink, her young renter had probably not noticed it at all, or not realized it was a serious problem. She would have to explain some facts about plumbing to them, as well as have an expert check the house completly for other potential problems. If there was one weak area like that, undoubtedly there would be others. While Carla drove home, she pondered what additional maintenance emergencies she should anticipate.

Preoccupied with making a mental list of things to do about her two properties, Carla had pulled into the alley leading to their garages before she noticed the lights on all over the house. It startled her immediately, for she was not aware that she had left that many on when she had hurried off. She parked in the garage, punched the radio signal device and stepped quickly under the closing overhead door just as a taxi pulled up alongside the drive. She was trying to see who was arriving, when Brigg came running out the back door like a madman.

"What's going on—" she started, before Brigg grabbed her in a rib-crushing hold.

"Carla, darling!"

She couldn't get a word out because he was holding her so tightly her face was buried against his shoulder. She was struggling to get free enough to breathe when she heard a raspy voice behind her.

"Are you all right?" Confused, she recognized Jody's anxious words.

Brigg suddenly held her away from him, looking her over carefully just as Jody was doing, even as she hobbled toward them from the waiting taxi. She had her hair up in pin curls, and a disreputable bathrobe hanging below her winter coat.

"Jody, what's wrong?"

"Are you all right?" the housekeeper asked again, seeming to think Carla's appearance was anything but reassuring.

Self-consciously Carla freed a hand from Brigg's anxious grasp and tried to smooth back her hair. She was certain she did look a mess after all the mopping up she'd been doing. And if she looked as tired as she felt...

"Well, I'm a little soggy, but—"

"Where have you been?" Color was returning to Brigg's ashen face.

"Is something wrong?" Carla asked pleadingly, thinking there must be news about her parents. Why else would they be so concerned?

"You've just about given us heart attacks, that's

all," Jody said, still peering at her. "We expected you to be home."

"Well I was, but there was this plumbing problem at my house, and I had to—"

"What house?" Brigg exploded.

Before Carla could answer, there was a loud clatter at the back door, and they all whirled around to see Jane and Ann plummeting off the porch.

"Dad, have you heard—Oh! Carla?"

"Where have you been?" Jane parroted Brigg's question.

Carla simply stared at everyone, stunned. It was finally dawning on her that she was the object of all the hysteria.

"Look, I'm sorry. There was a plumbing problem at this house I own, and I had to run over and take care of it."

"You could have at least left a note," Jody said in the same admonishing tone she used on the girls. "You knew we'd worry."

Carla knew nothing of the kind.

"What house?" Brigg asked repetitiously.

"Darling, I'll tell you later. Couldn't we go inside or something?"

"Lady, are you going to pay me?" The taxi driver was becoming impatient with waiting for Jody.

"Daddy, pay him. We can give Jody a ride back with us," Ann said breezily.

"I don't understand why everyone's home." Carla was still disbelieving.

"Daddy called the Meads to see if we knew where you were. We got to thinking about it and figured we'd better come home and help look for you. Billy Mead and his sister are along."

"What do you expect people to do when you disappear?" Jody snapped. "Just sit around and do nothing? Next time you go off, you leave a note like everyone else."

"But I didn't expect anyone to be home tonight."

"Well I was home," Brigg snapped as the taxi backed out of the alley. "At seven. You really have no business being out alone like this, anyway. The stores have been closed a long time. Your bedroom looked like a cyclone struck it. What was I to think?"

"Brigg, I only left a few sweaters thrown on the bed. And, besides, who's going to attack *me*? I'm almost six feet tall."

"Size has nothing to do with attraction," Brigg snarled.

"Carla, you *are* kind of flaky," Jane said seriously. "I mean, sometimes we think you need a keeper. You'd trust anybody."

Carla could see that Brigg was still shaken. She took his hand as they walked up the steps and through the long first-floor hall toward the front of the house. Billy Mead and his sister were waiting for them by the door.

"I just didn't think anyone would be worried," she ventured an apology again.

"Weird!" Ann shook her head. "Well, since we don't need to go hunting for you, we might as well go back to the Meads'. Jody, you want to go to your cousin's, don't you?"

"Might as well. Although my visit's probably ruined after this scare. If she'd left a note, it—"

"I'll leave a note from now on, I promise," Carla interrupted brokenly, tears beginning to swell. She was crying openly by the time they drove off.

"I suppose now we've hurt your feelings by yelling at you," Brigg said roughly before taking her into his arms. She cried all over his shirt front.

He, too, had calmed considerably when she finally got herself under control. "We didn't mean to hurt your feelings," he said tenderly, wiping at her face with his handkerchief.

"It was the nicest welcome I've ever had." She was smiling.

Brigg looked at her a moment, puzzled. Then his mouth quirked.

He leaned over and kissed her tentatively, as if uncertain of his reception. She returned his kiss, just as tentatively at first, then wholeheartedly, in enthusiastic welcome. She was trying to kiss him again, trying to press herself against him completely, when he held her away from him. It surprised her to see him smiling mischievously, as if he had some trick up his sleeve. She cocked her head suspiciously, not knowing what to expect next. But she followed willingly enough when he took her hand and began to lead her up the stairs.

"By the way"—he turned casually toward her when they reached the top of the stairs—"I have a great new idea for family togetherness."

Her expression of insult was extremely brief. "Very funny," she mumbled.

He laughed aloud and lovingly drew her into his arms. Everything else about the telling of his news went exactly as he had visualized it. Only better.

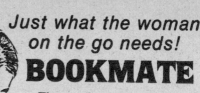

Just what the woman on the go needs!

BOOKMATE

The perfect "mate" for all Harlequin paperbacks!

Holds paperbacks open for hands-free reading!

- **TRAVELING**
- **VACATIONING**
- **AT WORK • IN BED**
- **COOKING • EATING**
- **STUDYING**

Perfect size for all standard paperbacks, this wonderful invention makes reading a pure pleasure! Ingenious design holds paperback books OPEN and FLAT so even wind can't ruffle pages—leaves your hands free to do other things. Reinforced, wipe-clean vinyl-covered holder flexes to let you turn pages without undoing the strap...supports paperbacks so well, they have the strength of hardcovers!

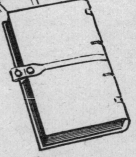

Snaps closed for easy carrying.

Available now. Send your name, address, and zip or postal code, along with a check or money order for just $4.99 + .75¢ for postage & handling (for a total of $5.74) payable to Harlequin Reader Service to:

Harlequin Reader Service

In the U.S.
2504 West Southern Avenue
Tempe, AZ 85282

In Canada
P.O. Box 2800, Postal Station A
5170 Yonge Street,
Willowdale, Ont. M2N 6J3

Yours FREE, with a home subscription to HARLEQUIN SUPERROMANCE™

Now you never have to miss reading the newest HARLEQUIN SUPERROMANCES... because they'll be delivered right to your door.

Start with your **FREE** LOVE BEYOND DESIRE. You'll be enthralled by this powerful love story...from the moment Robin meets the dark, handsome Carlos and finds herself involved in the jealousies, bitterness and secret passions of the Lopez family. Where her own forbidden love threatens to shatter her life.

Your **FREE** LOVE BEYOND DESIRE is only the beginning. A subscription to HARLEQUIN SUPERROMANCE lets you look forward to a long love affair. Month after month, you'll receive four love stories of heroic dimension. Novels that will involve you in spellbinding intrigue, forbidden love and fiery passions.

You'll begin this series of sensuous, exciting contemporary novels...written by some of the top romance novelists of the day...with four every month.

And this big value...each novel, almost 400 pages of compelling reading...is yours for only $2.50 a book. Hours of entertainment every month for so little. Far less than a first-run movie or pay-TV. Newly published novels, with beautifully illustrated covers, filled with page after page of delicious escape into a world of romantic love...delivered right to your home.

Begin a long love affair with
HARLEQUIN SUPERROMANCE.™
Accept LOVE BEYOND DESIRE **FREE.**
Complete and mail the coupon below today!

FREE!
Mail to: Harlequin Reader Service

In the U.S.
2504 West Southern Ave.
Tempe, AZ 85282

In Canada
P.O. Box 2800, Postal Station "A"
5170 Yonge St., Willowdale, Ont. M2N 6J3

YES, please send me FREE and without any obligation my **HARLEQUIN SUPERROMANCE** novel, LOVE BEYOND DESIRE. If you do not hear from me after I have examined my FREE book, please send me the 4 new **HARLEQUIN SUPERROMANCE** books every month as soon as they come off the press. I understand that I will be billed only $2.50 for each book (total $10.00). There are no shipping and handling or any other hidden charges. There is no minimum number of books that I have to purchase. In fact, I may cancel this arrangement at any time. LOVE BEYOND DESIRE is mine to keep as a FREE gift, even if I do not buy any additional books.

NAME _____ (Please Print)

ADDRESS _____ APT. NO. _____

CITY _____

STATE/PROV. _____ ZIP/POSTAL CODE _____

SIGNATURE (If under 18, parent or guardian must sign.)

134-BPS-KAP6
SUP-SUB-33

This offer is limited to one order per household and not valid to present subscribers. Prices subject to change without notice. Offer expires March 31, 1985

Harlequin reaches into the hearts and minds of women across America to bring you

Harlequin American Romance™

YOURS FREE!

Enter a uniquely exciting new world with

Harlequin American Romance™

Harlequin American Romances are the first romances to explore today's love relationships. These compelling novels reach into the hearts and minds of women across America... probing the most intimate moments of romance, love and desire.

You'll follow romantic heroines and irresistible men as they boldly face confusing choices. Career first, love later? Love without marriage? Long-distance relationships? All the experiences that make love real are captured in the tender, loving pages of **Harlequin American Romances.**

What makes American women so different when it comes to love? Find out with **Harlequin American Romance!**

Send for your introductory FREE book now!

Get this book FREE!

Mail to:
Harlequin Reader Service

In the U.S.A.
2504 West Southern Avenue
Tempe, AZ 85282

In Canada
P.O. Box 2800, Postal Station A
5170 Yonge Street, Willowdale, Ont. M2N 6J3

YES! I want to be one of the first to discover **Harlequin American Romance.** Send me FREE and without obligation *Twice in a Lifetime.* If you do not hear from me after I have examined my FREE book, please send me the 4 new **Harlequin American Romances** each month as soon as they come off the presses. I understand that I will be billed only $2.25 for each book (total $9.00). There are no shipping or handling charges. There is no minimum number of books that I have to purchase. In fact, I may cancel this arrangement at any time. *Twice in a Lifetime* is mine to keep as a FREE gift, even if I do not buy any additional books.

154-BPA-NAWE

_____
Name   (please print)

_____
Address   Apt. no.

_____
City   State/Prov.   Zip/Postal Code

_____
Signature (If under 18, parent or guardian must sign.)

This offer is limited to one order per household and not valid to current Harlequin American Romance subscribers. We reserve the right to exercise discretion in granting membership. If price changes are necessary, you will be notified.

Offer expires March 31, 1985

AMR-SUB-3